thanks for Your support.

The Great Deceiver

ANDREW CORMIER

ISBN: 1497568048
ISBN-13: 978-1497568044

DEDICATION

To my family.

CONTENTS

ACKNOWLEDGMENTS

To my friends Francis and Beti – you both took the time to read this novel as I developed it. Your suggestions and feedback along the way were invaluable. You helped make this novel work.

PROLOGUE

The corruption of a soul doesn't happen overnight. Nobody aspires to be evil. Even the worst humans in the history of the world didn't grow up thinking, "I hope I slaughter an entire race of people when I'm an adult."

Yet sometimes that's what happens.

It happened to me.

Growing up, I certainly didn't intend to be responsible for the maniacal, ruthless, and wholesale slaughter of innumerable souls. I was raised with a belief in a supreme being. I was raised with good moral values and taught right from wrong. There is no way in good faith I can utilize the pitiful defense that I didn't know what I was doing was wrong. Nor can I claim insanity or something like that. I knew damn well that murder was a crime - an abomination in the eyes of the Lord, or whatever God it is you believe in, assuming you have such faith. Mass murder, therefore, is a more heinous crime, and, logically, genocide would top that filthy list.

It was I who had to go and add genocide to my resume of destruction.

I wasn't just a bystander or a faceless dictator issuing orders that I'd never see carried out. I was a willing participant in my horrific atrocities. I watched families put to death right in front of me, at my explicit command. I had the power to change my mind and spare their lives. Yet I chose not to exercise my power in that manner. To my great shame, this scenario repeated time and time again.

What put me on this path? Well, aside from my theological instruction in a higher power for the good of all, I was also made well aware of the importance of an evil, malignant being. Surely there cannot be good without evil? The universe constantly seeks a natural harmony. Things must remain balanced.

I wish I'd paid more attention to that evil, malignant being: that is what I believe took possession of me. I am of a firm conviction that the devil twisted me into a person who I don't even recognize anymore. I have retained enough sanity to see that I am not who I once was. I couldn't have become such a monster without some overpowering force of evil acting upon me.

I have turned into a living symbol of the darkness the can reside in the human heart. I am hated by all. I am feared by all. My name is one best whispered in terror in a dark corner. I will be remembered as the greatest butcher to ever live. With the fury of my armies, I barbarized entire countries. I left landscapes for hundreds of miles barren and charred. Whole cities became nothing but smoldering piles of rubble and their streets were littered with the dead with no one even left to bury them. I owe the world a debt I'll never be able to repay.

So it is that I shall tell the story of my life. Fear not! It is not just a tale of war and death (though I'd be a liar if I said it wasn't full of both). My life is more complex and interesting than that. I have had my share of steamy romances which always make for interesting gossip! In my youth, I even found a storybook-like tale of true love.

There once was a time when I felt real emotion. I was not always an empty shell of a vessel made from flesh; back then I was like a prince rescuing a princess. We ran off happily ever after.

It didn't last, but I cherish the memories of the good times, which included other personal triumphs. Indeed, I overcame adversity through hard, diligent work to become a staggering success in my business. I made many long-time friends and I had a family to call my own. These, and other independent chapters, are the sum of my experience. They ultimately shaped all my actions. MY decisions claimed billions of lives.

This is a shame that I shall have to live with for the rest of my days.

It is only through hindsight that I can observe the consequences of my actions. My background played a large role in everything that transpired. I know history lessons are boring. No one wants to sit through a drawn-out tale any more than they want a third nipple. However, by detailing where I went wrong, my hope is that no one will ever follow a similar path again. Through careful analysis I can almost pinpoint the exact times and dates where I've, 'screwed up royally.'

I think of it like this: every decision we make affects a future decision and also affects the future. For example, if you were to kill a mosquito today it might not spread a fatal strain of bacteria like EEE (eastern equine encephalitis) to a horse it otherwise might bite tomorrow. That horse, in turn, wouldn't die from EEE, and potentially win the Kentucky Derby a week later.

I doubt all decisions have such black and white consequences, but I've definitely seen movies and read books where the hero went back in time and changed something in order to save the world. Everyone makes choices they wish they could change. Yet we only regret it after the fact. What I find really intriguing is the underlying reasons for the choices people make. I believe there are several common factors that cause people to act the way they do: in general, people want material, financial, and emotional security. They want to feel wanted and appreciated. Whether or not they know it, people really want these instinctive demands fulfilled.

I think it's the quest to satisfy our own demands that lead us to poor decisions (or at least, selfish ones). I can only speak for myself, but I know that many times I've only considered what I'd gain from any given situation. I won't lie by saying I have never made a selfish choice.

Most of the decisions that average people make involve business, politics, personal relations, or education. Not all of them are easy. Perhaps the toughest decisions are the ones that impact the lives of other people. What if you had to choose whether someone was to live or die? What if you were asked to take your brother off of life support after a terrible accident that left him brain-dead in a coma? The doctor said there's little chance he'll come through. If he does, he'll certainly have brain damage and likely will never be the same again. The doctor does know what he's doing, right?

For that moment, you'd have to play God. What a difficult task that must be. Imagine having infinite power, infinite knowledge, infinite responsibility; the ability to give life and take it. Yet, you'd just be playing God, not being him. How would you know whether or not you made the right choice?

I know I've made decisions I regret, and I played God many times.

ONE: THE STRUGGLES OF YOUTH

I was an only child born in Bloomfield, Connecticut to a loving mother and father. My dad had always wanted a son, and he finally had one at the age of thirty two. With a new addition to the family, my parents needed a larger place to live. The problem was that they couldn't afford one. They searched for a home within their price range for over a year. Meanwhile, the three of us crowded into a two-bedroom apartment.

Eventually, my dad found a larger, four-bedroom Victorian on the other side of Bloomfield. Calling it a fixer-upper would be a gross injustice to true fixer-uppers. This was the shack of the ages, so far as I can remember it. Of course, I was so young that most of my memories came from an old photo album that my parents had kept. The faded, yellowed Polaroids, contained inside of a thick, bound book, didn't paint the old house in the prettiest of lights.

The tiny, backyard was a mess, and it had no front-yard to speak of. My dad later told me it took him three weeks to clean all the trash out of the yard and to get the landscaping to look like more than just dirt with a stump and some weeds.

The actual house was built in 1870: both the exterior and interior were putrid shades of green, likely redone in the 1970's. The outside was complete with chipped clapboards that probably contained asbestos. Whenever the wind blew, a cold draft came in from just about every window. The roof leaked in spots, which was only bad when it rained, and the only floor which didn't sag was the basement (though it did pool with water on occasion).

Probably the only good point to the house was that it had enough bedrooms for everyone, and at least a yard for me to play in, regardless of the condition. We didn't need all four bedrooms, so my dad used one as his office. The other, extra bedroom was used for guests. I felt bad for anyone desperate enough to stay with us. Thankfully, we only lived there until I was eight.

Throughout my youth, the family never had a lot of money. Truthfully, we had very little money. Some weeks, my father just managed to put food on the table and get the bills paid. Sometimes, that wasn't even managed. On at least two occasions, I remember going without electricity or heat for several weeks straight. One of my earlier memories as a child is of my father embracing my mother in the cold darkness of our electricity-deprived home while sobbing. I remember him telling her, "We'll pull through somehow." This was during a lengthy period in-between jobs.

Although my parents couldn't provide the best material things, they showered me with love and care, which I suppose is something no amount of money can buy. I am grateful to have had that.

Prior to the bouts of unemployment, my father worked as an engineer for a local company. For over a decade, he worked hard, and managed to rise through the corporation. He was well liked, and respected by his co-workers. Unfortunately, the company made several unwise investments. They lost a vast sum of money and started to lay people off. My father survived the first three rounds of layoffs, but fell victim to the fourth. Eventually, the whole company went belly up. My father was one of many left jobless, the casualty of corporate incompetence and incredible, staggering greed.

For the next six or seven years, my father worked various jobs he hated. None of these paid very well, but they gave my father the capacity to at least provide the necessities for my mother and myself. This was a miserable period for the whole family.

It affected my father the worst, but I also felt the repercussions of being poor. For one thing, I had to attend public schools and kids were just plain mean. I was constantly mocked for wearing shabby clothes. I had a tough time socializing with people anyway, but this made matters worse. The first time I tried to make friends was when I invited a kid named Brian Redding over my house to play. While he was visiting, everything seemed fine. However, when I went back to school the next Monday, I discovered that he had told everyone I was poor and dirty. It turns out he was from a rather well-to-do family. My home, to him, looked like a ghetto. I became a regular subject of jokes and ridicule. Often, I heard other kids liken me to a white Oscar the Grouch (a few of them even nicknamed me Oscar). Also, I was skinny and full of irrational fears (I was scared of a monster living under my bed until I was twelve). All these factors piled up and left me feeling very insecure.

Perhaps my largest childhood trauma was inflicted upon me by a fairly large bully in elementary school. His name was Monroe, and he tormented me every chance he got. Monroe was always red-faced. His eyes were sunken in his face, and his hair was dark, cut short, and spiked. His nose was bulbous, like many depictions of Santa Claus. Aside from all these traits, there were two additional characteristics that really distinguished Monroe from the rest of the class: first, his breath always smelled of garlic. I don't know why, but that's how it was. At the time I assumed he was a vampire or something. Second, Monroe wore the same navy-blue, hoodie every single day. I used both of those identifiers to avoid him.

In those days, when I entered school in the morning, the first thing I did was look for the blue hoodie and get far away from it. If I didn't see Monroe, I could usually smell him coming, though usually once he was that close it was too late for me to do anything about it.

Monroe was your typical bully in many regards. He thoroughly enjoyed taking my lunch money, or throwing rocks at me during recess. Another regular torture he inflicted upon me was to take my book-bag and dangle it over my head, out of my reach. I then jumped up frantically, and flailed my arms to try to get it, but Monroe always raised it higher and laughed harder. Knocking my books out of my hands and onto the floor was another common occurrence.

Then there were the miscellaneous 'one offs' that were just as bad. As an example, Monroe once stabbed me in the arm with a pencil when the teacher left to copy some papers. It was bad enough to draw blood, and I hollered out loud. The whole class looked at me and pretty much knew what had happened. Monroe just laughed hysterically and threatened to pound on anyone who dared to tell on him. He never got caught for it.

There was one other thing I knew for certain: Monroe would call me "stanks" at least ten times a day. That was the nickname he made up for me. Looking back on it, I find it ironic that the boy with the worst breath in the school called me stanks. I suppose he did it to cover up some deep-lying inferiority. Monroe likely wanted to draw attention away from his own problems. Whatever the case, he focused on making fun of me at every opportunity.

At first, I ignored Monroe. I assumed he would grow bored of being cruel. Much to my chagrin, this caused him to harass me more. As the days went by, my frustration festered like an outhouse during a Jamaican summer. Eventually, a confrontation was inevitable. I remember how it went down as if it had happened yesterday.

It was early in the school day. I was walking the hall on my way to a class. Monroe, in his navy-blue hoodie, was strutting down the hallway arrogantly, and coming towards me.

"Hey stanks," he said as he got close and shoved me into a locker.

I don't know if it was my fear, but I saw red. For the first time, I stood up for myself.

"Monroe," I growled as my voice filled with venom and my fists clenched, "Call me stanks one more time. I dare you."

Monroe burst out laughing. He reminded me of a donkey. He grew even more defiant, "Yeah right," he sneered, "You're a little shrimp. What can you possibly do to me? I will rip you apart. Maybe I should call you little shrimp from now on, instead of stanks? What do you think of that, little shrimp?"

By now a small crowd of kids had gathered. They knew I was about to get my ass beat and were eagerly awaiting a fight. My anxiety level was through the roof. So was my fury. I was tired of being a laughing-stock. I was tired of being afraid. With an animalistic scream, I hit Monroe with all my might. My fist connected right into his nose and there was a sickening crunch. Blood spattered in all directions. It was nauseating. It was the first time I ever hit anyone. I was shocked. I'd seen fights in movies and on TV all the time, but they were nothing like real life.

Monroe fell backwards after that punch. His head collided with a locker on the way down. The reverberations of the impact echoed through the corridor. His head even put a sizable dent in the locker! As

Monroe hit the tile floor, he convulsed for a moment, like an ant you had stepped on that wasn't quite dead yet, but maybe just half-mushed.

The shock of hitting Monroe went away and an immense fear overcame my sensibilities. If I let Monroe recover, I knew he would beat the hell out of me. Motivated by that fear, I lunged at Monroe. From a sitting position atop him, I pummeled his head with alternate lefts and rights. I was in such a rage when I did this that I only remember what was told back to me later: I guess the built-up rage and frustration inside me poured out on him all at once. I was told that I was swinging full force at Monroe with tears welling up in my eyes at the same time.

I think this same fear later motivated some of my adult reactions. It is, perhaps, some of the reason behind the utter annihilation of my enemies as soon as I had the means to do so. I knew if I did not wipe out particular groups, and eventually extended groups of people, they would come back with a vengeance.

As for Monroe, the sound of his cries and the crowd of cheering kids fortunately alerted two teachers. They pushed through the crowd and forcefully pulled me off Monroe. At that point, I remember snapping back into reality. I was in trouble. One of the teachers escorted me to the principal's office while the other brought Monroe to the nurse.

This was my first taste of violence.

TWO: THE START OF SOMETHING GRAND

I sat in the principal's office for probably close to an hour as I waited for my parents. I cried the entire time. I wasn't upset about getting in trouble. Monroe deserved that beating and I deserved to be punished for it. That was all logical and reasonable to expect. Even as a child I grasped the idea of actions and consequences. That was one lesson I learned early in life: I am responsible for my actions. My father drummed this into my head for years.

I also wasn't upset because I beat Monroe up. It was more of a relief for me. I think that was why I'd cried. For so long, I'd held all of my emotions inside as I tried to block out Monroe's abuse. The fight released them. It ultimately showed me how unhealthy it was to bottle up my feelings.

My parents came in and met with the principal that afternoon. It was decided I would have to miss school for a few days. The car ride home was as silent as a solitary mime on a life-raft in the middle of the Atlantic Ocean.

Both parents made up for that when I got home.

I was screamed at, scolded, and chastised for a solid half-hour. The highlights of that are quotes along the lines of: "What were you thinking? You're going to ruin your education. What would possess you to hit that poor boy?" These comments were followed by my dad ranting and raving as he paced around the room. At that point, I likely cried some more and murmured "yes sir," which I would bet money was followed by the number one phrase I always heard when in trouble: go to your room for the remainder of the night.

I don't think I was there long before my mother finally calmed down and came up to talk. Through teary eyes, I explained to her how Monroe had been picking on me. When she heard this she gave me a big hug and said something along the lines of, "Oh sweetie, I'm so sorry I yelled. It isn't nice to hit people, though. Violence is never a solution to anything. Why don't you try to reason with him next time? I'm sure he'll understand."

My mother was such a kind and compassionate person, ever optimistic. She always did her best to try and understand the problems I went through. Whenever I had any questions or confusion growing up, she was there to comfort and assure me. No matter what, she stood by me. Even when our family's financial difficulties were at their worst, my mother had remained serene.

"God will get us through, trust in the Lord," she used to say. The degree of faith that my mother possessed amazes me. It was a faith that revolved around weekly attendance at Sunday mass.

Every week I was forced to wake up early and go to church. At the time, I resented this. I think most young boys who are woken early and dragged off to church on a non-school day feel the same. Regardless, I had no choice. Mom would always threaten me with damnation and groundings if I missed church. Under those ever-present and lurking threats, I'd roll out of bed half-asleep and complain the whole way. Mostly, my intent had been to convince my parents that God wouldn't care if we missed a day. I never had any luck with that. Nor was my willpower sufficient enough to have the car mysteriously turn around for home. My mother had a pretty straight-forward way to respond to my complaints. She used the age old, "We're going to church, and that's that. Now hush you."

If I didn't shut my mouth when she told me to, dad would threaten to slap me for talking back to her. I was then slapped. I learned rapidly not to argue with my mother.

At church, I always sat and fidgeted anxiously. I couldn't wait for it to get over. Although I never paid much attention, something must have sunk into my subconscious: I believe that because for many years, I devoted most of my life toward fulfilling religious duties. Or, maybe I picked up those habits from my mother. She spent much of her time organizing activities and giving to the "less fortunate," as she called them.

I felt like one of the "less fortunate" as I dealt with the repercussions of the fight with Monroe. School officials met with my parents and discussed a plan of action. Part of this plan involved me being forced to attend a school counselor every week for the next several months. There was also a brief suspension before I was allowed to return to school. The trouble when I came back was that the teachers watched me like weathermen tracking a hurricane. They wanted to make sure I didn't cause any more trouble. I got the impression they didn't want me around. Everywhere I went they looked down on me. I was ashamed to look anyone in the face.

The first time I saw Monroe again was at lunch in the cafeteria. I was terrified of his reprisal and my body shook with fear. I prepared myself for the worst beating imaginable. Monroe, however, was in rough shape. His broken nose was covered with a large bandage and packed with gauze. His right eye had swelled shut.

I hoped he wouldn't see me with the one good eye he had. I wasn't so fortunate. What happened next was not the beating that I had anticipated. Instead of storming up to me in a rage, Monroe froze up. The expression that crossed his face was one of absolute terror. I decided to apologize. As I approached him, he shied away.

"Please leave me alone," be begged, "I don't want any more trouble. I'm sorry, I'll never bother you again."

The day was mine!

It didn't take long until other students came up to me in the hallway and thanked me for standing up to Monroe. He had been bullying everyone for years and everyone had been afraid to do anything about it. One of the kids who approached me introduced himself as Tommy. He shared the same fears of Monroe. On that basis we became friends. Within a few weeks, there was hardly a time when I wasn't with Tommy. It was as if we shared an invisible leash, and our friendship became something I treasured.

After so long, I had finally started to make friends. People were beginning to accept me. I found myself being invited to other kids' houses after school, or we'd go to the park. This time of pleasantry, this golden spot in my difficult childhood, was short-lived.

I should mention now that my father had started his own business when he couldn't find work. As it happened, it exceeded his expectations. Within a year of me meeting Tommy, my father's business was booming. The workload outpaced his ability to do it, and the business had to expand. The end result was that my father moved the entire operation to Chicago, for a variety of factors I was too young to understand.

The move happened so fast that it really shook me up. One second the moving date was four months away, and the next thing I knew we were packing up and preparing for the long drive. Like many people, I don't think I fully appreciated what I had until I'd lost it all. The last time I saw Tommy we were hanging out in the park, eating candy bars and talking. I told him that we were moving soon, possibly in the next few days. I let him know that I had a lot of fun hanging out with him. I promised that when I got to Chicago, I'd call and tell him all about it.

I lost his number somewhere thereafter, and don't think I ever spoke to him again. My first real friend was gone forever. He was like the brother I never had.

Chicago was much different from Bloomfield; I never lived in a big city before. The buildings reached into the sky, almost challenging one another in a contest of height. There were more man made structures than natural ones. The only trees to be seen in my neighborhood were fenced with metal, like a fortress; the last defense against the encroaching man-made world. Constant beeping emanated from the traffic, while foul language and middle fingers seemed more common than "hello" or "thank you." Every morning around the same time, a siren would be heard. It was a daily reminder for me to eat breakfast. The rare gunshot at first was incredibly eerie and unnerving, but it soon became just another part of city life.

I entered high school in Chicago. There I excelled in all my classes. I made honor roll every semester. Teachers no longer looked at me with wary eyes. Instead, their faces and tonality revealed a great deal of respect. Additionally, I participated in various after-school sports. Due to my fairly slight build, I wasn't about to become a football player. I was also too uncoordinated for baseball and too short for basketball. Finally, I enjoyed my teeth too much to play hockey (plus I couldn't skate).

Therefore, the sports I picked up included track, archery, and lacrosse.

I never became an incredible runner or lacrosse player. Actually, I was merely an average lacrosse player and a rather sorry excuse for a runner. I was winded after jogging just under a mile and a half and I didn't even smoke. The only thing I had reasonable success with was archery. I could shoot a bow with moderate skill and I enjoyed doing it. In fact, the more I practiced, the more I enjoyed the sport. I bought a bow and set up a target in my yard. Every day after school, I shot a few volleys of arrows into a target. My routine practices allowed me to maintain consistency and gradually improved my aim.

I never felt that I was very good at anything throughout my childhood, even though I always did well in school. I never considered myself to be as skillful as everyone else. Therefore, it felt amazing that I had finally found something I enjoyed that I was good at. This really helped boost my confidence. One day, out of the blue, the gym coach came up to me and told me about an archery tournament that was starting soon. He told me to consider signing up. He thought I would be an asset to the school. If I won, he said it would help the athletics program, and I'd also take home a cash prize.

It didn't take much for him to talk me into it. I agreed that the regional tourney sounded like a good opportunity. To prepare for it, I doubled my practices. The end result was that I finished second and was awarded $500! I received my first trophy (it had a little guy aiming a bow on it), and the school was awarded $1,000 as well. The gym teacher loved me after that. He praised me every chance he got.

The biggest benefit I received from all these after-school activities and praise was that a young lady took notice of me. Her name was Jessica Bianchi. She began to flash me pretty smiles and talked with me in Geometry class about archery related stuff. I was happy to talk with her, mostly because she was really cute. I actually took notice of her perhaps a month earlier when I saw her wearing a tiny, hot-pink t-shirt, a matching cowboy hat, and tight, white yoga pants that truly did wonders for her ass.

Dressed as she was, I hadn't had the guts to speak to her. Quite frankly, she was intimidating. Even when she spoke to me in Geometry class, I was still really nervous. I think I must have stammered a lot. Whenever I met someone new, my anxiety always seized me as if I were a smuggler being detained by customs' agents at an airport. This was especially true when I met girls; I always worried that I'd say the wrong thing or do something stupid and blow my chances with them. The anxiety was even worse when the girls were attractive. I definitely classified Jessica as attractive. She kept playing with her silky, shoulder-length, brown hair and I found it hard to focus. However, Jessica's cheery nature and caring, friendly smile made me feel comfortable around her. It didn't take me long to get over my nerves.

Jessica asked about my archery stuff. I vaguely suspected she didn't really know anything about archery or even really care about it, but if that was true, she feigned interest very well. She then told me some stuff about herself, and the next thing I knew we were talking about our similar interests. She actually made the first move, and asked me to hang out after school with her. I told her I was busy. I think in hindsight this made her like me more. It was a few days until she asked me again to spend some time with her. In a very sultry tone, she told me that she was so bored after school sometimes that she just wanted company. She said she thought I was nice and we'd have a lot of fun together.

This time, I took her up on the invitation.

Jessica made it worth my while.

Before I knew it, we were kissing in her bedroom.

Maybe a week after the kissing she came over to my house while my parents were away for the weekend. She was wearing what I can only describe as a Japanese school-girl outfit complete with a plaid skirt and her pink cowboy hat. Best of all, I immediately took notice that her nipples were poking through the white fabric of her top. She asked if I liked her outfit. I probably said yes, but who the hell knows: my hormones were raging so hard that I couldn't put a coherent thought together.

It was that night that I lost my virginity to Jessica Bianchi.

I think it only lasted a minute or two. It felt like more.

Jessica said not to worry about it. From there on out, I don't think we left my bedroom the rest of the weekend and I improved. It was a blur of sensations and experiences that still bring a smile to my face, even so many years later. I went to school that Monday feeling like a stud, and of course bragged about it to all my friends.

It wasn't long until the whole school knew, but it was okay with Jessica and we ended up dating throughout high school, going to all the dances and eventually the prom together.

I graduated high school 18th in a class of 211. I had a few close friends and my relationship with Jessica was wonderful. I was only nineteen, yet I had almost everything a young man could dream of. I had no way of knowing what I would become.

THREE: YEARS OF ACCOMPLISHMENT

With all educational opportunities available to me following graduation, I pursued an interest in law. My reasoning was that I could supply justice to those who were deprived of it through no fault of their own. Having been subjected to the torment of Monroe as a kid, and also having been poor and bullied by other kids, I really wanted to make a difference in the world. Hence, a law career seemed like a good avenue.

I obtained numerous student loans, and received other financial help from both my parents and other relatives. I was accepted into the prestigious Yale University. There I began the life of a burgeoning college student with the zest of youth and aspirations aplenty. My studies were difficult. The scope of my courses went far beyond any I had taken in the past. Each assignment averaged several pages. I had at least two hours of homework every night. This forced me to spend most of my time in my dorm room, studying for various tests and being relatively isolated, unable to afford much of a social life.

This was okay with me, though. I discovered that in college many of the other students were heavy partiers. A few resorted to occasional drug use in their partying atmospheres. They were all from well-to-do families and had what seemed like limitless funding to pursue whatever sort of lifestyle they wanted. I saw a lot of cocaine on a lot of coffee tables in that time. I wanted little to do with those illicit activities. My studies were of utmost importance. I think I derived a disdain from such substances from my mother's religious devotions. She drilled it into my head when I was young that alcohol and drugs were the tools of the devil. I was full of fear that I'd go to Hell. Therefore, I only drank on special occasions, and never to excess.

Because of my isolated studying, lack of wild partying, and the fact that none of my old friends went to Yale, my college life was often lonely. Most difficult to bear was the absence of Jessica. She had been accepted to the University of Arizona. I only saw her when we both returned home on breaks, which we turned into frantic, passionate love-making sessions. Jessica even played 'naughty teacher' with me once and procured a yardstick for the occasion!

Other than a few untamed moments, I was otherwise a boring student and have no regal or exciting tales to share. I was at Yale for the long-term gain and to forge a career. I knew what it was like to grow up poor. I knew what it was to feel ashamed in school as a kid. I didn't want that again, and if I had a son or daughter someday I didn't want that for them. No child of mine, I vowed, would ever be nicknamed Oscar (unless it was for a good cause, like boxing legend Oscar De La Hoya).

I was rewarded for my intense effort and sacrifices when I graduated from Yale with a Doctorate Degree in the Science of Law. Concurrently, my parents moved out of Chicago and into a nice house in the suburbs nearby.

My parents held a marvelous celebration for me at their new house when I graduated. The affair turned out to be a catered pig roast that lasted throughout the afternoon, and it was followed by a live band and dancing later in the evening. All my relatives, old high school friends, new college friends, associates from work, neighbors, and of course Jessica, attended. My friends patted me on the back and joked they'd contact me if they needed a good lawyer. My male relatives expressed their pride in my accomplishment, wished me well, and shook my hand to congratulate me. My female relatives hugged or kissed me, told me what a success they thought I'd become, and asked me what I had planned next. This was one of the greatest moments in my young life.

With all my schooling completed, I moved back in with my parents. It was time to apply my education to real-life. I was off to earn my keep. Easier said than done. For the next four years, I worked at various law firms, and paid rent to my parents while I studied to pass my BAR exams. My parents only asked for $125 a week, but the jobs I had were terrible: they either demanded more time than I could possibly put in, or they didn't pay what I felt I was worth. The worst part of all this was that I was getting nowhere. I searched desperately for a way to get my career into full swing.

This opportunity came my way shortly after I passed the BAR exams. I located a firm called Whigham and Fosworth Associates, located in Fort Lauderdale, Florida. Both Frederick Whigham and Barnaby Fosworth were well known and respected lawyers. They were in need of a Specialist Lawyer for Serious Injuries. It matched my qualifications so I applied. Within a few weeks, I heard back: they were impressed with my resume. We held a phone interview and then a second interview via web-cam shortly thereafter. About a week later I received a phone call from Mr. Whigham. He offered me the job!

Florida was to be my destination in the very-near future. I reviewed my financial situation. There wasn't much to review. It became clear that I needed some help to get off my feet. I had to ask my father for it. He was glad to chip in. It was easy for me to talk Jessica into coming with me once I acquired my father's aid. She had studied Biochemistry at the

U of A and hoped to land a career in that field. At that time, she had no luck finding a relevant position in Chicago and figured a Florida search couldn't hurt. In truth, her alternative was the same as many other, recent graduates: flounder about from job to job if she was lucky enough to work at all.

We began the thorough search for a place to live. It was about as painful as an ingrown toenail. Neither of us could afford anything too extravagant. Nor did we want to live right in the middle of the city, where there'd be traffic and more crime. As luck would have it, we secured a pleasant, garden-style condo about five miles from where my office was located. The condo was close to I-95, had an attached, one-car garage, and was only eight years old. The only owner had been an elderly man who'd passed away.

His misfortune was our gain. When everything was said and done, Jessica and I co-signed the mortgage, plunked down a down payment, and were moved in by the end of that week.

Fast forward another year or so, and my life looked idyllic: my job at Whigham and Fosworth was going well, Jessica had found work, and our relationship was wonderful.

It was on the day of the seventh anniversary of our first date that we celebrated with a nighttime boat-cruise around the harbor. After we danced for a while, and had a few drinks, I asked her to meet me at the bow of the ship. I said it would make our experience like the movie Titanic, with Leonardo DeCaprio and what's her name. Jessica giggled, reminded me that the actress's name was Kate Winslett, and followed me to the bow.

There, I presented her with an engagement ring. It glittered under the moonlight. I was so nervous that I almost dropped it into the ocean! She began to cry as I asked her to marry me. As she said yes, she threw her arms around me and we shared a passionate kiss. We later planned our wedding day to be held on the first day of spring.

The only trouble was that neither of us belonged to a church. We didn't know where we'd get married and wanted to have a suitable venue. I had stopped attending church when I turned eighteen and my mother couldn't force me to go anymore. Jessica, in contrast, had never belonged to a denomination. She claimed to be Catholic, but just a non-practicing one (which is basically none at all as far as I was concerned). Either way, neither of us felt that it would be right to get married in a church we didn't attend. We located a friendly Presbyterian parish called The Church of Goodwill, and began a weekly ritual of Sunday visits. The man who held each sermon was truly captivating. His name was Reverend Gregory Morokio.

By the time our wedding came around, Jessica and I had made a host of friends and acquaintances among the church. Its parishioners became a familiar and friendly community. Our wedding day was picturesque and held on a beach. It was complete with shining sun, a cloudless canopy for a sky, and glistening ocean waters. A slight breeze blew through the palm trees; not enough to blow anyone's cup over, but enough to cool us in the warm sun. Over thirty people from our church attended the wedding. Many of our co-workers also came, as well as our friends and relatives from back home. We even had one of Jessica's little nieces' as our flower girl. She was most adorable.

After the wedding, we spent our honeymoon in Paris. There, we toured the Eiffel Tower. It involved climbing several hundred steps: you have no idea how big that thing is until you have to physically climb it. We also toured the royal palace at Versailles. The grounds there were enormous. Every feature of the palace was exactly what you'd expect out of royal monarchs, too. Just about everything was made of marble or decorated with gold. Every ceiling was painted with its own unique work of art, and each chandelier was made from expensive crystal. The palace went on for what felt like miles.

In addition to those sights and places, Jessica and I ate at expensive restaurants, enjoyed unique French cuisine (especially the deserts which I would rank as marvelous), toured Notre Dame with its elaborate stonework and exquisite stained glass, and spent a whole day at The Louvre where we saw all of its famous treasures.

We returned home and settled into a routine as we adjusted to married life. I spent the next few years working ever increasing hours, sometimes seventy a week. This allowed for a substantial, base income, and I also received bonuses and raises. Jessica landed a job in her field as a Lab Technician for a company called Krynos Medical Supplies.

During this time, I came home from work one evening to a surprise.

Jessica announced that she was pregnant! I laughed in disbelief at first, and said, "Oh good one. What's for dinner?" She quickly made it apparent that she wasn't joking. As this life-altering news set in, so many emotions went through my mind that I thought my head would explode. When I calmed down (after my third gin and tonic), I called everyone I knew and informed them of the news.

In a short while, we were coming up with names for our new child. If it was a girl, I wanted to call her Lisa Marie. Jessica wanted Susan. If it was a boy, I thought we should call him Louie. Jessica wanted Kurt. In the end, we narrowed it down to Susan or Kurt. Over the next nine months, we prepared our home for the new baby, and Jessica's mood swings became more erratic than they already were (which I hadn't thought was possible).

When my son was born, both our parents and Reverend Morokio were present. I stayed to watch Jessica give birth until I fainted. I know they call it the miracle of childbirth, but frankly it's pretty disgusting and disturbing. With that said, I do think it was a marvel when I first saw Kurt. He looked like a little wonder, to say the least. He had a little pudgy face, little pudgy hands, little pudgy legs....and so on. He was a little porker. When he looked at me, our eyes locked; I couldn't believe I had created this little, chunky guy! The look in his eyes was of pure amazement. I felt like he was thinking something like 'holy moly I'm here all of a sudden.' Jessica said, "Say hello to daddy," and even let me hold him although I was afraid I'd break him somehow! He was so tiny. He fell asleep in my arms.

The next few years were filled with typical new parent issues, as well as professional success in both Jessica's industry and my own. Jessica was promoted. She had a team working for her. I left Whigham and Fosworth to embark upon my own law business. It expanded until I had a whole office staff. My work hours increased, and so did Jessica's. As this happened, we both started to feel tremendous stress. In spite of the hardships, we were blessed with material success. My son was healthy, my wife was still beautiful and nurturing, our jobs and family were great. I felt on top of the world. For the first time, I finally felt like I was winning at the game of life.

Our combined success brought extravagant wealth to our fingertips. We could afford just about anything we wanted, even with a young son to care for.

We paid off the condo then tried to be prudent. We only made small purchases to improve our quality of living. Yet, as many people who've experienced it will attest, with more wealth comes more stuff. In turn, all of these objects and bills precipitated a need for more wealth, and so the cycle went.

I was soon purchasing things just because I could: I replaced our old furniture with an attractive new set from Germany. I bought a new, 55", 3D TV, and the latest stereo equipment, complete with surround-sound. I bought several European paintings at auction, to decorate our condo. Jessica enhanced her wardrobe and accrued more jewelry than she knew what to do with. She acquired about as many pairs of shoes, too. Kurt was also showered with gifts. He received all the newest toys and electronic games. My wallet continued to grow. So did my family's desires.

I opened my 3rd office shortly thereafter, and Jessica received a substantial promotion. We decided to buy a nice, new house that befit our status. We were, after all, becoming socially elite. We agreed that a contemporary home on the beach, with an oceanfront view, would be more suitable.

Our new mansion had an indoor pool, greenhouse, solarium, and even a movie-theater. It had so many rooms that we didn't know what to do with them all...at first. Eventually, it was decided that one would be a playroom to hold Kurt's stuff; it would provide a place for Kurt to spend time with friends, where he'd be out of the way, and wouldn't destroy the rest of the house. Another room was turned into an exercise gym. Jessica used it to help keep her ass looking great.

As an excuse to show off the house to friends, I decided to collect rare (or expensive) firearms. My plan was to convert another, extra room into a veritable museum. Jessica wasn't too keen on this idea when I first mentioned my plan. She took some convincing. I had to assure my wife that all my guns would be safely locked inside of display cases and would remain unloaded. She was still hesitant, so I promised I wouldn't buy any ammo for them. I let her know that the only ammo I would purchase would be for the few guns I took out hunting. Those guns were kept locked away in a safe, up in our attic. She finally gave me consent for my gun museum. I was ecstatic.

I filled my showroom with rifles and muskets from the civil war, various firearms from both world wars, and some additional firearms from the fifteenth century. These pieces were splendid, but I wanted to really show off my prestige, and in my mind, that required some really big, badass guns.

The first was a 1901, .30 caliber Gatling gun. It took me forever to locate, and cost a small fortune. My second trophy was a 38", bronze-cannon from Mexico. The cost of shipping alone was staggering. Plus, procuring it involved U.S. Customs, paperwork, a special license, a train, and several other vehicles. Yet together, these two, massive weapons completed my museum.

With my hobby, family, and work to occupy me, my focus turned toward material success. I lost track of my childhood values (though I didn't notice at the time). I began to worry unreasonably about my status in the community, and about how others viewed me (and my wealth). My pride controlled all my choices. I forgot the things my mother had taught me. I stopped going to The Church of Goodwill. I began to neglect my son and my wife. I became a self-made man, or so I thought.

FOUR: THINGS THAT MIGHT FULFILL

During my childhood, I had always believed that money would bring happiness. Were that true, now that I owned a new house and more material possessions then I knew what to do with, I should have been one delightful fellow. I mean, I owned a Mexican Cannon, for God's sake! What could I really be lacking?

The reality was that inwardly, I was a very unhappy person. I was full of discontent, though I was careful to hide it from others. I was trying to fill a spiritual hole inside of me with more physical things. No purchase on Earth could buy me true happiness. I couldn't identify this as an issue at that time, but I now believe that was the crux of my problem.

When my unhappiness reached a climax, I decided that a vacation was in order. I was stressed out from work. So was my wife. Her consistent nagging was really wearing me down. I would really have preferred a vacation where she didn't have to come along, but being married made that a challenge.

As I planned our vacation, I got to thinking about all the priceless art I owned; it adorned my hallways and had been crafted from all around the world. Yet I had never been to many of the places the artwork was from. World travel to exotic locales, I decided, was the ticket to my happiness! I picked Australia as the first place I wanted to visit.

Kurt was ten at the time. He was my spitting image: lean, in average shape, with short, dark hair, and brown eyes. He had Jessica's chin and her cheery personality. He was a genuinely nice kid, but Jessica and I figured he was still too young to bring along on our travels. Plus, we didn't want him to bog us down every step of the way. Another consideration was that we hadn't spent much time to ourselves since his birth. We knew it would be refreshing to get out again, like we had done in high school and college. I contacted my parents. They agreed to let Kurt stay with them in Illinois until we returned from our trip.

Our Australian adventure started with a very, very, very long flight in which I felt the icy grip of insanity drawing ever closer until we finally got off that Goddamned plane in Sydney.

While in Australia, we toured a variety of places along the East coast. They included Sydney and Melbourne. We also enjoyed sailing and scuba diving. We delighted in fine dining at Kings Cross and Newtown. We took a jeep-safari ride to Broken Hill, the gateway to the outback. I saw countless species of exotic birds, and a bunch of other animals that were unique to Australia. I even tried kangaroo pizza. It tasted like chicken.

When this trip concluded, I was filled with a sense of deep gratitude for a number of weeks afterwards. I was happy. I had solved my problems.

The feeling was short lived.

When the gratitude wore off, the same unfathomable sense of utter discontent boiled back up inside of me. Jessica turned into a shrill harpy once more. Kurt was a nuisance. Work was futile and routine.

As I grew more frustrated, I planned another trip. My new goal was Japan. Steeped in ancient tradition and customs, I figured it would be the medicine for the ailments of my displeasure. Plus, Japan had Samurais. Around this time, Jessica's father took ill. She wanted to support him. I almost canceled my trip in order to go with her to North Carolina to see her father. Luckily for me, she knew I was feeling down, and insisted I go enjoy myself.

I was thrilled.

Japan provided a chance to experience a vastly different culture. I indulged in its traditions and did my very best to adapt to them. From eating different foods to relaxing in their soothing hot springs (which acted as communal baths), I think I adapted very well. One day, I watched a Kabuki show where actors wore colorful make-up and danced around on stage. The next, I visited the Otokoyama Sake museum where I learned a lot about the history of sake and the brewing process. The day following my visit to the Sake museum, I was too hung over to do anything. I laid off the sake for the rest of the trip.

When I returned home, my wife was still helping her father. His condition had degraded. Doctors gave him three weeks to live. I didn't even bother to unpack my luggage and immediately left for North Carolina. There, I shuttled Jessica back and forth to the hospital and did what I could to attend to her needs. It was around 4am on one of those mornings when she received a call from a doctor informing her that her father had passed away.

After the memorial service, we returned to Florida. Jessica was grief-stricken for the next several months. It was a trying time for us. I did my best to provide assistance as she went through the grieving process. Mostly, I kept my distance from her. I figured she had to feel whatever she felt and accept the loss in due course. I buried my nose in my work and tried to allow her to grieve. Soon, I reverted to my usual self. By that, I mean I grew more dissatisfied every day with all aspects of my life. I felt it was time for another trip to lift my spirits. Moreover, there was a chance it could help take Jessica's mind off her loss.

When I brought this up to her, she argued every step of the way. She didn't feel up for traveling. Nor did she feel like attending to Kurt in a foreign place. She was still mourning and depressed. I told her not to be such a naysayer and informed her I had already bought the tickets. This resulted in the most hellacious of arguments. Nonetheless, when it blew over, we traveled to Egypt in short order and brought Kurt with us.

There we saw Alexandria, the Apis Bull, and the Catacombs of Kom es-Shouqafa, which were tunneled into the rock around the second century. We saw statues that depicted the Egyptian gods: Horus, Thoth, Anubis, Osiris, Isis, and more. We visited a Roman Theater and then the Anfushi Tombs. Another sight to behold was the Caesareum: it hosted a temple and two columns known as Cleopatra's needles. It is believed to be the site where Cleopatra committed suicide around 30 BC. Ultimately, of course, we visited the greatest attractions in Egypt: the Great Sphinx in Giza, the Valley Temple, and the Great Pyramids.

I returned from Egypt with the same elation as when I'd traveled to Australia and Japan. The trip had been fun and exciting. It was a privilege to see exotic environments.

Upon my return from Egypt, I am confident that most people could have analyzed my life and, had they done so, the vast majority would have opted to swap places with me. After all, my success far surpassed the average person. Many people never even came close to my quality of life. I owned an expensive home with two, luxury cars in the garage. I was popular. I had good friends. I'd earned the respect of my colleagues. I had a wonderful wife, and an adorable son. I lived in what I still consider the greatest country in the world. The ideals of the US helped to provide the basis for my success. I had done everything possible to fulfill my dreams.

Why then, did I remain unhappy? It was utterly baffling that I could have so much, yet feel so bad. There had to be something in life that I was missing. I ransacked my memories to remember the good times, when I'd felt more complete. I found my missing piece through that in-depth analysis of myself.

FIVE: HUMBLED SERVICE

I remembered something my mother said to me shortly after I started my law business. One day, when I wasn't sure if the business would succeed and I had more bills than I could pay, I was feeling really depressed and hopeless. My mother happened to call me that evening. Something she said stuck with me: if I was being greedy, I was doing the work of the devil. Nothing good could come from serving the devil. If I aimed only to please myself, and did not concern myself with the plight of other people, than I would never truly feel peace.

She told me that only through serving God could I be happy and useful in this existence. God was either everything, or God was nothing. There was no in-between, no gray area. She then went on to say that in God's time, this life was but a blink. According to my mom, if I pictured the best this world had to offer, including the combined goodness within every person, it paled in comparison to the glory of God and the eternal life that he offered. She said that if I served God well, with all my heart and mind, and tried to align my will to his, he'd reward me in ways I couldn't begin to comprehend.

That was the answer to my troubling dilemma! It made perfect sense. I had lacked faith since my youth. Worse that that, I'd selfishly served only myself for as far back as I could recollect. The only unselfish thing I had really done over the last few years was to provide an excellent standard of living for my family. I had considered that an obligation.

After all, if a man couldn't provide for his wife and kids, he wasn't fit to have a family. Yet even while I had supplied food and shelter, I had often neglected Kurt. I had regularly dumped him off on babysitters or been too busy to spend quality time with him. Those were moments I could never get back.

Then there was Jessica. I had often ignored her needs. I had considered her an annoyance. She was a pain in my ass rather than a loving, devoted wife. Even during the death of her father, I'd pushed her away to busy myself in my business. I'd gone so far as to force her along to Egypt with me! I was stunned as this revelation hit me. My poor, grieving wife had just wanted to mourn the loss of her father and I could not have cared less! I had been more concerned with my own issues and escaping to Egypt than about helping her through one of the most difficult events that any human can experience!

What a fool I was!

My mind began to open up to the other ways in which I had conducted myself. I began to feel ashamed about much of my behavior. I never gave a second thought to those less fortunate. In that regard, I was a total hypocrite! I'd grown up with next to nothing, and had been called Oscar and stanks, along with a slew of other names. Throughout my whole, adult existence, I had maintained the delusion that if you wanted something, you worked for it. Anyone who wouldn't work to earn their living was merely a leech who benefited off those who did. But I hadn't even done this on my own: I'd received thousands of dollars in financial assistance when I attended Yale to get my degree. Even my business was only a success because of the many, good employees who worked for me; them and the wonderful training/guidance I received from Whigham and Fosworth.

Truly, I realized, that no one can do it all on their own. The sudden remembrance of my mother's words rocked me like the roundhouse kick of a UFC fighter. The concept of serving God and helping others changed my life from then on. I re-devoted my life to God.

Well, until the massacres began. Those weren't any of God's doing (though I did fault him for the reasons behind my actions when I later used religion as a crutch, and as an excuse to commit murder). It wasn't as if I was the first to kill for the sake of religion, far from it. I was well aware of the Spanish inquisition, the Crusades, and modern-day Islamic terrorists. All those people believed they were devout as they dedicated themselves to whichever cause they fought for. All of them have been misled. Regrettably, the scale of their violence was insignificant compared to the death toll I accounted for. I pulled off religious massacres to a degree that had never before been seen.

At the time of this reflection, however, I swore my service to God as if I were a man kneeling before a queen to be knighted. I began what I considered a new life. My leave of absence from the church had been very long. I had totally forgotten Reverend Morokio and the Church of Goodwill. Both had been a critical part of my early married life.

I reestablished myself there for a second time, and didn't miss a single service for over a year. On this go-around, I got involved in their committee meetings. I soon was placed in charge of a youth program. Most of the youth events were locally held at the church. There were many, planned dinners and organized fund-raisers. On occasion, the kids and I would do chores for members in the community who weren't able to do the chores on their own. We cleaned gutters for older couples, or walked the dog of a disabled woman, and things of that nature.

The kids in the group complained frequently. They didn't understand why they had to spend their days off working without pay. I didn't mind their complaints. These innocent children echoed my childhood sentiments. They provided me with the chance to look back upon the days when I had bitched all the way to church in my parents' car. Later on in life, I knew these young kids would appreciate their good works.

For the first time in my life, I gave to others and asked nothing in return. In doing so, I received a complete and meaningful sense of gratitude. My life had purpose. I was genuinely happy, comfortable, and whole.

As a result of my new attitude, I realized it was only right to share my wealth with others. I now sympathized with those who underwent financial hardship instead of condemning them. There had been many occasions when I'd run into a down-and-out person on the street and had hurriedly walked around them. Whenever they had approached me, I'd told them in no uncertain terms to get a job and stop looking for handouts.

Thanks to my new outlook, I found myself walking up to them on purpose to hand them a twenty dollar bill and offer some words of encouragement. Money wouldn't buy happiness, I'd learned that from experience, yet it could help a poor fellow buy a sandwich, or likely a bottle of booze. Either way, these people needed the money more than I did.

Another thing I did to help the community was to volunteer at the local library. I read for an hour each week to a small group of children while we sat in bean-bag chairs. I grew to love each child like my own son, especially poor, little Reginald, who was confined to a wheelchair. To think I'd been so greedy my whole life and had turned a blind eye to such unfortunates! My former mindset sickened me.

One afternoon, when Reginald's parents came up to me and told me their son thought I was one of his favorite people, it brought tears to my eyes. At that moment, I couldn't imagine doing anything different with the life that God had bestowed upon me.

Besides my work with children, I also performed charitable acts at the opposite end of the spectrum. I refer to elderly people and those confined to hospitals with terminal illnesses. Mrs. Winslow was one of these folks. She was a poor widow, in her mid 70's, who lived across town. I made it a point to visit her every other Thursday evening and brought Kurt along. Jessica graciously baked Mrs. Winslow a cake every time I checked in on her. I always allowed Kurt to present the cakes at her doorstep; both of them derived a lot of enjoyment from that. Mrs. Winslow was always delighted to see us. She loved the cakes, but let us know that she was particularly fond of the coconut ones.

Two other senior citizens I frequented were Berma and Claude Miller. This elderly couple owned about a dozen cats, give or take two or three. Kurt couldn't come since he was allergic to cats, but I gave the Miller's his best wishes. Nor could Jessica bake them a cake: Berma could only eat mush. Most of her jaw and her tongue were taken out due to cancer. Moreover, Claude thought frosting was too sweet and it hurt his teeth. I discovered the Miller's liked jigsaw puzzles, though, so I brought them one every week instead of a cake. Sadly, Berma passed away a few months after we met. As a result, Claude lost the heart to do jigsaw puzzles without her. We sent Claude a sympathy card and stopped by a number of times afterwards to see if he needed help with anything. He welcomed our aid, but eventually went to live with his son, who could take better care of him.

In addition to willingly-sacrificing my time as part of my newfound way of life, I began to be more charitable with my money. I looked into various charities to be sure they were valid. Ultimately, I picked three, worthwhile ones that helped the most families. I donated to them on a regular basis. The first was a program that provided toys for children during the Christmas season. Each year in mid-November I sent them a check for four-thousand dollars. In return, I received a letter of thanks that was signed by the heads of the organization. They each blessed my generosity and wished me a happy holiday season.

To most people, a simple, solitary letter wouldn't seem like much of a thank you. I, for one, was glad this organization didn't send a fancy gift to everyone who donated. In my view, such gifts only diverted money away from the people it was intended to help. I was proud that this charity was putting most of my money to work.

The second aid-organization that I assisted on an annual basis dealt with disaster relief. It was established by a southern minister and focused on helping families around the world who had been struck by natural disasters, or so called 'acts of God.' My annual donation of five-thousand dollars covered the cost of blankets, pillows, medical supplies, toiletries, and other basic items.

The final charity I chose to assist was called Love to Laugh: it was designed to help children who had various facial-deformities get reconstructive surgery. By working with Luisa, the kindhearted and cheery woman in charge of the program, I witnessed miracles. Through Love to Laugh, I saw kids who would never have normal lives get a new opportunity. Their before-and-after photographs were astounding! There were cases where the set of pictures didn't even look like the same person!

The best part of this experience was when I met the children in person after their successful surgeries. They approached me smiling from ear to ear, accompanied by their parents. I shared many rounds of hugs with blissful families. These joy-filled embraces were often impossible to come away from without a few tears in my eyes.

I gave three-thousand dollars a year to Love to Laugh and considered every cent worthwhile. Yet, my monetary contributions didn't stop with just those three charities: I sent periodic aid to local schools for new text books, donated to the local library, helped clothe the homeless, paid for needed repairs to The Church of Goodwill, and sent a massive, ten-thousand dollar donation to Dana Farber for cancer research.

All of these endowments were worth it to keep my newfound, emotional balance, and to serve the Lord. It was over the course of seven years that I wrote checks, visited the ill, and performed many, other, kind deeds. I did everything for the glory of God. I truly loved my fellow man. It was the happiest time of my life and I enjoyed every second.

Then, a terrible tragedy struck me.

I came home from a church board-meeting one afternoon while Jessica was getting Kurt at a friend's house. When two hours passed and they hadn't returned home, I began to grow anxious. It was unlike her not to call if she was running late. Even when she got sidetracked with other errands, I usually received at least a quick text message from her.

I tried to put the issue out of my mind as I made myself dinner. Just as I was setting a juicy, 12-oz porterhouse on the table, the phone rang. It was a police officer. He identified himself as Lt. Murphy and asked me for my name. My appetite instantly vanished. I stuttered as I replied.

My answer was followed by an awkward pause. It felt like minutes went by.

Lt. Murphy cleared his throat. He then informed me that he was terribly sorry, but that Jessica and Kurt had been in a gruesome car wreck. A newly licensed driver had lost control of his car, swerved across the median into their lane, and hit them head on. They were both killed upon impact. I was asked to go to the local morgue and please confirm their identities.

SIX: THE TRAGEDY

I prayed to God that this was all a horrible mistake. The accident hadn't involved my family. It was one big mix-up. The drive to the morgue was the longest of my life. One repeating thought went through my head the whole way: this can't be happening, this can't be happening.

I parked in a handicapped spot when I arrived, not really caring or thinking, and rushed into the main lobby. I informed a receptionist who I was, and what Lt. Murphy had told me. She picked up the phone and called for Lt. Murphy. He arrived momentarily. The look on his face was of utter sympathy and sadness. Without much of an introduction or small talk, he led me to the morgue.

After we passed through a pair of steel double-doors, we entered the coldest, most sterile room I think I have ever been in. The floors were lime-green and tiled. Rows of freezers for bodies lined the walls. A bald doctor with a beard and a narrow, pointed nose was standing at a table in the center of the room. Two bodies were on it, covered by a white sheet.

The doctor greeted me briefly. It seemed to me he was as cold and lifeless as the surrounding room. "Please let me know if these are them," is all I remember him saying.

He pulled the sheet back to reveal the faces of the bodies on the table. My worst fears were confirmed. My beloved wife and my son were under that sheet on that steel table, stiff and dead. My knees gave out. I grabbed the table to hold myself up and leaned forward, hugging my dead wife and child, trying to will the life back into them. I wept hysterically. It felt like I was dreaming. I prayed to wake up. This couldn't be happening. This couldn't be happening. There was no car crash. There was no hospital morgue.

I don't really know what happened next. The following hours became a grief-filled haze. I remember waking up the next day, however, and the dream was all too real. My bed was cold and empty. I was alone in my big, fancy house. The day before, in less than an hour, my life had crashed down around me.

I didn't have the strength to shower or put on new clothes. In fact, I noticed as I got out of bed that I was still wearing the clothes from the day before. I stumbled out into the hallway. My footsteps echoed noisily. The house felt so very lonely. When I made it to Kurt's room, I looked at his bed. Then, I looked up at all the posters on his walls. They were of various rock-bands. I fell to my knees, buried my head in the carpet, and sobbed.

It took a while for me to get somewhat composed. Prior to heading downstairs, I went into the bathroom to blow my nose. Next, I trudged down the stairs in my slippers. The little, red light on the answering machine was blinking; no doubt messages from concerned friends and relatives. I didn't have the heart to listen to them. I went straight to my liquor cabinet. My only thought was to get completely, insanely, rip-roaring, shit-faced drunk and forget everything.

I poured myself a glass of top-shelf vodka then added a splash of Coke for color. My last memory of that day is drinking that glass down in about three gulps.

I woke up on the floor of my solarium the next day. It was almost noon. There were more messages on the answering machine. Perhaps a day or two later, as I tried to function as a person, I listened to them half-heartedly. I mostly just hit delete as each well-wisher, sympathizer, or prayer-giver came on. I went through the motions of planning Kurt and Jessica's funeral and wake while still in a state of mental disbelief. Their funerals came and went, and I honestly couldn't say if they happened a week or a month after the accident. I lost the ability to feel. I was so numb that somebody could've used me for a pincushion, or a voodoo doll, and I don't think I would have noticed.

Over the next few weeks, I mindlessly completed whatever chores I needed to attend to. Business didn't seem important. Serving God didn't seem important. Life didn't even seem important. I was unable to accept the circumstance of my life and I grew incredibly angry with God. The same spiteful questions ran through my head over and over, in one form or another:

How could this happen to me?

Why did this tragedy befall the most loving, compassionate and caring woman I'd ever known?

Why was my innocent, little-boy violently taken from this world?

What had I done to deserve this?

What had my wife and child done to deserve this?

I began to curse God in fits of rage. Each day instead of saying 'thank you God for all your blessings,' I began to say 'fuck you God for being such a malicious son of a bitch.' I usually followed these so-called prayers with mocking and cynicism.

I was blanketed in rage and shrouded in grief. It got to the point where I had to force myself to get out of bed in the morning. It became an effort to simply get dressed. The only time I had any peace of mind was when I was asleep. I woke up every day, and turned my head to look at my wife, only to find the empty spot where she used to lie. The memory that she was no longer with me burned in my head like a tumor. I sullenly sauntered around the house, barely able to function. Every time I looked at anything, I'd somehow relate it to my wife or son, and curse God all anew. Things continued like that for months. Each passing day drove me further into depression.

It was on one of those bleak, despondent days I made the most difficult decision I had ever been faced with. I made the one choice that would forever change me. I couldn't go on living this way, so I decided to not go on living. I made the selfish choice to take my life.

Under normal conditions, the human mind and body are astonishing creations, which can recover from countless forms of abuse. The cells of our bodies can die or be damaged, but will regenerate over time, and are replaced with new ones. Even with serious abuse, the body can recover from grave injuries. In rare circumstances, I've heard of people who were declared medically dead but were resuscitated through nothing short of a miracle.

The human mind, likewise, can contend with a great deal of traumatic memories. Some people are bullied in school (like I was). Others are sexually abused. Some people put up with the rigors of war, either as a combatant or an innocent victim. Nearly everyone lives through the deaths of loved ones. How each person responds to mental trauma really depends upon the individual. Some people deal with their problems. Others run from them. Sometimes people try to file their problems away to the dark recesses of their mind to be dealt with at a later date. They purposefully forget. Often the mind can be damaged beyond repair and psychiatric disorders develop.

I'd heard over the years that suicide is a permanent solution to a temporary problem; a psychiatric disorder of sorts. Yet I was caught in the midst of my torment like a slave in a lion pit. I forgot about the business partners and employees who depended upon me. I forgot the organizations that used my monetary donations to help make the world a better place. I forgot the friends who'd stood by me through my triumphs and tribulations. Worst of all, I forgot the rest of my family members who genuinely loved me.

What I focused on was my own funeral. I wondered what it would be like. What would people say about me? Who would show up? I had been to three funerals of people who had committed suicide. Based upon my observances, the reaction from people who attended was either of anger such as, "Why the hell did he throw his life away?" or shock such as, "I can't believe he could have done that! I never would have thought he was that troubled. Why didn't he come to me for help?"

For some reason, people feel like they should all be the solitary-individual whom the deceased guy or gal in the coffin should have confided in. Many people assume the person's suicide was an issue of just talking out their problems, or seeking professional help. What they always forget when forming these well-intentioned rationales, is that perhaps the person in the coffin didn't want their help, or anyone else's. Maybe the deceased physically COULD NOT ask for help. Maybe they had too much pride to admit any weakness, especially given the 'do it yourself' mentality that is woven throughout mainstream society. This mentality is so often used to backup the illusion that 'everything is okay,' because God forbid it isn't, or you become a pariah.

I don't know which category, if any, of these things I fell into. I just know that I was spent as surely as the last staple in the stapler and I could do no more. I pictured Mr. Whighham at my funeral. He would likely shake his head in disbelief. He was far too proud a man to cry openly, but I knew he'd nonetheless be torn apart. He'd cry when no one was around. I suspected he would be morose for weeks and maybe months. I imagined him saying something along the lines of, "What a great guy he was, one of the best I ever met." I pictured him pounding on a table with his fist and shouting, "Damn it all! Such a waste. Son of a bitch!"

Next, I pictured Mr. Fosworth. He wasn't as proud as Whighham and would cry openly, but not to excess. He had been practicing law for so long that he had seen terrible tragedies and was thus a bit more repressed. As the few tears he shed rolled down his cheeks, he would dab them away with the red hanker-chief he always carried in his back-pocket. "How could he go and do that?" He would say, "He had it all. The man was brilliant, absolutely brilliant. He was the best damn lawyer I'd ever seen. God knows we'll miss you, you foolish bastard."

My next days were reserved for morbid reflections about my life. At the end of them, I drew the conclusion that it didn't matter whether I lived or died. I reasoned that everyone would be better off without me. After all, I wasn't helping my business anymore. I hardly showed up for work and often shirked my responsibilities. When I did show up, I couldn't concentrate on what I was doing. I often misplaced folders or copied inaccurate information. My clients no longer mattered to me. Due to my negligence, I lost several cases that I could have won, and did a number of clients more harm than good. I was on my way to becoming a washed-up has-been. Perhaps most tragic of all was that none of it mattered to me.

I spent a lot of this time thinking about the good deeds I'd done for people over the years. I recalled the youth-group kids from The Church of Goodwill, Reginald in his wheelchair, Mrs. Winslow, Berma and

Claude Miller, the families from Love to Laugh, and countless others. All of those people, baring Berma Miller who passed, would surely miss me. Nonetheless, I reasoned that someone else could always come along and take my place. There had to be plenty of people in the world who could do the good work of the church. If anything, I carried more than my share of the weight. It was other people's turn to make sacrifices. After all, the church would get along fine without me. It had been around for thousands of years before I came around. And besides, all my efforts had been rewarded with pain.

The desire to end my life ruled me like the dictator of a third-world country. I knew that if I was to follow through with it, I had to make sure I did it right the first time. I racked my brain as thoroughly as an IRS agent performing an audit. Planning suicide was more complicated then I thought. Important questions popped into my head.

The first of these was "what should I wear?" I knew there was a certain shame associated with killing oneself, especially in America. I wanted to maintain as much of my dignity as I could, given the circumstances. Had I lived in Japan, where they viewed suicide differently, there would have been a lot less shame associated to it. Yet I wasn't about to move halfway around the world now. While debating my final wardrobe, I first ruled out certain items: I wore a three-piece suit to work everyday. Therefore, I certainly didn't want to spend my last breath in one. I also ruled out a tie because I was sick of them. Shorts were out, as were any shirts with a zipper. My definitive option was a nicely-pressed pair of grey khaki's along with a dark-green, collared-sweater, a maroon vest with a breast-pocket, black socks, and black dress-shoes. The outfit was elegant enough that I figured I would make a presentable corpse.

The second question that I addressed was whether or not I should leave a note, and if so, what to say in one. I didn't want to write a standard, "goodbye world, I'm sorry, poor me," type of bullshit explanatory speech. Nor was I a discourteous bastard who would punch my ticket without so much as an explanation. I had to write a note. I owed the survivors that (I began to view my remaining friends and family as survivors, for some reason).

I sat down at my kitchen table and grabbed a pen and a spiral-notebook. My first attempt at a suicide note read like this: "To whom it may concern."

I threw that out because I didn't think it fit. It was much too informal.

I changed the intro to read, "Dear friends," but I didn't really care for that, either. I tried a few more headings, but couldn't come up with something I felt was appropriate. I opted to leave out the introduction and started to write the body. When complete, my letter read as follows:

This must come as a shock to you all. I bet you feel very cheated. I feel the same way, and I think with good cause. I ask you not to get too upset and will offer some reasons. The main one is that I have achieved a lot in the time I was given. I have tried my best to do something positive for society. I hope I have succeeded. There is nothing more in life I could have asked for. All my dreams have been fulfilled. I thank everyone who helped make this journey so interesting. Tragically, without my beloved Jessica and my beautiful boy Kurt, I am lost. They were my essence. Without their support and love I have lost interest in other things. I no longer possess the passion I once felt for life. I feel I have become a burden to all those I encounter. So without taking up more of anyone's valuable time, I wish you all happiness, prosperity and good health. There is nothing left for me in this world anymore, so I do not wish to remain a part of it. I am very sorry for all of you who may grieve me, but know in your hearts I shall always be with you.

I signed the letter and tucked it, along with my pen, into the breast-pocket of my vest. I knew the letter would be easily found there. Now, what about the method? What was the quickest way to end my life? I'd heard awful stories about people who attempted suicide and failed.

One acquaintance of mine, who was the brother of a friend, tried to put his mouth on the exhaust pipe of a car to inhale the fumes. He burned his mouth very badly and was rushed to the hospital. He had to eat using a straw for two weeks as he'd sat in a psychiatric ward. Another person I read about in the newspaper was paralyzed when they jumped out of a window. They too ended up in a locked ward.

If my attempt failed I would share that fate and my reputation as a good lawyer would be tarnished (I never considered that if I killed myself, my reputation would be tarnished regardless). I had to take my life on the first try, with as little pain as possible; I was never one to stomach pain well.

I ruled out death by hanging. I also ruled out drowning. Why anyone would drown themselves when other methods were available was beyond me, yet the thought entered my head, nonetheless. I figured I could drive my car into a river. I supposed that would do the trick. But, then it occurred to me that I might deter firemen (and other authorities) from a real emergency. Also, I figured once my car started to fill with water, I'd panic and come up for air.

Shooting myself was the least painful and definitive way to take my life. It made the most sense. I hardly mulled that thought over for long. With my choice made, I got up from the kitchen table and went up to the attic where I stored my guns.

I remember climbing the narrow stairs and flicking on the light. The familiar, musky attic smell filled my nostrils. The attic hadn't been cleaned since Jessica and I had first moved in. On the far side of the room was a very narrow, grimy window. It barely let in any light. A pile of old, cardboard boxes to my left contained the most random junk imaginable: Christmas decorations, skiing equipment that was useless in Florida and hadn't been touched for years, assorted lawn ornaments (which included gnomes of various sizes), Kurt's baby clothes, and old Halloween costumes.

The right side of the attic was lined with furniture and other important keepsakes. Closest to the stairs was a large, black trunk with a brass latch. It was full of things my mother had given me when my grandmother had passed away; I'd still been in high school at the time. Next to that trunk was a faded, yellow bureau with a mirror and three drawers. The bureau had once been white but time had gotten the best of it. Further down, there was a child's oak desk with an attached chair. It had belonged to me as a kid.

That desk was placed next to a newer, maple table. It was our original kitchen table from the condo Jessica and I had first purchased when we moved to Fort Lauderdale. We had planned to save it for when Kurt eventually moved out. I wondered where it would end up after my death. Perhaps another kid would get it and put it to good use. As an afterthought, I realized I had neglected to write a will! What kind of sad excuse for a lawyer was I?

I retrieved my suicide-note and the pen from my vest pocket. Writing on the dusty, wooden boards of the attic, I scrawled a few lines on the bottom of the paper. I gave all of my possessions to the Church of Goodwill, to allocate as Reverend Morokio saw fit. This was, as I saw it, my final, charitable act. I had helped the community even as I prepared to die. My possessions would serve a number of good purposes. I further hoped this good deed would take some sting out of my death. I returned the note and pen back to my vest pocket as I stood up.

I grumbled as I dusted my knees off, annoyed that I had sullied my death-outfit. I then looked beyond the kitchen table at an old, torn mattress. Springs were bursting out of it as if it were a sea-urchin that had gone into defensive mode. The mattress was only there to conceal my gun safe from Kurt, because Jessica worried he'd get a hold of my guns by accident. The likelihood of that had been slim, but having an only child had made both of us cautious to the point of absurdity. A more logical reason why I concealed the safe from Kurt was that it held a number of other, assorted valuables. Kurt was a good kid and I didn't expect he would try to take anything. Rather, I worried he would talk about the safe to the kids at school, and that one of them might try to break in.

I pulled the old mattress forward and pushed in to the floor. That stirred up a layer of dust. I sneezed a few times, then grasped the round dial of the safe. Years earlier, I had memorized the safe combination in case I had to access it in a hurry. Two turns to the right, 31. Three turns left, 22. One turn right, 44. I cranked the safe's wheel to the right and heard the bolts inside slide open.

I pulled the heavy safe door open wide. Inside it, I first saw two, twelve-gauge shotguns. They were fitted into specific, vertical slots on the right side of the safe. I didn't want to kill myself with those: they'd leave a terrible mess everywhere. In addition, I wanted my teeth intact in the event that someone needed dental records to ID my body.

My three rifles were next to the shotguns. The one furthest to the left was a Browning A-Bolt rifle. It had a walnut stock, a rosewood grip, and fired .243 Winchester rounds that were fed through a detachable magazine. I bought it for quick loading. Next to that, was my Ruger M77 Mark II Compact Bolt Action Rifle. It was my first hunting rifle. The stock was American Walnut. Although accurate, it held only four .308 rounds. My third rifle was a Remington Model 700 LSS that fired .260 ammo. The Remington had a stainless-steel barrel with a gray-colored stock to match. It was a superbly accurate rifle, and quite resistant to the elements. I knew the church would fetch a good amount of money just for selling these guns.

Below the rifle, there were two shelves. My handguns rested on the top one. I owned a Smith & Wesson .38 special, a heavy Ruger Redhawk Double Action Revolver, a Smith & Wesson .22 Magnum Revolver with a black finish, and an 1851 Colt "Navy" Revolver that used black powder. The Colt Revolver was handed down to me by my grandfather. It was silver, with a white handle, and looked similar to the guns George Patton once carried. Inscribed on each side of the barrel was my grandfather's name: *Howard*. It was a family heirloom, which is why I kept it in the safe and not with my collection downstairs. I had hoped to one day pass it on to Kurt.

Below the shelf with the handguns was a shelf that held a simple, wooden box full of bank bonds. Kurt's grandparents had bought them for him when he was born. Jessica and I had stored them away ever since. We figured they would make a good start to a college fund.

Other items in the safe were old photographs of my parents, a gold ring that had belonged to Jessica's great-grandmother, the pearl necklace that Jessica had worn on our wedding day, and a marble that Jessica's father had always carried with him. I had learned that he carried the marble because one of his friends had told him that he'd lose all his marbles after having kids. Well, when he learned that Jessica's mom was pregnant with her, he went to a local store and purchased a bag of marbles. He kept a bluish one that resembled the color of Jessica's mother's eyes. He'd kept it with him so he'd always been able to claim he still had one of his marbles left.

I stared at those sentimental items as I sat on the floor. Overcome with grief, I cried with my head in my hands as I thought of my wife and son. Their bitter loss was more than I could stand. I thought about how many memories were tucked away in this attic as I gazed around the room. Surrounded by memories and items that tied my life together, I realized my attic was a fitting place for my life to end.

I hadn't given the location of my final moments much thought until now. There were undoubtedly nicer places with better views I could have picked. There were even nicer rooms just downstairs. Yet the attic was really the one place in my house that connected the many aspects of my life. Besides, I certainly wasn't about to blow my brains out on some beautiful beach where someone's kid might see it.

When I was finally able to lift my head up, I reached into the safe and pulled out the Ruger Redhawk. The cold steel sent chills down my spine. The handgun felt dirty, in a metaphysical sense. My hand trembled as I reached into the bottom of the safe where the boxes of ammo were organized by caliber. I shook badly as I opened the .44 ammo. Fumbling as I attempted to load the gun, I dropped several of the rounds. They hit the old, wide-pine boards with a resounding echo in the nearly-empty attic. I heard them roll away while I continued to load other rounds in the Ruger. After I closed the cylinder, I gave it a little wiggle to make sure it was properly lined up with the barrel.

I rose from a sitting position to a kneeling one. My shaking intensified as I raised the barrel up to my head. A few drops of sweat ran down the side of my face. I pressed the cold end of the barrel against my temple. The Ruger felt so heavy in my hand.

"Why have you done this to me?" I asked God in between uncontrollable sobs. By now, mucus was running out of my nose. I wiped my face with my other sleeve. The Ruger was still pressed against my temple. I thought about my terrible predicament. It was cruel and unjust. I debated if I really should end it all in one final blaze. Was it right to just end my pain and be done with my life? What more did I really have to live for? I had been kind enough to everyone during my life to more than account for this one, heinous act. I hoped God would forgive me. Deep down, I don't think I necessarily wanted to die; I just saw no other way out of my pain.

Without further hesitation, I pulled the trigger.

SEVEN: WHAT LIES BEYOND

I couldn't be dead, right? What about the whole genocide thing? What of the billions of lives I said I snuffed out? What about the burning cities and mounds of the dead that were all killed on my command? I did say I pulled the trigger. Maybe the gun misfired.

A logical assumption, but incorrect. I had done it: I shot myself in the head, point-blank, with a .44 Ruger Redhawk. Life truly had become too much to bear following the death of my beloved wife Jessica and son Kurt. So how did I survive? Well, this is where things get very interesting. What now follows is as highly detailed a memoir as I can put together. Granted, I probably got some names wrong. Likewise, most of the conversations aren't word for word. My account is undoubtedly filled with errors and omissions. It's also probably safe to say I left out some sections of my life. I'm not entirely at fault for all these things. There are periods before, during, and after the genocide where events and people get a bit hazy at times, with good cause. I'm also documenting what happened long after the facts.

Here is what happened when I pulled the trigger: there was nothing but an empty void that overcame all senses. Everything went dark for an unknown length of time. I'm not just talking moonless night dark, or close your eyes dark. I'm talking the abyss of the dead dark, or bottom of the sea dark. I can't say how long that lasted. Perhaps it was seconds.

That empty void of darkness was followed by an intense white light.

It broke through the blackness and permeated every sense of my being. It filled me with peace. As the light faded, I saw my body. What was left of my mortal remains were sprawled across the floor of my attic, next to the old mattress. Blood poured out of the massive head wound I'd created. Not that much was really left of my head. The top of my skull was blown entirely apart. My blood was spreading rapidly. It was starting to form a large pool that was soaking into the side of the mattress. More blood, brain matter, and bits of skull speckled the walls and ceiling. The sight of my crumpled body with its half-missing head sickened me to the core. I was overcome with grief and regret.

Then, it hit me.

I refer to the realization that I was dead, but there was some sort of consciousness that remained. There indeed was some form of life after death! I could not reverse my decision, but I had retained all my memories and could still produce rational thoughts. The knowledge of my former life was still with me. It was as if I were alive, yet without a body! I supposed I was some sort of invisible ghost, able to observe the world, yet not able to interact with it. I tried to get closer to my old body, but I couldn't control my movements.

I then realized that my consciousness (for lack of a better term) was gradually being pulled upward, into the sky. My vision turned black once again, and disoriented me for a second before it returned to give me a view of the area between my attic ceiling and my roof. I saw a vent made from PVC for a brief second before a piece of insulation turned everything pink. When my consciousness entered the insulation, I was filled with a soft, cozy feeling but also itchiness, as if I was really touching it. The pink was replaced by more black followed by a variety of blurred colors and interesting sensations.

The colors momentarily came into focus. I was looking down on my house. From the outside, it appeared perfectly normal. Chances were pretty good that my neighbors didn't yet know of my grisly death. I alone knew of the gruesome scene in the attic which was hidden from the outside world by the walls I looked down upon. I knew my body would be discovered eventually, but wondered how long that would take. Would it be days or weeks? When I was discovered, I wondered about the stir it would create throughout the community. I hoped rats and bugs didn't eat me all up in the meantime. It would be gross if my old body was all filled with worms.

As I drew further away from my house, the homes of my neighbors came into view. Some of my neighbors were in their yards, watering the lawn or picking oranges. None of them seemed alarmed. Perhaps they hadn't heard the gunshot. Then again, my yard was pretty big. Or maybe if they had heard the gunshot, they weren't sure what it was. The thought occurred to me that I never really took the opportunity to get to know my neighbors. I'd lived next to them for years, but I was always working, traveling, or spending time with various charities. It would have been nice to have gotten to know them.

My consciousness was climbing in altitude. I could see around the block. There was a police cruiser speeding in the direction of my house with its siren on. If it were, in fact, heading for my house, I estimated that the officer would arrive in the next three minutes. I hoped he or she had prepared themselves for what they'd come across. I felt a tinge of pity flow through me as I thought about how tough a police offer's job must be in moments like those. I had no reason to doubt they encountered tragedies like mine on a regular basis. I hoped the officer who discovered my body wouldn't need therapy for the rest of his or her life because of my actions. Chances were, they'd have nightmares for a while. With any luck they wouldn't suffer from long-term effects.

My progression upward began to accelerate. Within seconds, I could see all of Fort Lauderdale and its surrounding towns. In another half a minute, I was treated to a spectacular view of the entire eastern half of the United States. I was miles above the Earth. Next, I saw the entire continent as I floated higher. I only had a moment to enjoy the view. Everything went blurry once more as I reached the outskirts of Earth's atmosphere. The whole universe seemed to collapse in on itself as it rushed towards me with unimaginable velocity. As this occurred, the intense, white light returned. I lost all sense of time or space. It was like I was drifting in a cloud with no worries in the world.

A black spot then appeared in the center of all that white. It gradually expanded into a circle as I drifted toward it. Was it a black hole? No, as I got closer, I then realized it was a tunnel. Its walls pulsed with a plethora of changing colors. The colors rotated clockwise inside of the tunnel walls. I serenely floated through the center of the hypnotic, flashing tunnel. I couldn't tell if it was rotating around me or if I was spinning. It felt a lot like an amusement park ride, but without all the dizziness, vomiting, and inevitable crying, little kids.

As I was drawn further into the tunnel, the flashing colors in the walls began to take on purpose. They merged together like cells joining on a molecular level. They then formed what I can only describe as movie screens which displayed short episodes from my life. I saw myself parting ways with my friend Tommy, my fight with Monroe, my first meeting with Jessica, and my graduation party. There were also viewings of my wedding day, moments of passionate love making, Kurt's birth, and my most pleasant memories from the many trips I had taken. The final clips were the terrible scene at the morgue, Kurt and Jessica's funeral, and then my own suicide. Each played with full audio! The sound was better than even my home-theater. Another discovery even more amazing was that every physical sense I'd experienced in life (during those times) came rushing back to me! It was a wave of senses and emotions that sometimes blurred together and felt exhilarating but also very overwhelming.

As the clips ended, the little movie-screen things faded into the background of the tunnel, which continued its random color patterns. I emerged through the other end of the tunnel as the last screen disappeared.

Searing white light and a sense of overall peace once more surrounded me. The light vanished as quickly as it had appeared. A solitary object became visible in a sea of white. It was a giant, golden platform that looked about half a mile away and about as far below me.

The platform was a perfect square that floated in emptiness. It was maybe a mile in diameter but only a few feet thick. A magnificent catwalk began at the far end of the platform and extended into the distance as far as I could see. The catwalk was of equal thickness to the platform, and looked to be about ten feet wide. The catwalk made me think of a vast variety of board games. I say that because it appeared two-dimensional and turned at 90 degree angles every so often (though its path looked random). I imagined the giant hand of God moving game pieces along it and chuckled. Then, I wondered if I was one of the pieces, and suddenly it didn't seem so amusing. What was to become of me now?

I floated down to the platform and its connected catwalk. As this happened, I immediately become aware of a change in my physical state.

Until now, I had only been able to perceive what was going on around me. I began to feel as if I had pins and needles all over. A body (I wasn't sure if it was my original one or a different one) become ever-so transparent around me. My consciousness was being injected into a body! Or at least that's what how I would describe it.

I first noticed my fingers and hands outlined in a faint, blue glow. After that, my entire outline appeared. The glow began to dissipate as color returned to me. As near as I could tell, I was back in the same body I'd had while on Earth! I flexed my fingers for what felt like the first time in decades. I was now able to control my movements. I had form.

Of equal curiosity was the fact that clothes mysteriously appeared on me. I suddenly looked down, and WHAM, to my amazement, I was wearing a plain, white t-shirt. I also had white khaki pants, a white belt with a square, golden buckle, and, to go along with that motif, comfortable, white slippers. No socks though. And I wasn't sure about the underwear situation. In any event, I never dressed that way on Earth but I was grateful I didn't have to roam an unfamiliar afterlife in the nude.

With both my feet planted solidly on the golden platform, I glanced behind to get a look at the vortex from which I'd emerged. It seemed miles away. I was shocked to see other people floating out of the vortex toward me. Just like I had done a moment before, they started off as transparent outlines that glowed with faint, blue light. Within thirty seconds they became more opaque and were fully colorized by the sixty second mark.

Some of these developing people only appeared as parts until they had completely materialized. It was totally bizarre to see the upper section of a torso, or just a head with shoulders floating through space.

Something I found equally bizarre, was that when each person finally, fully materialized, no one had any facial features! Instead of faces, everyone just had the pinkish outline of a face. It was as if they were all wearing a stocking over their heads. I wondered if I looked the same. I could only assume that I did. Likewise, I wondered how I was able to see without eyes. I had to file that one away as an anomaly of the afterlife.

I turned around and noticed four people ahead of me: three men and one woman. The men wore identical clothing. The woman's clothing was nearly identical. The only difference was that instead of khakis, she had a white skirt that went to about her knees. These four headed across the platform toward the catwalk. I had no idea where they were going, or if they knew what they were doing, but I felt it would be best to have some company. After all, I wasn't sure whether I was in Heaven, Hell, or some alternate dimension of existence. For all I knew, I was waiting to be regurgitated back to Earth as a lima bean or some weird shit like that.

I was anxious to talk with someone else. I hurried in the direction of the blank-faced people. To my surprise, my footsteps made no sound against the smooth, golden floor. I paused to adjust to this oddity and tapped my foot a few times to make sure I was still sane. I felt my foot strike a solid surface but it was like being stuck in a silent movie.

I was unnerved but undaunted. Twenty silent steps later, I reached the small group.

"Excuse me, do you know what's happening?" I tried to ask this simple question. There was a problem: I discovered I lacked a mouth! Consequently, this made speech impossible.

The woman in the group looked my way, shrugged helplessly, and pointed in the direction of the catwalk. It was evident she was going to follow it to wherever it led.

In the direction she pointed, I then noticed a giant, muscled figure. I knew I was crazy now because he wasn't there a moment before. He blocked the entrance to the catwalk, which was consequently, my exit. The large figure wore Romanesque-style armor with a centurion type helmet. Both were of solid gold, like the catwalk and platform. In massive hands the size of catcher's mitts, he wielded a vicious looking spear that was at least three feet taller than he was. The figure looked like he'd been chiseled out of stone, like a surreal Calvin Klein underwear model.

I wanted to turn around and run but another person came from behind and gently urged me forward. I had no choice but to press on, which was okay because there wasn't anywhere else I could run to.

The eyes of the roman-looking figure were intense, bright-red, and they glowed at me from under his helmet like the fire of two lanterns. They reminded me of the eyes of The Terminator, though these were worse: they seemed alive with fire and felt like they burned into my soul. I shuddered. I wished his face were blank like everyone else's.

The people in front of me reached the entrance to the catwalk and stopped near the figure. He remained motionless as he stared off into space. I noted that he hadn't made an effort to kill anyone just yet. That was a good thing. Although, if he decided to do so, I wasn't sure our whole group together could stop him.

I took a deep breath and decided it was safe to move closer, though I prudently positioned myself behind the other, four people; I was brave but not stupid. No one attempted to pass by the gladiator and it was clear he wasn't going to budge. We stood there in absolute silence as more people emerged from the vortex and filled up the platform. It became so crowded that there was hardly room to move. It reminded me of a concert, a veritable sea of people. And we all looked alike.

When there was no more room for anyone, I watched as the swirling vortex closed in on itself. This interrupted the total silence. It was like a thousand freight trains. The platform shook from the vibrations of the collapsing vortex. An ethereal wind tore at me. I was quite glad I wasn't near the platform's edge because the wind easily could have pulled me off. I didn't know what would happen if I fell and had no desire to find out.

The rumbling and wind both stopped at once. The giant figure then spoke, "Proceed down the skywalk one at a time." His voice was like a thunderclap. It shook the platform and commanded absolute obedience. Reacting as one entity, the crowd moved forward like a herd of cattle being ushered out of a pen. I fell in line behind the four people that were in front of me.

Our procession of featureless people marched down the meandering sky-walk. We eventually formed a line that stretched for miles. We reminded me of a trail of ants that I had seen when I foolishly left the sugar-bowl uncovered one summer. Onward we walked until the platform was no longer visible behind us. Ahead, there was nothing but the golden skywalk and an expanse of white. Time felt like it stood still in this place. Perhaps we were outside the realm of time.

My new body never tired during this trek. Not a single muscle ache or cramp did I feel. In fact, I'd felt no pain or physical discomfort (other than the pins and needles) ever since I'd been granted this new body. Even the old aches and pains which usually plagued me were gone. Could it be that I would never again struggle to put on a pair of socks for fear of blowing out my back? I could only hope! This lifted my spirits.

I then caught a glimpse of something that filled me with jubilation. It was a massive, golden archway that was supported by two, spiraled columns that shimmered with brilliance. Could it lead into Heaven? If so, another giant figure waited for us at the base of the archway. He was identical to the prior gladiator, but held no weapon. Now, I only had to fear being pummeled or ripped into pieces; though I reasoned that if I were assaulted, maybe it wouldn't hurt?

The figure waved for the leader of our line (who was only six or seven people ahead of me) to pass. Whoever the guy at the front of the line was, he went forward and disappeared into a silver fog that enveloped everything just beyond the golden archway.

As for the Roman beef-cake, he raised a meaty palm and ordered everyone else to stop. Our movement came to an abrupt halt. Several minutes ticked by before the figure motioned for the next person to go through the archway.

The third person was allowed to pass him soon after, then the fourth. I trembled with apprehension as my turn drew near. I still wasn't sure whether I was in Heaven, Hell, or maybe Narnia for all I knew. I was afraid I would enter that silver, mysterious fog and be lost in it forever.

The fellow in front of me was motioned in. I fidgeted nervously. The fog was so close I could almost reach out and touch it. The gladiator signaled that it was my turn. I went under the archway and into the fog with carefully measured steps. I mentally steeled myself for the worst. Maybe I would vaporize.

Instead, my body filled with ecstasy. The silver fog was pure bliss! Every one of my nerves felt like it was having an orgasm! I wanted to stay in here forever but was either being pushed or pulled onward by an unseen force.

Once through the fog, I saw the most elegant gate ever imaginable. It was easily over a hundred feet high and decorated with fancy scrollwork of flowers, vines, and little cherubs. The beauty of this gate surpassed even the one I had seen at the royal palace in Versailles. In fact, I dare say that this gate totally trumped Versailles! Prior to setting my eyes upon this masterpiece, I would not have thought such a thing was possible (the French really know how to design a palace). In addition to being made of gold and elegantly crafted, these gates had one, specific enhancement that Versailles also lacked: in what I considered almost cheating, they actually glowed with golden, vibrant light!

As if that weren't embellishment enough, I heard heartfelt laughter and delightful music emanate from the other side of the gate. The aroma from a variety of fresh baked goods also wafted past. If I had a mouth, it would have started to water. I smelled cakes, brownies, cinnamon, and more. As I continued to stare at the gate, the two most beautiful women I'd ever seen strolled past. Both were naked and holding hands! One of them looked my way and giggled then teasingly blew me a kiss. Her friend giggled as well and gave the first girl a playful tap on her firm, perfect bum. They both skipped off together.

This was the entrance to Heaven. There could be no doubt. Again, if I'd had a mouth, I would have smiled from ear to ear.

As I stared dumbfounded where the girls had just pranced by, I heard someone clear their throat. Shaking my head, I realized there was a stern-looking, old man standing right in front of me. The man had a pointy nose and tufts of white hair that sprouted out from his ears. He wore a crimson robe that had golden trim on the sleeves and neck. There was a golden pedestal positioned directly in front of him, and his head barely came over the top of it. Small of stature though he was, he had the air of authority about him. He looked to be some sort of sage.

"You are now granted speech," the sage explained. "You will need it to explain some of your deeds and perhaps ask forgiveness for them."

I reached up to my face, and now felt a mouth. I also felt eyes and a nose. I had a whole face! It was unnerving to experience such rapid alteration, but also pleasant to feel normal again. I decided to test my new mouth, "Thank you," I replied simply.

The sage nodded then pulled out a large scroll. He unrolled a portion of it. In a monotone, nasally voice he then told me, "This is the book of life. The Lord knows your works. He knows the actions you performed in his name. If one lives, one lives for the Lord. If one dies, one dies for the Lord, as it is written. No one passes through this gate except for those whose names are found in the book of life. Within this kingdom, is only bliss. There is no suffering. We experience no pain. This is a joyous kingdom. It is overflowing with the love of the Lord. Let us now see if you have been one with the spirit."

The sage's eyes glanced over the scroll. As he scanned it, he recited a large number of things that had happened during my life. I wasn't sure whether he was talking to me or reading aloud to himself. "Hmm, this is most excellent," he praised as his eyes worked their way down the scroll, "I see you did a lot of work for your church. You helped many of the Lord's children."

"Yes, I did," I replied, "I admit I was greedy for a long time and ask forgiveness for that. I was misguided. I tried my best to correct those personal flaws."

"Mmm, yes, that is most excellent of you," the sage replied. Then he smacked his lips together a few times and went on, "Mmmm, you will be forgiven for that greed. You realized your wrongdoing and have repented. So it is written, as you have done to the least of my children, you have done unto me."

Excellent indeed, I thought. I could hardly wait to get through that golden gate. Those prancing, naked women and all those tasty baked goods waited for me!

"Mmm, this is excellent as well," the sage nodded.

"What is?" I asked eagerly.

"It seems you have a recommendation from a Berma Miller. She mentions all the good things you did for her in your life. She also makes it known that you helped her husband Claude after she passed. These type of recommendations go a long way here."

I smiled in approval. "That is so kind of her," I beamed. It felt like I was already through that gate. One all-important question buzzed around in my head as I listened to the sage. I had to ask it, though I was afraid what the answer would be. "Tell me sage," I asked curiously, "Is there a chance I will see my wife Jessica and my son Kurt on the other side of that gate?" I pointed to the glowing gate. The prospect that I could see my family again was so exciting that I totally forgot about the naked, prancing girls.

The sage hesitated for a moment as he unraveled some more of the mystical scroll that he'd called The Book of Life. "Mmm, why yes, yes they are both within the kingdom of the Lord," he answered. "Pending final approval, you should most certainly see them."

I almost jumped over the pedestal and tackle-hugged the sage to the ground (made of clouds). It was all I could do to restrain myself. As I thought about my wife and son and wondered what they were doing within the glorious kingdom, the old sage suddenly shook his head in disapproval.

"Oh, what is this?" He said with a bewildered look on his face.

"What?" I stammered. A feeling of panic set in.

"You took your own life." It was more a statement than a question. I had no answer for him, and could only look down at the cloudy ground in shame. "I am truly sorry," the sage continued a moment later, "But our rules strictly say that anyone who takes his or her own life shall be denied access to the kingdom of the Lord. We appreciate the amount of goodwill and service you've done. However, your final act was one of extreme selfishness. The Lord created you. Therefore, your life isn't your own to destroy. When you did that, you were playing God."

My jaw dropped.

"What, you can't be serious?" I asked in stunned disbelief.

The sage looked at me with a critical expression and continued, "Mmm, but I am afraid so. As it is written, you are bought with a price. Therefore, glorify the Lord in your body and your spirit. These are the Lord's. You failed to do this. Thus, your faith wavered. Your choice became one of evil."

"But surely there are exceptions?" I argued.

The sage shook his head and raised his hand at me, "One cannot play God and also serve him. I'm dreadfully sorry, but I'll have to turn you away. It seems your last decision was indeed an unfortunate one, and one that cannot be reversed. This decision is final."

The sage looked over his shoulder and signaled with a hand motion that looked as if he were asking for a check at a restaurant. Two, giant, gladiator figures appeared from seemingly out of nowhere. They grabbed my arms in vice-like grips. I was lifted up with seemingly no effort at all.

"Wait, please reconsider!" I pleaded as I thrashed about in a pitiful attempt to free myself. "I need to see my wife and son again!" If I could just get loose from their grip, I could perhaps run by the old sage and sneak through the gate. Even If I had to knock him down, then so be it! The sage remained silent. He stared at me with all-knowing, gray eyes. He looked me over with what I would say was pity before he turned to address the next fellow in line who approached him.

Rage filled me.

"Fuck you sage!" I cursed at the top of my lungs as I struggled with the giant, unyielding figures. I could just as easily have been a small puppy for all the effort I put into fighting them. "You fucking heartless bastard!" I continued to swear, "I'll get you! I'll make you pay!"

The sage ignored me. The two figures showed no emotion whatsoever. My resistance didn't appear to have the slightest impact on them. Regardless, I twisted and kicked with all my strength until they dragged me over to the edge of the platform.

"Let me go you sons of bitches!" I cursed them, "You fuckers! I need to see my wife and son, damn you!"

When I looked down, I saw another raging, swirling vortex.

Unlike the first one (which was bright colored), this vortex was black with swirls of the darkest red. Bolts of lightning lanced out at random inside of it. The vortex reminded me of a hungry mouth and the lightning of flicking tongues. I wished I chose different words than 'let me go' a moment ago: the figures did let me go. They unceremoniously dumped me over the edge of the platform. I screamed.

EIGHT: TRAIL OF THE LOST

As I spun through the air toward the raging vortex of black and red swirls, I closed my eyes. It felt and sounded like a roaring tornado and I couldn't bare the sight of it. The maelstrom threatened to tear me to pieces as it sucked me into it. The noise was deafening. As soon as I entered the vortex, an icy chill rippled throughout my body. The cold was so intense that I instinctively opened my eyes.

I had passed through the vortex and was now falling down, into what I would call the mouth of a cave. The walls around me were red clay. I imagined they looked much like the surface of Mars. The atmosphere was stifling. It was like being stuck in a poorly-ventilated attic in the summer. I started to sweat as I plummeted, and I slammed violently into one of the red-clay walls, which sloped inward. The jarring hit took the wind right out of me.

It became brutally apparent that I could feel pain again. I gasped for air as I continued to fall. My body spun out of control. I drifted toward the center of the tunnel briefly, then smashed against another wall. My knee took most of the impact this time. I howled in excruciating pain as I clutched my wounded leg. I was sure something was broken.

I smashed against the walls a few more times, which scraped me up rather badly, before I landed with a hard thud against a gray, cracked, stone slab. I was barely conscious. I breathed in and winced in pain. It felt like I had a few broken ribs. The clothing that I'd been wearing was now shredded and soaked in my blood. For a few minutes, I couldn't even move. I tried to labor to my feet but pain shot through my leg. It was so intense that tears welled up in my eyes. I screamed and gritted my teeth so hard that I was lucky I didn't bite off my tongue.

I wanted to remain immobile until the pain subsided, but more people began to fall from the vortex far above. Each one landed with a hard thud. The bodies slammed into the floor all around me. I was forced to crawl out of the way to avoid being hit by them. Using what little strength was left in my arms, I managed to move an agonizing fifteen paces across the uneven floor. I made it to a spot where there were no bodies falling nearby and passed out from the strain.

When I came to, I lifted my head off the cold stone and looked around. I had entered into a nightmare. Instead of being admitted through the golden gate of Heaven, I could only believe I was now at the entrance to Hell. I was in a massive cave that had to be a holding chamber or waiting room of some sort. It was about the size of a football field. Red-clay walls rose high around me. There were many tiny holes in each wall. Every hole acted like a vent. Hot steam billowed out from them. The ceiling was funnel shaped. It culminated with the swirling vortex in its center, high above me.

People were sprawled out on the floor below the vortex. Some were twitching and barely conscious. Others clutched broken limbs and screamed. Others were motionless, either unconscious or dead. The ones who were able to move were painstakingly trying to get out of the way of falling bodies. I watched in horror as a screaming person fell through the air and landed on someone who was unable to get out of the way in time. The crunch echoed loudly in the stone chamber.

I puked and then I fainted. The conclusion that I was likely in hell and the horror around me was too much to take in.

Upon waking, I had a very unpleasant stream of vomit coating the front of my white t-shirt. I found it a bit odd that I'd been able to throw up. I hadn't eaten anything and I figured that I hadn't physically existed (as far as I knew) until I materialized out of the original vortex onto that golden platform. Then again, prior to all this I hadn't known what happened after death. I guessed anything was valid from here on out. Later, I learned that Hell had precise rules, which were much different, and more complex than any Earth religions had imagined.

I rose to my feet and looked around for my white slippers. I wasn't sure if I'd lost them in the fall, if they just vanished when I went through the vortex, or what. Unable to find them (or even a trace of them), I resigned myself to the fact that I'd be walking around barefoot.

I took a few steps and discovered another anomaly: I was no longer in as much physical pain. As I moved about, I immediately noticed that the severe pain in my knee now just a dull ache; I had been certain that I'd broken it in the collision with the tunnel wall. In addition, my ribs felt fine. As for my other injuries, they were entirely gone! This miracle of healing brought me some measure of relief.

It was short-lived.

My pleasant discovery was interrupted by the most dreadful smell that I have ever encountered. It reeked of decay, like a tomb, but was as if someone had lit a pile of hair on fire as well. I hadn't noticed the stench before, likely because I had hardly been able to breathe without wincing. The aroma assaulted me now.

I immediately searched for the cave exit. I quickly found a tunnel that was marked by a black gate that looked as if it were made from twisted, jagged metal, and covered in foot-long thorns that protruded in every direction from its vertical bars. I didn't want to go through there, but I also couldn't spend another second in this awful cave with that putrid stench.

On the other side of the black-thorned gate stood another massive figure. He had the same enormous stature and rippling muscles of the gladiators I'd seen in Heaven, but otherwise bore no resemblance to the Heaven gladiators. This creature was far more menacing.

Its skin was a dark shade of gray, like the color of asphalt. It was covered in horrible burn scars. One large scar ran diagonally down the length of its massive torso, from just below its right shoulder, to its lower, left rib. There was also a visible gash, maybe four inches long, down the creature's left forearm. This wound was crudely sewn shut with black wire. It was still seeping pus. Instead of a Romanesque-style helmet, this figure wore a rusty, iron mask, which had just a narrow slit for its wicked eyes. Gazing out from inside of the eye slit was the blackness of death.

This was a monster of the foulest type. The tremendous, barbed club in its hands looked just as menacing as the monster itself. Although I couldn't see its face, I was willing to bet the face inside of the mask was hideous.

To my surprise, the monster spoke to me, "Get moving," it growled. Its voice was like that of rusty gears grinding together. It resounded harshly in the chamber. I hurried through the black-thorn gate and kept as far away from the creature as I could. I basically sprinted past. I desired to put as much distance between us as my body could manage. This turned out to be a good move: behind me I could hear other people getting bashed with that club. Their pained yelps chased me down the narrow tunnel I had entered.

Just around the bend, this new cave split into two. Another guard stood at the fork. He looked nearly identical to the one I had just seen. Above him, etched into stone above each tunnel was a sign. One read 'men,' the other 'women.' It appeared the guard was there to make sure everyone entered their correct tunnel. Although it wasn't necessary, I noticed him shove everyone hard in the right direction, even the women, who now wept and clung to each other for support.

I felt sorry for them but was in no position to play hero. Following a vigorous shove by the guard, I headed down the appropriate tunnel. It descended steeply into absolute darkness. I stumbled my way down as I tried to navigate its pitfalls. I scraped against the wall many times. More then once I lost my footing and fell flat on my back. I soon learned to plant my front foot solidly before I lifted my rear foot off the ground. It was impossible to keep from slipping entirely, but this technique helped a little. Unfortunately, it didn't do anything for the sharp rocks I continued to step on.

Another painful lesson was learned when I hit my head very hard against the low, rough ceiling. I kept my hands up ahead of me from then on as I fumbled along. The ceiling only seemed to get lower as I progressed through the cave.

Deeper underground, the air got thicker and staler. It became an effort just to breathe. I soon became disoriented and nearly passed out. I probably would have done so, except that someone came from behind and shoved me hard. I fell forward and slid ten or fifteen feet down a sharp slope. Before I stopped my tumble, I scraped both my palms up pretty good.

My desire to find the jerk that had pushed me so I could bash him in the face was great, but my desire to get out of the cave was greater. I had been stooped over for so long now that my back was really beginning to hurt. The only way I could tell I was even going the correct direction in the pitch-dark cave was by listening to the cries of pain as other people ahead of me fell, stepped on jagged rocks, or hit their heads. These cries continually reverberated up towards me. I found myself wondering if the cave would ever end. I thought that perhaps I made a wrong turn somewhere. Maybe everyone else was in another tunnel. What if this was just a dead end?

Much to my relief, I eventually saw a dim light. It could only be the exit to the cave. I crossed my fingers and made my way toward it. The light expanded and soon revealed a definite exit. I whooped joyfully as I left that horrible cave behind me and stood up straight. I was now standing on a high ledge that ran along the side of a cliff, along the circumference of a massive, underground cavern that seemed endless.

I was now officially in Hell. I know that because there was a faded, wooden sign that literally said, "Welcome to Hell." It was painted with blood and someone was crucified above it. He was still alive and moaning feebly.

Other than the horror I felt at that moment, the first thing that hit me about Hell was the wretched stench: it was even worse than the smell inside the vortex-room. If you can imagine a dozen rotting corpses, a mountain of recent feces, a skunk, and some rotten eggs, then you're on the right track. Or you've been to the same place.

The intense heat hit me a second later. I can't say that surprised me: I had always believed that Hell would be full of fire and brimstone. Nonetheless, the combination of smell and heat was nauseating and I could already feel sweat dripping down my back. The one thing which prevented me from passing out was I didn't want to fall off the ledge.

I decided it would be a good idea to rest for a few minutes until my body got accustomed to this new place. I also really needed to give my back a rest. I headed down the trail a bit so I could get beyond the crucified man and the sign. When I could no longer hear his pained moans, I sat down.

While I took a break, I looked around. The cavern ceiling was about half a mile above me. Bolted to the ceiling, in a disorganized manner, were giant spherical lights. They were held in place by fixtures that resembled the talons of vultures. Each sphere pulsed in a slow rhythm as it changed colors from very dark-green to a kind of Dijon-mustard yellow. The lights did a piss-poor job of illuminating anything through the thick haze that permeated the cavern. I wondered how the lights were powered. There didn't seem to be any sort of wiring or pipes attached to them.

After I watched the sphere-lights pulse between their two states for a minute, I glanced downward. A valley stretched endlessly in every direction. Running the course of the valley, all the way to the horizon, and weaving between the Mars-like terrain, was a crimson river. From where I sat, I estimated it to be well over three miles from bank to bank in some places. I could only imagine how deep it was. Aside from being the color of blood, and in all likelihood composed of blood, one other characteristic about the river struck me as odd: its path was very unnatural. The course it took was jagged. It had many sharp turns instead of smoother transitions that marked the path of least resistance, like the rivers on Earth. I wondered, perhaps, if it was artificial. Eventually, it rushed into a natural tunnel and disappeared underground.

Along the right bank of the river, I noticed what appeared to be ominous, black buildings through the haze. I squinted and tried to focus on them but from this distance it was hard to make out any details. I could see that the buildings occupied a rather large area. I figured if it was a city that I was looking upon, that this city was at least the area of Manhattan, and maybe larger.

Directly beyond it, and dominating the landscape, was a massive mountain that nearly reached the top of the cavern ceiling. It towered well above everything else in the region, dwarfing even that city in its shadow. The darkest of storm clouds lingered around the peak of the mountain, in constant, swirling motion. Fierce lightning blasted in rapid succession from within those swirling clouds. The bolts appeared to often strike the peak of the mountain. They lit up the darkened sky all around it.

I stared at that ominous storm for a moment. Meanwhile, a few other people emerged from the cave and continued past me. I drew my attention back to the city. A solitary road led out of it. I traced its path from my vantage point. It seemed to lead right up to the cliff I was on. However, I couldn't tell this for certain because the cliff curved outward further ahead and blocked my view.

I swallowed hard. Deep in my gut, I knew that city would be my destination. The path I was on would lead to that road somehow. I felt a shiver move down my spine when I thought of what might greet me when I arrived. There wasn't much left to do but get up and keep going, so that's what I opted to do.

Less than a quarter of a mile later, I came across another large Hell-guard. This one was creepier than the one with the club that I'd passed at the thorny gate earlier. He was of approximately the same build as the prior guard, and his skin was the exact same shade of gray. His eyes were also black and empty. This one didn't wear a mask, but I wished that he had one.

Where his left eye should have been, there was nothing but a raw, empty, pink socket. Additionally, a disgusting boil grew out of the side of his face! It was throbbing, and purple, and about as large as a walnut. I had to turn away from that abominable sight. I felt about as sick as if I'd just seen my parents having sex.

I walked in front of this guard with my head down and my eyes averted. Before I could make it past the guard, I felt rough hands on my back. With one massive thrust, I was shoved to the ground. I got a mouth full of dirt which I spat out and gagged on. I was fortunate that I was pushed forward, and not to my left, or I could have gone right off the cliff! As I struggled to my feet, the guard laughed at me and exposed a mouthful of crooked, blackened teeth.

"Such a weak human," he boomed with his arms crossed in front of his broad chest and a sinister looking whip clutched in one hand. "Be good to break you. With one hand, I could."

I shuddered. I had no doubt of this beast's claim.

The guard continued in broken English. The phrasing was bizarre. "Lucky for you, weak human, I told not to break. You get on your way now. Follow path to the bottom. Long road ahead of you. You're such a weak human that I thinks you won't make it. Be better if I break you now."

The guard then clutched his belly and laughed with raucous enjoyment at my expense. A blast of hot, vile breath hit me in the face as did the flakes of spit that flew out from between its teeth. In that moment, the creature reminded me of Monroe. I thought of opening my mouth to defend myself, but pushed the thought down. My instincts told me it was best to get away from this boil-faced monstrosity with no delay.

I stumbled away and felt like a coward. After a few steps, I heard the guard's whip cut the air nearby. The tip of it cracked just inches from my face. With a yelp, I ran along the ledge for the next few minutes.

When I turned around and noticed the guard hadn't pursued me, I breathed a deep sigh of relief. I was quite glad the whip had missed me and also pretty certain the guard had not meant to miss. In that instant, I wanted to sneak back up to him and push him off the ledge. Yet as much as I didn't like to admit it, the cruel guard had made one good point: I had a long road ahead of me. I was physically exhausted from the treacherous ordeal in the cave. That, along with everything else, had really tired me out. It was best to get going and conserve my energy.

I walked onward and began to adjust to the smell. It still made life (or afterlife, rather) uncomfortable, but like living next to a garbage dump, in due course it became tolerable. The heat was the most difficult thing to contend with. Sweat poured off my body. I already felt quite thirsty. A bright flash in the distance caught my attention. It was a jet of flame, like a geyser, that shot forth from a huge hole in the ground. The fiery eruption that burst forth rose several hundred feet into the air. Several other flame jets followed it from other holes. Each one seemed alive, like the mouths of dragons waiting to roast their dinners.

I watched those flaming geysers go off as I made my way down along the ledge ever so carefully. My feet kicked small rocks down the cliff-side on occasion. I glanced down once to watch them tumble to oblivion far below. I then decided to not look down so often.

Soon, I caught up with some of the people who'd passed me earlier.

These people looked like the living dead. For all I knew, they were. Each person wore the same white clothing that we'd been granted up in

Heaven. However, the clothing no longer looked pristine. Everyone was now covered in dirt. Many of their garments had tears or holes. One guy had a blood stain down the front of his shirt. Another guy was missing the knees to his pant legs.

Our bedraggled group carried on with our arduous journey. Time and again, someone collapsed from exhaustion. I fell several times myself. We worked together to help one another back to our feet. In a stupor, we traversed the steep incline. No one really said much. I suppose there wasn't much we felt like talking about. Our progress was slow. At places in the trail, we had to step over an unconscious or dead body. People were lying immobilized in the path. They begged us for water, though it was clear we had none. If anything, their labored requests only served to remind me of how parched my mouth already was. I hoped to find something to drink when I reached the valley floor.

In addition to these woes, the steepness of the trail put a tremendous strain on my already sore ankles. This made it difficult not to stumble. One false move would be a catastrophe. Often times, the ledge got so narrow that I had to slide sideways with my back pressed against the cliff to make any forward progress. On these occasion, I felt like a circus tight-rope walker. The worst times were when sporadic, fierce winds ripped at me and tried to claw me from the ledge. These violent gusts almost sucked me into the chasm a number of times. It was during one fierce flurry that I watched in dumbfounded awe as one of the people accompanying me dropped out of sight with a chilling cry. When he finally hit the ground below, it was so far down that his impact didn't even make a noise.

There had been a time in my life when witnessing such a thing would have brought tears to my eyes and perhaps called for psychiatric treatment. Now, however, I had my own survival to worry about. My focus was on the descent.

A few minutes later, and I was very thankful to be off the cliff. The path here widened. That afforded an opportunity for a needed break. I sat down in the featureless dirt, along the spacious trail, and stretched my tired legs. For the first time since I had entered the cavern of Hell, I saw a sign of what once may have been plant life; dead branches grew up from the cracked ground in a number of spots. In my mind, they counted for something, maybe just a glimmer of hope that things wouldn't be as bad as they so far appeared.

As I looked at the remnants of what was once perhaps a shrub, I began to hear terrible screams rising up from the valley floor below. My hope was dashed to pieces as surely as the man I'd watch fall from the cliff. The pure, unholy agony of these wretches pierced my ears and made the hairs on my back stand up. I was forced to cover my ears to block them out.

I sincerely hoped I wouldn't be subject to the same fate, whatever it was. The people near me heard the screams as well. Everyone looked concerned and afraid.

"You think we'll get tortured like that?" A guy next to me asked.

I shook my head. "I don't know," I told him. "I hope not."

He then introduced himself as Joe. I said hello and introduced myself as I rubbed my sore, swollen ankles and examined my blistered feet.

"What did you do to get sent here, Joe?" I asked (I later discovered that this was the most commonly asked question in Hell).

Joe snorted and replied, "I committed adultery. My neighbor's wife was so hot, man. I mean, big rack, killer face, great ass. A total knockout. When I finally got the chance I just had to tap it. I couldn't help myself. I still can't say I regret doing it, though it looks like I may soon enough. This place sucks my ball-bag."

I nodded in agreement. Then I gritted my teeth and stood up. The blisters on my feet screamed. "Well, Joe," I said, "I'm going to keep pressing on. If you want to accompany me you can."

"May as well," he shrugged.

We continued together for the last leg of the journey to the valley floor. It seemed to take forever but I was grateful for a companion. My feet gave out just after I reached level ground. I fell to my hands and crawled over to a large rock to rest. How I missed the luxury of an ice-pack. I doubted I'd ever see one again. I even started to miss granola bars. I wasn't much of a hiker, but always had a granola bar or two when I went on a hike. Most of all, I missed water. It felt like someone had rubbed sandpaper inside of my throat. With no means to relieve my thirst, I plunked myself down and did what I could to alleviate the soreness in my ankles. Joe sat down next to me.

We hadn't been resting for more than a few minutes when a raspy voice shouted from right behind us, right in my ear.

"GET UP! GET MOVING!"

I almost jumped out of my skin. Full of terror, I turned to stare up at another Hell-guard who hovered over me. If his lower body hadn't been covered by an impressive, black, plated cuirass, that extended down to his knees, I would have been staring right at his genitals. I was quite pleased that the cuirass was there, but not so much about the guard.

The fact that he was here to harass us could not be a good thing. In addition to the cuirass, he wore black gauntlets that had a silver stud embedded in each knuckle. His boots were a matching shade of black and made of the same twisted metal as the thorny gate. They went to about his knees, and had individual toes made out of forged-silver. This guard carried a menacing bullwhip in his right hand.

All these things made him intimidating. They couldn't match the look on his face. It was one of absolute hatred. He looked about as angry as a person who'd just planted new grass in their lawn and then had watched as someone had driven right over it. In equal proportion to the anger in his face was an unnecessary amount of ugliness. This was a face that would curdle milk. The nose was too big. One nostril was huge. The other was tiny. One eye was higher than the other. The crown of his head looked dented.

"Little human, your feet hurt?" He taunted as he noted my obvious discomfort. This guard, much like the others I had encountered, had an uncanny knack for picking out weakness. "Bad for you. Get your ass up."

I groaned as I rose.

"You fragile human. I'm strong. I'm strong and you're weak and useless." He laughed and slapped me hard in the face with a black-gauntleted hand. The force of the impact knocked me to the ground. I was fortunate that the metal studs missed me, or I probably would've lost an eye. As it were, the slap opened up a cut on my left cheek.

"I hardly hit you and you bleed, har har," the guard laughed as he flexed his fingers.

Joe reached down to help me up. The guard used this as an opportunity to abuse him.

"Little, weak human, who told you to help this one to his feet?"

"Cut me a break, man," Joe answered with indignation. "We just want to get on our way. We don't need any trouble."

Joe's response must have been a trigger for the guard. Or, maybe the guard was just in a bad mood. I'll never know. Whatever the case, the guard's reaction to Joe was extreme and merciless. Without so much as a word, he reached out with a massive, gloved hand and squeezed his fingers around the top of Joe's head.

"Hey," Joe shrieked as he tried to pry an enormous thumb away from the side of his face.

The guard applied more pressure.

Joe cried out, "Please...let me go...I didn't mean anything!"

The guard spun Joe around and wrapped his bullwhip around Joe's neck. Just like that, he began to strangle Joe. All I could do was look on in terror. Joe flailed around wildly as he struggled to break free. He began to gurgle. His hands tried to break the guard's death-group, but the guard was just too strong.

As Joe was choked, his face turned blue. The arteries (or maybe veins, I wasn't sure which) bulged out from the sides of his head. His eyes looked like they would pop right out of his face. His flailing became feebler and stopped entirely, along with his hideous gurgling. Joe twitched a few times and then stopped moving altogether.

With his bloodlust apparently sated, the guard dumped Joe's lifeless body on the ground. He looked at me in a threatening manner then coiled up his bullwhip and went on his way as if nothing had happened. I wasn't even given an explanation as to why Joe was killed.

I seethed with nearly uncontrollable rage. I wanted nothing more than to push that murderous bastard into one of the fire geysers I had seen and watch him burn. My only option, though, was to trudge along the dusty, barren road. I was all alone, very deflated, and very helpless.

NINE: ROAD, RIVER, DUST, AND BONES

The road that I now tread upon was indeed the same one I had spied from atop the cliff. The city was still far off in the distance. My only companion was dead. Or maybe his soul was dead. At this juncture, I wasn't sure what happened once a person died while in Hell. I assumed they went to another level of Hell, or maybe they encountered infinite blackness. I banked on the former for the simple reason that infinite blackness would be welcome compared to this. We had been tossed down here as a punishment for sinful lives. That made me think we couldn't escape it.

I gazed out over desolate terrain that spanned as far as I could see as I contemplated such things. Everything seemed to have turned a brown color. The few shrubs that existed were withered. Their crisp, blackened, dead branches remained motionless except when a dust storm billowed through. I felt about as depressed as the landscape looked.

The dust storms were the worst part of this trek. They threw sand in my face and mouth and made my already difficult journey even more arduous. I dared not travel while the dust blinded me. If I wandered off the road, I might never find my way back. When a storm started, I learned to lay face-down on the ground and wait for it to pass. At one point, I was on my stomach for so long I felt like a sun-bathing lizard. By the time the worst of the storms passed, I was covered in an inch of sand.

In order to reach the city, I had to cross the crimson river, which I was still betting was made of blood. The terrain was very flat, much like Florida, so I could see the river long before I reached its banks. When I got there, I first noticed a shoddy, wooden, rope-bridge that spanned at least a quarter mile. It looked a thousand years old. Boards were missing in many places. Other boards hung by a single nail and waited to entrap an unfortunate soul who would set them free with the slightest motion. Even when no stale wind was blowing, this bridge swayed dangerously above the river's churning waters.

Not only was the water churning as it flowed with great force past the banks, but it was also boiling! I presumed it was heated by the fire geysers. Large rocks, that may as well have been saws for how perilous they looked, jutted out from the bottom. They waited hungrily for an unlucky sap to fall into the river so they could feast upon him.

It was certainly not possible to swim across the river. The bridge didn't seem like a viable option, either. For lack of alternatives it would need to be crossed. As far as I could see, to my left and right, there was no other place to ford nor any other bridge.

I put my right foot on the first, rickety step. I pictured myself falling through a hole into the crimson water and being torn apart on those rocks. As the scene played out in my mind, I finally got the nerve to take a second step. My knuckles were white from the tight grasp I had on the bridge's railings of rope. The entire bridge shifted uneasily as I made my way across. I tried to tell myself I wouldn't look down but couldn't help it. I had to be insane to be doing this!

I came to a large gap in the bridge where a number of boards were missing. I had to jump it. The river was twenty feet below me. It roared past the rocks with a supernatural fury, as if it wanted me to fall. I held my breath for a moment. I counted to three.

I made the decisive leap.

When I hit on the other side, my feet nearly slipped out from under me. I fortunately held on tight. I hastily got across the rest of the bridge and didn't rest until my feet were on solid ground once again.

I laughed with the hysteria that only someone who just dodged a terrible death can know. My nerves were toast. I put the bridge and the river behind me. As the city got closer and closer, and the buildings grew ever larger, I felt a renewed surge of energy. In the back of my mind was the hope that I could somehow find a way back to Heaven to see Jessica and Kurt again. I walked with purpose and could soon barely make out a fence on the city outskirts. The stark whiteness to the fence was a sharp contrast to the dismal darkness of everything else.

When I was got closer, I realized that most of the fence was made from bones. They were all haphazardly arranged and held in place with wire. It was actually more of a mesh than a fence. When the wind blew, foul as it was, it shook the whole mesh and the bones clinked together like some sort of voodoo chimes. In some places, whole skeletons were piled up to form what I supposed constituted posts. In other places, I noticed actual posts of dried-up, hole-ridden wood. Each post had a skull nailed to its top with what appeared to be a railroad spike.

I scurried over this mishmash of bones, wiring, and wood. It left me with no desire to look upon it for a second longer than I had to. Now, the twisted, blackened buildings of the city loomed in front of me. They were a blacksmith's project gone bad. Nothing about these buildings spoke of any logic behind their construction: walls were warped and twisted as if forced into place. Beams jutted into the air at random. Parts of walls didn't appear to connect to anything at all. Windows were misshapen, as if the glass had melted and then solidified again. A feeling of immense dizziness came over me like a lunar eclipse.

This feeling may have been caused by the distorted view, but it was more likely a combination of hunger, thirst, and exhaustion. Everything was finally too much for my body to bear. My knees buckled. I collapsed in the middle of the road. With a gasp, my eyes rolled back in my head as consciousness faded.

TEN: LABORIOUS AETERNUM

When my eyes at last opened, I was greeted by the dirty faces of some ragged-looking people standing over me. Terror struck as I realized I had no clue who these people were or what they wanted from me. I sat up and tried to stand, but a rather large, bald fellow with dull, gray eyes put a hand out and signaled for me to relax.

"Easy there," he said, "You need to get some of your strength back." The fellow then handed me a light-tan, leather pouch with a wire belt-clip on it. "Drink up," he instructed, "You need water."

I removed the unusual cap from the pouch (which didn't fit very well) and took a hearty swallow. The water wasn't cold at all but I was happy to have it. I drank some more and looked around.

The scenery had changed a little. I was now in a city square. The ominous, black buildings that had been far away now surrounded me on all sides. Some looked as if they were made out of obsidian; others looked iron, and some were a combination of the two fused together. The buildings ranged in height from just a few stories to perhaps thirty. There seemed no logic to their placement: some had many yards of room between them, others had inches, and some were placed at odd angles or offset so they jutted halfway across the unpaved road. These buildings, and the road that ran alongside them, made up the border of the square. I estimated the area to be a few hundred yards in each direction.

The square's middle area began at the other side of the road and was marked by a knee-wall of carved, stone blocks. Like the buildings, each block looked randomly placed and their shapes and sizes were nothing close to consistent. In some places, the knee-wall curved in or out by as much as ten feet.

The middle area of the square inside the knee-wall was what I assumed they considered a park in Hell. It looked more like an old war photograph. The area was all but empty from what I could see, except for a few traces of withered shrubs, and sporadic, dead trees that looked like they could've been pines at one time. These trees also looked ready to topple over any second. The only other objects in the park were some jagged, rusted pieces of metal. These reminded me of the hedgehogs that the Germans used to hamper allied invasions along the beaches during World War II.

As I took this all in, the gray-eyed man gently broke a piece of moldy bread from a loaf he had wrapped in an olive paper. "Here, eat this," he said as he handed it to me, "It's not much, but it's all we can spare."

The bread looked disgusting but I took it anyway and gradually chewed. It felt like I hadn't eaten in weeks. When I finished, there wasn't even a crumb left. My stomach hurt just from having food in it.

"Where am I and who are you?" I asked at last.

"You're in Slaver Square, part of the Residential Area. I'm just another unlucky fuck stuck here."

"Okay," I nodded. I didn't quite trust him but my head was filled with questions. Any answers he could provide were better than none. "So you guys found me?"

"Yes, we did," he replied. "We were just doing our job. We came across you during Routine March Duty, so we picked you up and carried you back here."

"What do you have routine marches for?"

"That's the duty we've been assigned. The marches are setup to find new arrivals, like yourself, or to find unrecovered bodies. We go out in squads all day and night because people get sent here continuously. Often, the new people don't make it to the city. We find most of them along the road. The majority of people die before they can get put to work. That's no good for the economy here."

I scratched my head. "I'm sorry," I told him, "But maybe you can clarify some things. How can we die when we're already in Hell? I've been wondering how that works for a while. Aren't we in our soul forms....or....or something like that?" I then blurted out a number of hurried, semi-rational comments before he could answer, "I thought I was going to drop dead. I saw a number of bodies on the way here. My friend Joe was even strangled by one of those....monsters. And what is this economy you mention?"

"Slow down buddy," the guy chuckled, "Let's answer one question at a time." He appeared quite used to panicked, newcomer questions like mine. "Yes, you're already dead, and we receive bodies in this realm. They are technically our soul-bodies, but we don't usually call them that.

"Everyone is granted a soul-body when we first enter Hell, and it can die. This happens in much the same fashion as on Earth. Think of it like this, friend: Earth is to your body as Hell is to your soul. Your soul-body here is affected by pretty much all the same things that your flesh-body on Earth once was. The consequences of death, however, are not the same. If your soul-body dies, you get revived in a new one. This takes place at a Communal Room, in the center of the Residential Area."

The gray-eyed guy then pointed to a four-story, black building with a number of long, misshapen windows in it. Steam poured forth from multiple smokestacks of different lengths in its roof. "That building," he went on, "Is the Communal Room where your soul gets pumped back into another body."

So far, I was following this fellow's explanation. I indicated as much with a simple "okay" and a nod. Then, I inquired, "Does it hurt? When you get put in a new body, I mean?"

He tapped his fingers over his lips for a second and replied, "You won't even notice that process. It's like being born, I suppose. You'll just suddenly be there. What really hurts is the dying part. Usually because it's a brutal death. Now that's a true bitch, but that's Hell for you."

I processed that knowledge for a moment then asked, "If we get a new soul-body every time, what does it matter if you guys go out to find us or not?"

The gray-eyed fellow thought about this for a moment then answered, "Well, as near as I figure, Hell doesn't like to waste soul-bodies unnecessarily. Usually the old, dead, soul-bodies get reused in one way or another. Granted, no one knows all the ins and outs of this place. We all just have scraps of info and we put those together. I'm sure there's a greater picture to things than what we see."

I nodded my head. The rush of information was a lot to take in. Hell was nothing like what I had anticipated. Suddenly, something disturbing occurred to me. With timid curiosity, I asked, "What do you mean the old bodies get reused?"

The guy laughed and smirked. He creeped me out.

He raised an eyebrow and asked, "What do you think that canteen that you were just drinking from was made out of?"

It took me a moment, but soon the dreadful realization hit home.

Skin. It was made from Human Skin. And the cap was some sort of bone.

I shuddered and began to gag.

"Don't puke up that bread!" My associate lectured, "Or you'll be lucky to get dead rats in the future! Oh, and yes, we do have rats in abundance here. We also have spiders, snakes, earwigs, maggots and the like."

I felt sick to my stomach. He wasn't being much help. Changing topics seemed like a good idea.

"When I first entered Hell," I stated as I tried to get my mind off the disgusting truth that I'd just been drinking from a container which had once been a person, "I fell down that big tunnel. I know my knee was broken when I landed. The weird thing was, when I woke up, it was fine. Do you know anything about that?"

"That one's easy," my associate responded, "Your soul-body will heal from most injuries very fast. That is accepted as a universal truth here. In my time on Routine March Duty, I've seen this in action a lot. Man, I've brought people back from near-death in an hour or so with only a little water and bread."

"Any idea why we heal so rapidly?" I inquired.

"Can't say exactly, but I think it's because of the extreme abuse we take from day to day. It's more of a curse than a blessing: I think the Overseers and Overlords here use our fast healing as an excuse to beat us more."

"Overseers and what?" I asked.

"Oh, right. No one's told you yet. Allow me to explain. You've already met the Overseers; they're the big, gray guys who are mean as fuck, and that's on a good day. They watch us all the time. Your Overlord is like their boss. You haven't been assigned an Overlord yet, but you'll know it when it happens."

"Oh, alright. I guess that makes a little sense. What exactly goes on here from day to day? Do we just get tortured all day and stuff?"

"Yes."

I stared at him dumbfounded.

A second later, he added, "Though Hell is a lot different from what most people expect. It's not just a place where we're stuck for eternal damnation, suffering, fire, heat, and that kind of stuff. Hell is really more like its own society. You will quickly find out that everyone has a place. If you aren't in your place, you pay the price. We each have a job. There's really no set duration to the jobs here. I have seen people switched around, but it doesn't happen often. I've had this job since I arrived. I have enough trouble making sure I do it well, so I can't tell you much about what anyone else does."

"What is your job like?" I asked. Mentally, I noted that my question was ironically similar to small talk on Earth. Perhaps some things never truly change. I welcomed any sense of the familiar.

"As far as Hell goes," he said, "It's one of the better jobs to have." He paused for a minute than extended his description, "It gets me away from the watchful eyes of the Overseers and my Overlord. That saves me a lot of terrific beatings and torture. My biggest pain is when people die on the cliffs, or real early on, like before they cross the River of Blood." He snapped his fingers and added, "Oh, and by the way it's also been called The River Styx by the Greeks. Here we just call it the River of Blood." He grinned and seemed really pleased with himself to throw that scrap in. "But anyway," he continued, "When people die on the cliffs, we need to assemble special expeditions that we call Corpse Finders. Their job is to locate hard-to-find bodies. These specialized groups are given extra food and supplies so they can stay out in the wilderness for longer periods. The men sent out as Corpse Finders have a little more leeway and freedom than most of us.

"As for my own history in case you're curious," he added (I wasn't really, but I listened as a courtesy since he'd been so helpful thus far), "I don't remember my life before Hell. It really was that long ago. I couldn't tell you what I did for a living, my name, or even if I had a family. It's like none of that stuff ever happened. I can't even recall the reasons I was sentenced here. I do remember that when I arrived, I fell off the cliff on the descent down. I fell a few thousand feet. I remember screaming as the ground rushed up at me. The next thing I knew, I was in the Communal Room with a bunch of other people. I was given this job later that day. I've had it ever since."

"That sounds like a tough entrance, but your job sounds pretty respectable," I commented. "It's not unlike search and rescue teams on Earth."

"Definitely," he agreed, "And there are some duties you absolutely don't want."

"Like what?" I wondered.

"Well, let me think." The gray-eyed man paused for a second and scratched his chin. "I certainly wouldn't want to be stuck in the 'Satisfaction of a Lower Nature' department. Those people have to provide sexual gratification for the Overseers."

"Ughhh."

"It's just as bad as you'd think," my friend confirmed, "I've heard stories I won't even repeat. And I've also heard that the people who did those jobs and didn't do them well received an even worse punishment."

I didn't want to know what was considered worse. I was thoroughly revolted at what I had just heard. Hopefully, he was stretching the truth. The gray-eyed man must've realized I was sick of hearing about the duties Hell had to offer. "I really need to get back to my duties," he let me know. "You can keep this," he added as he tossed me an extra water pouch.

"Thanks for your time and help," I said, still in a stunned state of disbelief. I had the feeling that helpful people would be few and far between.

The gray-eyed man walked away and motioned for the other members of his crew to join him. I looked at the canteen made from human skin and grimaced. After some hesitation, I decided I'd have to get used to drinking from it eventually, and I was thirsty now. Gathering all the gumption I could muster, I took a swig then corked the top (which looked like a knuckle bone or something). I then attached the canteen to my belt with the wire clip that was built into it.

Alone once more, I wandered the Residential Area of Hell. The next person I came across was a rather sickly individual with lesions on his face.

"Hi there, I was wondering if you could tell me more about Hell?" I asked as I tried to be polite. Perhaps I could make a friend. The guy turned and looked at me with a blank expression on his face. "Fuck off," was all he had to say.

I decided it was smart to walk away. Moving to a new area, I found a nice place to sit where I didn't see any Overseers or any signs of potential trouble.

A moment later, another person approached me. "Hey, since you're new I'll tell ya a few things," he informed me as he sat beside me and tried to look nonchalant. His voice was gruff and he seemed irritated, but

I welcomed advice. "I don't like associatin' much wit' people down here. We're all in hell for a reason," he let me know.

I nodded in agreement. I was still unsure what, if anything he expected from me, but my intuition said he was up to something.

"The temperature here surprises most people," he rambled, "I always thought Hell would be ridiculously hot. Ya know, like skin-searing. The truth is the thermometer maintains a steady reading of 92 degrees Fahrenheit at all times. It's still hot as a bastard, though."

"I noticed that."

Great, I thought, *I have to get stuck with a nut job.*

He spat into the dirt and slapped the ground with an open palm a few times. After an uncomfortable pause, he simply stated, "You're gonna get punished here."

I didn't know if he was threatening me or just stating a fact. He wasn't looking at me so it was hard to read him.

"The punishments are usually whippings or floggings," he droned on. "They depend on ya Overlord. Hopefully, ya get a decent one. The nice ones will only whip, beat, or stab ya."

"And the bad ones?" I asked. I also tried to act nonchalant and somewhat disinterested. The man was a loon so I didn't want to seem as if I cared too much about what he was saying.

"Praying won't help ya here, but I'd pray ya don't get a bad one. They'll enjoy coming up with creative punishments."

"Such as?"

"Ya really wanna know? Well, just remember ya asked." He spat on the ground again as he rambled, "They may have ya set on fire. Maybe they choose to hang ya. Either way, sooner or later they take a punishment to the point where it'll kill ya. Then, the bastards bring ya back in another body and put ya back to work. WA-BAM." He clapped his hands, "Just like that," he said and nodded his head up and down rapidly. I almost got up and found a new spot but he wouldn't shut up, "When ya get a new body, enjoy it while it lasts. They'll mangle it up again, real good, soon enough."

I think my face turned pure white. The guy must have noticed my discomfort because he finally turned to look at me. He reached out and grabbed my face roughly with both of his hands and pulled me toward him. I was so petrified that I didn't even resist.

"It's fuckin' horrible!" He blurted out. His lips quivered and his face twitched nervously. He began to talk faster, almost to the point where I had trouble making sense of his words, "I've been lucky so far. Lately, I've only had my left arm shattered...maybe a few weeks ago. Just last week I had my toes torn off, see?" He turned my face toward his dismembered foot, which he raised up so I could get a good look at it.

I wrenched myself free of his grip and stood up. I just wanted to get away from this madman. When I started to take cautious steps backward, to my amazement, the guy started to tear up.

"Please don't go," he whimpered. "I haven't had a chance to talk to anyone who gives a shit in so long. I just want someone to have some sympathy...if only for a minute."

I truly felt sorry for the wretch. I exhaled nervously and sat back down. As tears rolled down the guy's cheeks I asked, "What did you do to have your foot mangled?"

They guy shook as he answered, "I was two minutes late for mornin' march to work."

"Oh Jesus!" I exclaimed.

A look of panic crossed the guy's face and he glanced around apprehensively. "Never let an Overseer hear ya say that," he whispered. "That's a punishable offense. They have zero tolerance for the J word."

"Thanks for telling me."

"I mean it. That is serious shit here. The same goes for saying 'God bless ya' if someone sneezes. Never say that, either."

"What should I say?" I inquired.

"Probably nothing," he conceded. "Sympathy don't get ya nothing here. If people and Overseer's think you're weak, they'll make ya pay for it. I swear the bastards can smell weakness."

"Got it."

"I'm gonna have to get going soon, but there's a few other things that will be good to know. I may as well be the one to tell ya," he let me know. "Hell is divided into four parts that I know of. First one's the Overlord Dwellings. That's where they stay. We ain't allowed there. Got it?"

"Got it, " I confirmed again.

"The second is the Residential Area. It's the safest part of Hell. We sleep on the ground here at night, though if ya get lucky maybe you can make a bed from garbage. There's a few garbage piles at the other end of the square," he pointed. I couldn't see them from here but took his word for it. "I usually just dig myself a hole, though," he let me know, "Things are safer that way. Then no one will try to kill ya for ya bed.....or worse."

"What do you mean?" I inquired.

"Ya see any women?" He asked.

I looked around. It dawned on me that I hadn't seen a woman since the two tunnels split up when I'd entered Hell. I had been so preoccupied with everything that I hadn't given it any thought until now.

"No, I don't," I conceded.

"Neither do I," he let me know," And I ain't seen no woman ever."

"None at all?" I found it difficult to believe.

He nodded and looked annoyed. "The women are kept separate from us. Rumor is that Satan keeps them all for himself, lucky prick."

That was depressing news. I was sure the women weren't too happy about it, either. Who knew what terrible things Satan was doing to them.

"My point being," my associate continued, "Is that ya should get used to the idea that sooner or later, someone is going to fuck ya ass. Oh, and it'll happen more often than you'd like."

After a moment of being dumbfounded, I shouted with astonished revulsion, "I'd like it never!" Then, for good measure, I added, "And you're kidding, right?"

I was answered with a shame-filled explanation that quickly turned to rambling. "Oh, I wish I was, boy. It's a lot like prison down here, but a lot worse. With no women around for eternity some of the guys just go crazy....ya start looking like a woman to some of 'em. More so if ya don't cut yer hair. We don't get much in the way of razors or scissors here, but there's always sharp objects laying around....."

"Wait, wait, wait," I interrupted, "You really are messing with me, right? You're trying to scare me."

The guy sneered at me and rolled his eyes. "You'll find out what that's like soon enough, boy. That's why I told ya before, the best bet is to dig ya-self a little hole before ya go to sleep. Try to bury ya-self in it. I've found that tends to keep the bastards at bay." After a brief pause, he added, "Most of the time. It's probably cause we're worked like dogs during the day. Most guys won't go through the effort to dig someone out of a hole when there's plenty of easier victims around, know what I mean?"

I was flabbergasted. "Can't say that I do."

He looked at me as if I were a liar or else crazy and told me, "I've had a lotta nights I wish I could forget. Many mornings where it hurt just to walk, too."

I almost cried. There was an awkward silence. I had to find something to say and managed a simple question, "How long have you been here?"

"Since 1967."

My jaw dropped.

The guy chuckled, which I found almost more disturbing than when he had started to cry. "Don't worry, it only feels like eternity."

It was a feeble joke. My heart sank. I realized the gravity of my situation. This guy was still relatively new to Hell and he made it sound like he'd been here for a few centuries.

"Oh, but in all seriousness," he continued, "Joking is a punishable offense. That's the first one I've told in a very long time. I should know better. Never let an Overlord or an Overseer see ya making anyone laugh. They'll march right up to ya and tear ya tongue right out, lickety split."

"I'll be careful," I assured him. "So what are the other parts to Hell that you were talking about?"

He grumbled something unintelligible and went on, "The third part of Hell is called the Work Area. That's where we spend most of our time. It's the largest part of the city. We go there to perform our duties. The only time we get to rest is at night. The best advice I can give to ya is this: make every second of rest count. The work here's worse then any job ya ever had, even if ya shoveled shit."

"What do you do?"

"I work in The Hospital."

"That doesn't sound so bad."

"Wouldn't be, cept' it ain't much of a hospital. I'm in the Research and Development Department; The Overlords test different diseases on me. They infect me with stuff and lock me in a room to see what happens. Sometimes, I'm left there for days. The only reason I'm not at work right now is cuz they're makin' something new. It ain't ready for testin' yet."

"Shit, that's pretty bad."

"Told ya the jobs are bad. At least I didn't get put in the Unnecessary Surgery Department."

My stomach churned. "How...how do they p-pick your job?" I mumbled.

"Basically, the more sinful ya were in life, the worse the job they give ya."

"Oh, ok," I breathed a sigh of relief, "I wasn't that bad. I just made a dreadful decision at the end of my life. In fact, I shouldn't be here at all."

"Heard that before," the guy said with a shrug, "But what'cha do?" He raised a disheveled eyebrow.

"I committed suicide."

"That's it?"

"Yea, for the most part, anyway. That's what the robed guy in Heaven said at the gate. I'm sure I've done other things as well. We all make mistakes. That's the only one I really regret."

"Shit man, that robed guy was a mother fucker." My companion yelled and punched the ground. "I ever see him again, I'll break his face. I think you got a raw deal, man. Most everyone down here's done worse."

"What did you do?" My eyebrows rose this time.

"I'm here cuz I robbed a store. The police came. I tried to escape n' accidentally ran some pregnant bitch over in my truck."

"Oh shit."

My face must have shown my disgust because he hung his head in shame while he continued, "Yea, I hit that fuckin' bitch good. Kept drivin' too, 'til the cops forced me off the road. When I got out, I pulled out a knife. They shot me dead. I was drunk, ya see. I deserve this, as much as I hate it."

"We've all done things we regret," I tried to reassure him.

"Yeah, well, fuck it," he exclaimed. "I guess, even if I hadn't been killed by them cops, I wouldn't have been able to live with myself afterwards...once I sobered up, ya know?" His voice cracked as he went on, "That family must be torn up. Was a terrible thing I did. Wish it had been me instead of that fat bitch."

"Just because she was pregnant doesn't mean she was fat," I let him know. As I saw it, there was a definite distinction between the two.

He laughed a moment and told me, "Know what man? You're alright. Damn shame ya ended up here."

It was my turn to laugh, though mostly out of self-pity. "No need to remind me."

"Well, good luck to ya. Hope I saved ya some unneeded sufferin'. I'm glad ya listened to me but now I gotta get back to work. I'd shake ya hand, but ya might catch somethin." He stood up and started to leave.

"Oh wait," I blurted out as he turned away, "You didn't mention the fourth part of Hell!"

He turned back and stared into my eyes. His tone became dead serious, "The Pain Fields. They're the Punishment Section. Don't end up there, no matter what."

And, just like that, he was on his way. His disturbing response normally would have sent a shiver down my spine. As things were, I was stunned into silence. I decided to take his advice: I would get some needed sleep. But, before I did, I would dig a hole first.

ELEVEN: MY NEW OWNER

Much to my relief, I awoke from my hole unmolested. I hadn't slept well, which was understandable. Aside from the other problems on my mind, and the fact I couldn't get comfortable, I had spent much of the night wondering about what Jessica and Kurt were doing in Heaven. Were they playing hide-and-seek among the clouds together, as they had done when he was four? Maybe Heaven had a pool and they were playing Marco Polo. Did they know I was dead? And if so, were they waiting for me to arrive, or had someone told them I'd been sent to Hell? What would they think of me if they knew I had been sent to Hell?

The night was rough, but I had a feeling this day would prove worse. As I dusted myself off as best I could (which hardly mattered because my clothes were now filthy), I noticed a multitude of people had joined me during the night. They were scattered around at random. Many slept in the dirt, facedown, and rested their heads on their arms. Others were like gophers, and had dug a hole to lie in horizontally. Only their heads were visibly jutting out of each hole. These gopher-imitators often used a pile of dirt as a pillow. A few people had constructed a bed of assorted garbage, which I had been cautioned against.

I wasn't awake for long when the breakfast frenzy began. It started with a distant bell that rang five or six times. As if on cue, everyone began to scurry to the road. The next thing I knew, a bunch of gray Overseers appeared from between a few buildings. Each carried a five gallon bucket. Another drum that looked like a pickle barrel was strapped to each Overseers broad, powerful back. They walked down the road and reached into their buckets to throw handfuls of stale biscuits around at random, as if they were in a parade throwing candy to little children.

All around me, people swarmed to the Overseers in a violent rush. I watched as people knocked each other down, pulled hair, and tripped to get as close as possible to the Overseers and their stash of stale biscuits.

I tried to position myself to catch some. This became a difficult task given my circumstances. Foremost, the biscuit throwing was so random that many biscuits never even came close to me. Secondly, the throng of hungry people grew so large that it became a problem to move through them so I could intercept a biscuit. Lastly, when biscuits did come my way, someone in front of me would always jump up to snatch them out of the air or bat them down. It was as if a thousand people were playing defense on a football team and I was the only receiver trying to get open.

Every time a flying food-item was grabbed or knocked to the ground, it prompted a melee between a number of people who fought for it. It was like they were brawling over a baseball that had been hit into the stands. Usually, these biscuits were destroyed into no more than crumb-components in the process.

I knew I couldn't rely on eating anything if I hung back and let the biscuits come to me. That was akin to being the one person who got a random t-shirt shot at them from a t-shirt cannon, or perhaps a guitar pick or drumstick from a concert. The odds were weighted against me. I did, however, notice another means to get them: each time an Overseer tossed us a handful of biscuits and brought their arm out of their bucket in a throwing motion, many biscuits were pushed out by accident. These un-thrown treats landed around the Overseers' feet. That was the reason that many people swarmed right amongst the Overseers. My cohorts risked life and limb for a chance to eat. It dawned on me that I would need to do likewise, unless I wanted to go hungry. It was a risky proposition.

These Overseers were on a humanitarian mission to feed us. Even so, they remained just as brutal as the rest of the Overseers I had encountered. While they tossed biscuits at us, I watched as they lashed out at random to punch or kick anyone who happened to be in the wrong place. They also stepped on hands and fingers with seeming indifference as people reached among their feet for the fallen biscuits. I watched a great many people come away with broken digits, clutching a hand or a wrist.

The individuals who had the most success were lithe and quick. Perhaps they'd been pickpockets or street-urchins on Earth. They darted in and out like hummingbirds hitting flowers for nectar. I observed their technique and decided to mimic them. I forced my way through the crowd until I was close enough to an Overseer that I had a shot at falling biscuits.

The moment his hand came out of the bucket, and some biscuits tumbled out to the ground, I was diving. I grabbed one in each hand and was out again. Like that creepy little Lord of the Rings goblin guy, I slunk back into the crowd and mawed down my little precious's before anyone could steal them from me.

I was going back for more when I watched one, unfortunate fellow get pushed from behind by someone else. He fell at the feet of an Overseer, who then stepped right on his head. His scream was brief and the cracking of his skull under the colossal weight of the monster was sickening. I lost my appetite.

As if that weren't bad enough, once that same Overseer had emptied his five-gallon bucket, he callously whipped it into the crowd. He could have easily been an all-star pitcher. With tremendous velocity, the empty bucket slammed into the face of a guy who hadn't seen it coming. He dropped instantly. The bucket clattered to the ground nearby. I didn't know if he was unconscious or dead.

That was how breakfast was served in Hell. Refreshments came immediately after.

When every Overseer had emptied and disposed of their bucket, they gathered in a group about fifty yards away. I noticed that everyone followed them, so I kept pace. The Overseers stopped when they came to a series of wooden troughs which were lined up along the knee-wall. These had been obscured by a bend in the knee-wall, so I hadn't noticed them the night before. I also hadn't been adventurous enough to explore given everything I'd been through.

The Overseers reached the troughs. Each one removed the pickle-barrel from their back. They hefted the barrels up and proceeded to fill the troughs with filthy, brackish water. Like everyone else, I was now running to get some. We were like teeny-boppers rushing a boy band. The frenzy for water surpassed even the biscuit brawl. There simply wasn't enough room at the troughs for everyone, and it didn't look like the water would last. People man-handled one another out of the way, punched, kicked, bit, and clawed to get a spot. I forced my way in after getting a finger poked into my eye.

Right next to me, a person had drowned in the trough. Perhaps they'd been crushed by someone else. It was also possible they'd been knocked unconscious. The only reason that anyone had the decency to move the body was that it took up valuable room.

Like a farm animal, I leaned my head in and gulped down the

disgusting, communal water as fast as I could. Bits of dirt, debris, and hair floated around in it. I ignored those deterrents as best as I could. I also had to brace myself against the trough with one hand as I drank. That made it very difficult for anyone else to dislodge me. I simultaneously used my other hand to fill my canteen so I'd have water for later.

I was punched and kicked a few times while I did this. Once, I caught a knee to the ribs. In any event, I came away from the trough feeling rather fortunate.

The breakfast fiasco was over minutes later.

That was when the Overlords appeared. They thundered into the Residential Area to relegate duties. I learned this happened every day after breakfast. The Overlords were pear-shaped, naked beasts with scarlet skin. They shook the ground with each step and towered over us: the smallest were ten feet tall. Each had two fat, greasy legs with disgusting toes. Each toenail was long, cracked, yellow, and so long they curled at the ends.

The body of each Overlord was bloated and engorged, like someone whose kidneys had shut down. They had two, stubby, t-rex-like arms which extended out of what would have been pecks if they had any muscles under those layers of fat. Each arm had three, blood-stained talons instead of fingers. Although those arms were puny, and the claws looked worse than any imaginable case of carpal tunnel syndrome, I had no doubt that each talon was razor sharp.

Instead of a belly-button, the Overlords had what appeared to be a tiny, toothless mouth that opened and closed at random. A thin layer of what I hoped was saliva coated around the lips of it. The belly-mouth would have reminded me of a vagina except for the snake-like, forked tongue that darted in and out. It reminded me of the little, mini-mouth from the aliens in the movie with the same name. I saw no visible sex-organs as part of the Overlords, but that didn't mean much; any organs could easily have been covered up by the gross fat that hung down in front. They definitely had what I would describe as front-asses. This made it impossible to tell their gender.

I watched as the Overlords looked us over like a pack of hungry wolves. Their eyes were yellow and jaundiced. There was something feral about them. Each pair of eyes was sunk deep into a swollen, hairless head that was much too large for the greasy, deformed body it rested on. Every Overlord had a bulbous, twisted nose that reminded me of Monroe after I'd smashed him. The few teeth within each monster's snarling mouth were chipped, pointed, and twisted. No amount of dental work would fix them. Their heads reminded me of mushy jack-o-lanterns that had been left on someone's front step a month after Halloween.

Many people walked over to a specific Overlord as if they knew exactly where they were supposed to meet. I had no idea what to do. I remained in place near the troughs, frozen with terror and amazement. I noticed a number of other people were doing likewise. Maybe they, too, were new to Hell.

Moments later, one of the gargantuan beasts lurched my way. A long, flickering tongue darted out of its mouth as it stared at me. My knees started to shake. The Overlord then spoke slowly, as with great difficulty. Its tone was guttural and barely tangible, "Slave," it croaked, "You belong to me now. You will work. You will call me master when you address me." It then looked me up and down as if it were sizing up meat at a deli.

I stared up at the monster and tried to determine how I would tell it apart from the other Overlords. I also tried not to piss my pants. I wasn't very successful at either.

My Overlord snorted, and then simply turned away from me. It's fat, pock-marked ass jiggled grotesquely as it shambled toward another person who stood alone, apparently unclaimed. I noticed my Overlord had a long, rat-like tail which snaked behind it and carved a trail in the dirt as it walked. I looked at the other Overlords nearby. None of them had a tail. I could only assume that each had its own distinguishing characteristic. At least a tail was easy to spot.

After all the new people were accounted for (or made property of), my Overlord informed our group that anyone who already knew their job could head off to the Work Area so they could get started. The majority of the people in our group departed. The rest of us, who were all new to Hell, were told that we would be taken on a guided tour. My Overlord then signaled for us to follow it. The creature then headed towards the rest of our group.

Our gaggle numbered about forty. I watched the other Overlords as we moved. They were each headed a separate way and were also accompanied by their own flock of wretched souls. I presumed each was going to a different section of the Work Area, where different facilities and jobs were located.

I cautiously followed my Overlord. I didn't want to get too close to the monstrosity in case it got violent with us. Plus, I didn't want to stare at its disgusting ass or catch a nasty fart to the face. I also tried not to lag far behind the Overlord because I didn't want to look like I was being disobedient. This was a fine tightrope to walk. I was only concerned about it for a few hundred yards, however. It was then that we came to a thorn patch.

"You will now cross this," My Overlord told us. Then, very slowly, it explained, "It is called The Thorn Patch."

They're so creative here, I thought.

"You will cross it on the way to work, and on the way back from work, everyday."

I stared at the impossible tangle of vines and barbs with disbelief. It went on for as far as I could see.

"Get going!" My Overlord roared when it noticed that many of us hesitated. It wasn't even patient enough to finish speaking before it grabbed the closest, hesitant person in its talons and tossed the guy, head over heels, into the thorn patch.

The poor guy flew twenty feet before he landed amid some long, painful spines. He hollered like a two year old who'd been put in a time-out. My Overlord ignored his yells as he sneered at us and said, "The Thorn Patch is only two miles. It is of no trouble at all."

The monster, in fact, seemed to have no trouble with the millions of tiny barbs that jutted out from the tangled vines under its feet. I, by way of comparison, had enormous difficulty as I started out across it. Every step was worse than the one before it. The jagged points pierced into my toes and the balls of my feet. Some lanced my blisters. I screamed and fell down into the patch, amid a tangled mess which scratched up my arms and face. Some of the thorns had clearly broken off and embedded themselves in my feet. I picked them out as best as I could. I had no choice but to keep moving.

There were only a few safe places to step along the entire walk. The other, new people, who accompanied me, had just as much trouble. Their faces also twisted in pain with every footstep. Blood-chilling screams made my ears ring. Whereas at first I'd tried to contain my tears, by the end of the walk I was visibly weeping and I didn't care. My feet were shredded. With every step, I had to grit my teeth. I could feel the foreign objects force their way deeper into my flesh.

In a hushed voice, a guy next to me whispered, "Don't worry, man. Your feet will toughen up over time. If you can keep the same soul-body for five or ten years, maybe twenty, you'll be able to step on the smaller thorns without much of a problem. Either that, or your feet will just lose all feeling."

He didn't do much to lift my spirits.

After what seemed like an eternity of the worst pain I'd ever felt, we finished traversing that torturous expanse. My Overlord showed no sympathy. In fact, my new owner seemed to enjoy our misery. This was evident because it pressed us harder as we entered the Work Area.

TWELVE: THE TASK AT HAND

The streets within the Work Area were cobbled. My bare, bloody feet slapped noisily against the stones (which felt cool compared to the surrounding air). I wished I could lie down for a while. My Overlord began to address our group as I entertained the foolish hope.

"I explain this once for new people," It thundered in its slow, deliberate speech, "Prepare your sound-holes, stupid, weak humans, or you will miss out on vast things. Know that I am in charge of this section and all facilities within it. You will be led past the areas where you will be assigned work. There is no compromise. The duties you receive are to be carried out to maximum efficiency. You will also see many wonders. You will consider it a reward. This is impressive, good work," my Overlord pointed with an outstretched talon to a massive tower on the left, "This was built after the Night of a Thousand Wails."

It seemed my Overlord's perspective on good work differed from my own. The tower had a base that was about a city block in circumference. Rings of iron spikes were positioned every few feet around the tower's circumference. The only windows in the tower were high up in its parapet. They were oval shaped and covered in bright red, stained-glass. The tower roof was hexagonal shaped. It came to a point in the middle. A lengthy, curved-spike ornamented each corner of the hexagon like the horns on Viking helmets. Each spike extended two feet beyond the edge of the roof. These adornments made me think of the Thorn Patch. I was still in great pain from crossing it.

"It is called the Tower of Sleepless Nights," my Overlord continued, "The idea for it was conceived after all the screaming and wailing of many tortured souls kept us masters awake. The workers inside never leave. They are monitored at all times and never allowed to rest. In that way, they serve our master. For the punishment of being lazy on Earth, and sleeping their days away, this is where they go."

I was pleased that wouldn't be my destination. I hated being stuck in any one place even for a few hours. Being assigned there would be like being trapped at home during the Illinois winters (except sleep deprivation obviously made it worse).

My Overlord pointed across the street with its other talon. "That building is known as Packaging," it said.

I looked over at the Packaging building. It was seven stories tall with warped walls. It was shaped like one of the dragon's teeth that were once placed to stop tanks. The metallic walls were so bent and creased they reminded me of a crumpled automobile.

Unlike an automobile, the building had no windows and only one door set into an enclave. There was a body nailed to the door. Two wooden spikes through the eyes held the head in place while its legs and arms were each nailed to a corner. Centered above the door, in the middle of the building, was a crimson, rectangular banner. It had an upside-down, white cross in the middle.

"Any removed limbs are brought there," my Overlord informed us, "The limbs are sorted by workers. This is how we punish those who were ungrateful on Earth. People who took things for granted, and showed no appreciation for what they had in life, now work here. It is the job of these people to sort out limbs. Once all limbs are sorted by length, color, and type, they are brought to the Store Room, located next door, right there," my Overlord pointed right beyond the Packaging building to the next building on our right.

The Store Room looked like Hell's version of a pyramid. It was shaped exactly like the Great Pyramid in Egypt, and had to be almost as large, except it was built from piled skulls! An archway and ramp opened up to the inside of the pyramid. Through random chance, my Overlord happened to be looking at me as I gazed in horror at the skull pyramid. I think it mistook my horror for admiration because it nonchalantly spoke to me, "Most impressive skull pile. Took many years to make. Very scenic work, you agree, skin-bag?"

I wasn't about to disagree with the beast and not very pleased that I had drawn its unwanted attention. I quickly nodded but kept my mouth shut. I hoped at the very least that by getting on this thing's good side (if it had one) I could avoid future tortures. It was a gamble that made sense to take.

When my Overlord saw that I agreed (for lack of a better option), it smiled in a way that made me want to gouge my eyes out. Bits of rotted food were visible in between many of its teeth. Its smile was utterly heartless. It then talked about the function of the Store Room, "The limbs that arrive from Packaging are stored here until they are needed. There are many uses for limbs and they are often in high demand. Also many tasty rats to eat in there." Its long tongue flicked in and out and it smacked its lips together in a sickening display.

I gagged.

"Sometimes," my Overlord explained to our group, "Limbs are sewn back on workers here if they lose one from injury. They heal up in time and become functional again in a few days. Other times, we want to give someone extra arms. They can do extra work with more arms. This happens in the area within the Store Room called Customer Service."

I wasn't sure if my Overlord was being sarcastic about people doing more work or if the statement was really true. Or, perhaps, it was a sick farce. Either way, the concept was dreadful.

"Other times, it is amusing to sew a foot or hand onto someone's face. RAA-HA-HA-HA!" My Overlord's laugh was cruel and laced with malice. It was worse than any movie super villain. When my Overlord stopped laughing, it assigned a number of people to the Store Room and Packaging buildings. It then issued more instructions, "Look across the street, fragile worms. Over there is The Hospital."

With the mention of that facility, I thought of the man I'd spoken with the day before; he spent his days confined within its walls. I wondered what room he was in. From what he'd told me, The Hospital was a place of immense suffering. From the outside, the building was deceptively ordinary. It actually looked more like a prison because all the windows had bars. Other than that, it was a simple, square structure. The only real identifier that distinguished it as a hospital was an iron 'H' positioned above the main, obsidian doors.

"Workers go here for a number of punishments and for a multitude of sins that range from greed and envy to murder and rape," my Overlord explained. It then pointed with its talons to a number of men in our group. Those men were informed that they would be stationed inside of the hospital. One man groaned. Another turned white. One fainted. The last tried to run. He was picked up by nearby Overseers and beaten unconscious before he was dragged inside. The other men hung their heads and went willing but begrudgingly after that.

As we passed The Hospital, we took a right turn onto the next street and crossed an intersection. Once on the other side of the road, I could hear horrible cries of pain. They drifted through the windows of The Hospital and followed me for the next hundred yards.

"This is the Hall of Tedium," my Overlord said as it pointed toward a granite building on the opposite street corner. The building looked like a courthouse. I found that rather ironic given how much of my life I'd spent inside them on Earth.

The Hall of Tedium had the only pitched roof I'd seen thus far. A frieze faced the street and was carved into the triangular pediment that was formed by the roof. It depicted a brutal Overlord centered in the middle who towered over a number of slaves on either side of him. The disheveled slaves were pushing large, stone blocks across the dirt toward an area where the Overlord was pointing. For some odd reason, they looked up at the Overlord with reverent expressions as if they welcomed their slavery. The frieze appeared to be Hell's version of the Last Supper, or else was making a mockery of the event. Another consideration was that it was a biased, historical account of the Hall of Tedium's construction.

The building's roof extended beyond its walls and was supported by fluted granite columns with rectangular bases. Its steps were broad and made from bluish marble with swirls of black in it. The same banner with the upside-down cross that I'd seen on the Packaging building hung in between the columns from three, equidistant spots on the roof.

"There are two sections within the Hall of Tedium," we were told. "It looks small on the outside, but don't be fooled, dumb pink-skins. There is a floor level and also a lower level.

"The floor level is where repetitive paperwork is handled. Workers are forced to write all day. They sign and fill out the same documents non stop until their hands are cramped and their minds are numb. The documents shuffle back and forth. They never really go anywhere or amount to anything."

It reminded me of work back home. This sounded like the best place to be assigned so far. Until, of course my Overlord added more details a moment later, "These workers sit at the same desks all day. They are strapped into their desks. They perform their work while we fill the room with maggots. RAH-HA-HA!"

I knew there had to be a catch.

"Many of the souls that are punished within The Hall of Tedium were once selfish employers. These people inflicted similar, mind-numbing frustrations on others whilst alive. They kept their employees held down and shared none of their gains while they made other people virtual slaves."

Any sympathy I'd had for the souls in that room vanished. I was fairly sure some of them were CEO's and corporate big-wigs who deserved it. I would have bet that any former employees down here who knew them would have paid just to watch.

"The lower level of the hall is for similar sins," My Overlord droned on. It started to remind me of the very same corporate big-wigs who felt such over inflated pride in their own companies. Its belly-mouth opened and closed a few times. "Workers on the lower level go down to a broad cavern. There, they push around large rocks all day or move mounds of sand from one spot to another. They work until they collapse. When they recover, they do it all again. This is their punishment for excessive pride. They used to boast. Now they are humbled to menial tasks. RAAAA-HA-HA-HA-HA!"

I pondered their fates as we came to the next building in line. It was called The Ovens. Here, I learned they punished the gluttonous. It was a nine story, pentagonal building of obsidian. Circular, brass shields, about twelve feet in diameter, were mounted halfway up its walls every twenty feet or so.

"The Ovens are good for cooking," my Overlord said as its foul, snake-like tongue darted out of its mouth. "Overseers tie worthless humans to metal pans. Those pans heat up. Not fast, but very slow. The humans are cooked until they are a golden brown. They taste best that way."

As I realized the Overlords ate us, the only thought I was capable of was: oh fuck.

Three people from our group were then informed they would be 'working' within The Ovens. One puked instantaneously. The timing was unfortunate: we were all feeling rather queasy from this tour. Once people smelled vomit, a stupendous and awful chain reaction started.

I tried to exclude myself from the chain but could not. I lurched over and heaved up the filthy biscuits I'd eaten earlier. The pain was unrelenting. My stomach felt like it was being stabbed from the inside. I groaned and fell to my knees. I just missed landing in my breakfast.

As this wave of nausea overcame our crowd, My Overlord stood over us and laughed.

"You amuse me, humans but you waste good time," it said. "Lucky for you I laugh at your antics. Otherwise, you would pay for good time with good blood. Now, we move on."

At this juncture I stood up, took one step, and slipped on my own mess. I landed on the hard cobblestones with a shout and splayed out awkwardly. My Overlord noticed me fall. It laughed so hard its arms flailed about maniacally and its tail whipped around like a jump rope. It also passed gas so loudly that I swear I felt a breeze.

I felt a peculiar blend of embarrassment, disgust, and hatred.

My vile Overlord eventually stopped laughing at me and continued its guided tour of our specific section of the Work Area. It pointed out the purpose of various facilities we passed and periodically assigned people to them.

After a few more stops and lectures, we came to something called The Kitchen. To my surprise it was actually used as a kitchen! The building was square and windowless, with a single, obsidian chimney in the middle. Inside, other slaves cooked food for the denizens of Hell. This excluded our masters, who I'd just discovered ate people, rats, and who knew what else. As for the food we received, I had only seen moldy, stale biscuits. I wondered if the biscuits were fresh when first cooked and the workers either let it sit around on purpose to go bad, or more likely were forced to wait until the bread was nearly inedible to serve it.

One of The Kitchen workers eventually affirmed that my former assumption was, in fact, the truth. Such a sadistic policy wasn't really a surprise. I also learned that on special occasions, kitchen workers served rats, frogs, possums, and other vile creatures that looked and tasted hideous.

The last men within our dwindling group were assigned to The Kitchen for their crimes of gluttony. There, they had to work with food all day but could taste none of it. They were forced to smell delightful baked bread (which was the only pleasant smell in Hell) but could never taste it; even as the bread baked, and the workers imagined how good it would be, the Overseers found extra ways to amplify the torture of the workers. This was most often done by cramming sardines down each worker's mouth then punching their stomach until they regurgitated everything. The exception to this was people who liked sardines while on Earth: they were given other awful substitutes, or food that they were allergic to.

When the rest of the men in my group went into The Kitchen to begin their eternal chores, I was left alone with my Overlord. I felt very vulnerable and terrified. I followed my Overlord down the street like a well-trained puppy. I was ever-careful about my actions. The last thing I wanted to do was to upset the foul, evil monstrosity.

We hit a stretch where the terrain became barren again. My Overlord stopped talking. More buildings were ahead of us, only minutes away, and I had the feeling I was going to be assigned to one of them. Eventually, the silence became very awkward. I feared my Overlord would get bored and decide to torture me for fun. I decided to break the silence and did so in a manner I thought would be relatively safe for me.

"May I ask you something, master?" I tried to sound like a timid ass-kisser. This wasn't too difficult since I was scared out of my wits. My Overlord looked irritated with me but as far as I could tell it always looked that way. Regardless, I visualized a punishment coming on the horizon.

"No, there are no questions permitted," It scowled. "You have nothing worth saying. In the future, questions you think important will be met with punishments. Nothing less than strict obedience is tolerated."

"Yes master," I quickly answered.

The awkward silence resumed.

"Something strikes my mind," it said as it nodded at me just moments later. I feared my torture was about to begin. "You fell over and made me laugh," it commented, "Also, you are new. Therefore, I will permit you to ask one question based on those facts. It is the only question you will be allowed to ask that won't result in your punishment. Now, be quick, before I change my mind."

I breathed a sigh of relief that I was careful to hide. I wouldn't be punished for asking a question this time. In that way, I had gotten very lucky. At least I had learned to keep my mouth shut the easy way. I had one question to ask and a thousand I wanted answers to. I didn't have time to think so my question seemed ridiculous. It was actually more of an observation, but I was too afraid to put together something coherent, "I-I heard someone mention there is an ec-economy down here," I stammered. "Pardon me, master, but I don't understand how it works. All I see are people being tortured and it doesn't add up to me."

My Overlord hesitated for a minute. Its tongue snaked in and out of its mouth and it waved its t-rex arms around as if shaking them at me.

"You are not meant to understand," it told me. "You are a four-appendaged skin-bag. I will tell you about the economy in a moment. To better understand, first, look at the closest building on your left."

I did as I was told. I saw a pair of structures that looked very much like an industrial park. The two buildings were connected by a crumbling skywalk. A number of rusted, dangerous staircases led to different entrances and exits. Narrow, rectangular windows lined the walls along the top of each building. Every window was fitted with the same red stained-glass as the Tower of Sleepless Nights. To the right of the co-joined buildings, black, metallic cylinders were positioned in a row. Each was the size of a pickup truck. They looked similar to propane tanks.

"What do you think is the purpose of that facility?" My Overlord asked. I hadn't the faintest idea and told him as much.

"It is called The Refinery," it let me know. "Within its walls, all the torment of Hell is converted into useable energy. It is through suffering that we generate power. We use this power to combat the evil of God and his Angels. That is all you need to know about our economy."

I thanked my Overlord for answering my question and thought about the response. I recalled the words of the gray-eyed man: *Hell's more like its own society. Everything and everyone has a place. If you aren't in your place, you pay the price. We each have jobs to do.*

Our jobs were to suffer.

Somehow, that suffering aided these evil creatures and whatever vile purposes they served. The idea of Hell made more sense in that moment. The creatures here weren't being cruel without cause (though it often felt that way to me). Somehow, someway, they were serving a higher purpose. There was meaning behind the things they did to us. If Satan were truly the boss of Hell, then he must have a goal in mind. Did he plan to achieve it through the workers here? Had I alone deduced this, in only my second day in Hell, and nearly by accident? How many others had realized this mystery?

I would later be privy to those answers. In addition, I would also discern the exact mechanics behind the economy of Hell. I had no way to know it at the time, nor would I have believed anyone if they had told me, but I would ultimately play a crucial role as I served in Satan's chilling vision. The building blocks of my genocide were being laid and I was totally unaware of it.

"Here we are," my Overlord said as we came to a four story building, "This is where you will work for your sin of acedia, skin-bag. Acedia is recognized as a supreme lack of joy. It is what led to your despair and suicide. You shall now perform a joyless duty to pay for your crime. You will be filled with despair. RAH-HA-HA!"

I waited for more of an elaboration upon what my Overlord meant but

I received none. I crossed my fingers that what it considered a joyless duty wouldn't involve too much pain. I would have prayed for as much, but stilled fumed with rage about my sentence to Hell and knew no prayers would be answered, regardless.

Like the Packaging building, this facility had walls that were bent and crumpled. Several spikes wove their way in and out of the walls at random. They made me picture someone with a sewing needle having a seizure. The spikes eventually protruded through the roof to form a twisted spire in the center. There were no windows that I could see. The only door was over-sized and gothic-styled. It was also rusted, and had two, metal hinges. The handle was a pointy piece of scrap metal.

"The Overseers I supervise here will keep watch on you, weak human. They will watch you even though you're ugly enough to sicken us. The way your jabbering mouth moves up and down while your head bobs in all directions…it makes me want to slit my own throat. Now, enough talk of you. You are not worthy of my time. This is The Factory."

I looked at the building where I would be working, then back to My Overlord, then back to the building again.

"What are you waiting for, filth? Go inside!" My Overlord slapped the back of my head and caused me to stumble forward. I regained my balance in the same second that I grabbed the warped handle to push the door to The Factory open. The handle, with its many serrations and metal slivers, sliced into my palm painfully when my hand closed around it.

"Ahhh, son of a bitch!" I yelled and held my palm up to check the injury. It seemed alright, at first. Then, blood began to flow from the gash. Lots of blood. Within seconds, it was already dripping down my wrist.

My Overlord roared in amusement at my folly.

I suppressed my frustration and tried again. This time, I pushed above the door handle with my good hand so I wouldn't cut myself. The door was so heavy it barely moved. I heaved against it with all my might and the loud squint of metal scraping against metal made me wince.

When I got the door open far enough that I could see inside, I gazed into a darkened hallway full of thick, black smoke. My Overlord shoved me hard from behind. I fell through the doorway of The Factory with a shout. My landing on the rough, cement floor was awkward. I hit hard on my left side. My elbow absorbed most of the impact. I rolled over twice before I arose with a groan. I felt bitter and humiliated and could hear my Overlord laughing outside. The heavy, gothic door slammed shut behind me.

THIRTEEN: THE PUNISHMENT DUE

I made my way through the smoke-filled entrance to The Factory. The hot smoke made me gag and it stung my eyes. I pushed through it and into another room that was thankfully clear. Another disheveled worker was already there. He looked up from some type of control panel as he saw me enter. The look on his face was one of jealousy but also concern.

"Man, you're late for work," he let me know.

"I'm new," I told him as I sputtered from the smoke. In a sarcastic manner I added, "I just got a free tour."

"Oooh, yep, yep, yep," he reminisced, "They do that tour everyday for you newbies. Once you've done it once, you're not expected to need it again. I'd even advise against repeating it...you don't want to be around your Overlord more than you gotta. Not to mention it'll make you late. On your first day, it's a privilege to be late. You won't get punished this time."

"Okay," I said, "So what's with all that smoke?" I pointed back at the entrance with my thumb as if I were hitch-hiking.

"Oh, a dang exhaust pipe empties out into the lobby."

"Why don't they fix it?"

"It is fixed," the guy told me. "They ordered us to change the exhaust so it would vent poorly. That's what we did. The Overseers are happy with it."

I should have known the smoke was intentional.

"K, back to work for me," The guy said. Without another word, he looked down at his control panel again and pulled a lever. He didn't so much as give me another glance.

I looked around the room. It wasn't all that different from many industrial warehouses on Earth. Well, for the most part.

I first noticed a green chalkboard on the left wall; scratched into it, as if with a chisel, were the words, "This workplace has gone zero days without an injury." I wondered how they changed the numbers. The writing on the board looked permanent. Then, I realized what a foolish notion that was. It made me rather depressed in lieu of the understanding that I'd soon become one of those recurring injury victims.

Next, I noticed a ton of thick vines with vicious, three-inch thorns. They were pretty similar to the Thorn Patch vines, although must have been a different species of plant: the stems were much thicker and, thankfully, the number of thorns on them was fewer.

These thick croppings of vines broke through the cement floors and weaved their way up randomly throughout the building. Many broke through walls or meandered along the lengths of hallways. They eventually all worked their way upward until they protruded through the high, cathedral ceilings.

As I walked down a long hallway and looked for an Overseer (or some sort of hint to tell me where I should go), I had to frequently duck underneath or step over the vines. I inevitably jabbed myself on a thorn. My loud swear of, "Ahhh shit!" drew the attention of an Overseer who had been in an adjacent, side hallway.

The next thing I knew, I was looking up at a brute who was easily eight feet tall. He had a pig-like nose and beady eyes. He was also naked from the waist up and wore burgundy pants that appeared made from wool. One of his arms was about six inches longer than the other. And, most notably, a large, curved knife rested in a sheathe that hung from his belt. It reminded me of an Arabian scimitar. "You are making a distraction for others," he told me.

"I'm sorry," I rapidly apologized. Pointing to me injury, I added, "I just got stabbed by a thorn."

"You will be punished for being a distraction later, you worthless abomination. For now, protocol requires me to take you downstairs for merciful healing. That takes time out of my duties. You will be also punished for that at a future date."

I was making friends fast.

The Overseer growled at me and grabbed my wrist. He jerked me so hard that I lost my footing. He proceeded to drag me down the hallway as I tried to get to my feet. When we came to a set of metal stairs that led downward, he didn't even stop. I bounced behind the Overseer down three flights. My head clanged noisily off a great number of steps and I was painfully bruised when we reached the bottom landing.

I was immediately tossed into a tiny side-room with no windows and loads of spider webs in every corner. It looked like a cell from Guantanamo Bay. I collided with an immovable stone slab that was located in the center of the room. It served as a table. Multiple leather straps and some sort of head harness were connected to it. Another Overseer was already waiting within the room. Blood spattered his charcoal-colored surgical gown and a matching surgical mask that was about two sizes too small for his face. The pig-nosed Overseer followed me into the room and blocked the door to keep me from running (which I tried to do). I was now a trapped housefly that had been closed inside a window. Together, the two Overseers basically body-slammed me onto the stone table and soon had me strapped into it.

Pig-nose then stuffed a foul rag into my mouth. It tasted like oil. He watched in silence as the Overseer in the doctor outfit came at me with a red-hot brand.

I screamed into my rag and thrashed about as the Overseer with the brand pressed it onto the hole where I'd received the minor thorn stab just minutes ago. The smell of my crisping flesh filled the air. As I flailed about, I heard the doctor Overseer say, "You're just making it worse on yourself by moving."

I chose not to heed his advice and continued to strain against the leather straps.

When it was all over, I was unstrapped from the table. Out of instinct, I punched the doctor Overseer square in the jaw. I hurt my knuckle. He didn't move an inch. Pig-nose laughed at me and my wound throbbed.

"I take it you enjoyed your merciful healing?" The doctor Overseer chided. He laughed as well and turned his back to me. I swear I heard him call me a pussy under his breath, and then I watched as he placed his iron brand into an oven that I just now noticed. I hung my head in reluctant admission to the futility of my situation.

"What do you say to The Doctor for helping you and for providing his good services?" Pig-nose expressed with disapproval.

I couldn't believe it! I was expected to say 'thank you' for my torture. I kept my mouth shut. Pig-nose prompted me a second time. It became clear I was about to get punished if I didn't do as he asked.

"Thank you," I blurted out in-between sniffles.

I had many more unwanted visits to the Overseer simply known as "The Doctor" over the course of my work at The Factory. When this particular one was over, Pig-nose dragged me back upstairs, this time by my hair. My arm throbbed so bad that I hardly noticed the pain in my scalp.

It was time to discover what my work was going to be. I ended up with a duty that I considered fortunate: I collected the various skins they removed from people and packed those skins into boxes. Once full, I carried those boxes down to the first floor where I gave them to another worker. He was then responsible for reattaching the skin to living people who, for various reasons, had lost some (or most) of theirs. This procedure was accompanied to the tune of drawn-out, inhumane screams which echoed throughout the entire building at all hours. The end result of this (after the suffering was endured) was a lot of horribly mutated, grotesque-looking citizens wandering around in Hell with different colored patches of skin.

Over the next weeks, I learned the many pitfalls of The Factory, and hence saved myself many doctor visitations and punishments (in truth they were one and the same when it boiled right down to it). I also saved myself from a few extra deaths. Whenever I did meet with demise, the worst part, aside from the death itself, was getting revived all the way back at the Communal Room in the Residential area. This meant I had to cross back over The Thorn Patch an extra time on the long haul back to The Factory.

Oh, and speaking of pitfalls, there was a section of hallway within The Factory where most of the floor had collapsed. It had never been repaired, so there was a large pit in the middle of the hall. It was about a twenty foot drop for anyone who fell in. The only way around this pit was a thin ledge. Only one person at a time could traverse the ledge. Someone fell into that pit about every week. They usually broke an ankle or knee. No one paused to help any fall victims because we were punished if we took time out of our work.

I fell in on my third week and landed on my side. My head hit against a chunk of concrete at the bottom of the pit, and I was knocked out. I don't know how long I was there for, but I awoke to an Overseer yelling in my face. He called me lazy and asked why I was sleeping on the job. I explained what had happened and offered up a viable defense. As usual, my plight was ignored. I was punished for my actions. I'll spare the details of that particular punishment.

Regardless of what was done to me (and why), I was left feeling very bitter from the experience. There are few things worse than injustice. Having been a lawyer in my prior life, I had seen my share of it. Yet nothing on Earth could compare to the injustices of Hell. We were expected to get an unrealistic amount of work done. We were punished when we didn't complete our impossible burdens. We were subjected to horrific working conditions as forced laborers. Our work location had many hazards and impediments which prevented us from being effective. Yet, we were punished if we fell victim to these things. The Overseers were worse than any prison camp guard that had ever walked on Earth. They didn't accept excuses, even justified ones. Then, as always, was the unfaltering heat.

It was common for people to pass out from heat stroke several times a day. Our main, and only reliable means of hydration, was the little water we took with us in our skin-canteens in the morning (assuming we had a successful bid at the troughs). It ran out fast and had to be carefully rationed. Otherwise, periodic pools of water could be found in the basement. These pools formed as the result of a number of leaky pipes (yes, Hell had plumbing in places). The pipes ran upstairs to a variety of hydraulic machinery that the Overseers operated. We weren't allowed to touch those machines. Every so often, the pipes would break and leak into the basement. Of course, once workers discovered there was water inside those pipes, they ended up 'accidentally' broken at least twice a week.

The Overseers knew this was going on. As brutal as they were, they weren't stupid. If they caught someone drinking basement water, that person was punished so severely that it usually resulted in their death. Oh, and woe be to anyone who was caught tampering with the pipes! Under this constant threat, we filled our canteens with basement water at our own peril.

Other than the heat and lack of water, The Factory also had a number of burn hazards. These ranged from heated, escaping gas on the bottom floor (which I fortunately avoided in my regular duties) to scalding hot-water spills. There were also numerous open flames to watch out for. Then, there were the crushing dangers: grinding gears, compactors, and conveyor belts. It was common for someone to catch a hand in one of those on any given day.

In the section where I worked, one of the worst environmental problems was a dark cloud of dust that always filled the cramped, stifling room on the third floor. The dust got in my eyes and irritated them all day. It wasn't much different from when I helped Jessica's father build a deck once and got a face full of sawdust. This dust never went away and there was nothing I could do to avoid inhaling the particles. By the time work ended, I could hardly breathe. I often coughed up thick, black phlegm all the way back to the Residential Area.

These were the conditions I dealt with six days a week in twelve hour shifts. There was no OSHA to complain to. I could only imagine the conniptions an OSHA employee would have if they were required to file a report about The Factory! I worked all day in misery, and mentally tortured myself on top of it. I constantly thought about Jessica and Kurt. I couldn't help but wonder what they were doing. I longed to see Jessica's smiling face or hear Kurt's youthful laughter again. Those thoughts, and others like them, helped me to endure the long days.

FOURTEEN: ANTIPATHY AMPLIFIED

The only break I received while at work was a twenty-seven minute lunch. I am specific about the duration because I found it very irritating to be shorted those final, three minutes each day. Even the worst employers I'd had as a kid had given us a thirty minute lunch. If it was good enough for the federal government to need a law about it, I figured Hell should as least match their standards.

I mentioned that I only worked six days a week. On every so-called day off, Hell held a competition. The Overlords claimed it was designed to build community. It was more of an excuse to hold a free-for-all boxing match in teams, where four teams faced-off at once. Each team consisted of all the slaves who served under an Overlord. The competition was setup in a bracketed style: the winners advanced until only one team remained.

During each brawl, we had two official rules to abide by. There was also one unofficial rule in place. The first official rule was that we couldn't use any weapons. The second was that we weren't allowed to bite one another. The third, and unofficial rule, was: don't get caught using a weapon or biting. These rules sounded fundamentally sound, but in reality the Overlords didn't really care how their team won or what happened to us; they just wanted their team to win. They only established some formal rules to give these insane brawls the appearance of a real sport.

In actuality, the only winners were the Overlords themselves. The rest of us just came away with broken bones, missing teeth, bruises, cuts, concussions, and the like. We were never even told what the Overlords received upon winning, and therefore couldn't even get the slightest satisfaction from any victory. I only know that our masters always looked as close to happy as I ever saw them whenever their team won a match (and especially if they were declared champion of the entire tournament). I had to assume the Overlords received some sort of prize. At the very least, they came away with bragging rights for the rest of the week.

These matches were one of the few times when I found it beneficial to form an alliance with other slaves (who I normally wouldn't associate with). We did that too slightly improve our odds of not getting beaten senseless. In that regard, I suppose the idea of community building did come into play, if only for a short while. Regardless of what my team tried, we never won the tournament. We were usually destroyed by the third round.

On a personal note, I was often unconscious, or incapable of fighting, within two to three minutes after the start of almost every single brawl. I was never a fighter on Earth and Hell didn't turn me into one. If anything, it turned me into a better punching bag for others.

As for the rest of my week, I had my work assignment within The Factory, and that was that. The limited knowledge of everything else that went on inside my workplace was gained from the few slaves I interacted with each day. These interactions went only as far as they related to my specific job function.

The one time I stopped to try to discover what someone else was doing, I paid for it. I paused for only a few seconds to watch another condemned man. He was working alongside a few others who were stationed at a series of metal bins. These bins resembled coal-mining carts without wheels. In a stroke of bad luck, pig-nose entered the room at the precise moment when I was standing around. He pointed one of his stubby fingers at me and summoned me over. "Why aren't you working, you fetid heap of quivering soft-tissue!?" He growled.

I shook as I began my explanation, "I was just trying to see what that guy is doing," I said as I pointed to the slave I had been observing, "I…I hoped to further understand… um…the nature of his work to see how it uhhh….helps me." It was a plausible excuse and also the truth.

"Shut your flapping jaw, worthless aberrant. You will ask me questions instead of bothering others. Did you think I was too stupid to assist?"

I wanted to say yes, but I knew better. Furthermore, he didn't allow me time to say anything. As pig-nose shook his head with disgust, he commanded, "You will follow me." He moved in front of the metal bins. The other slaves stationed at them did their best to look busy and to remain unobtrusive.

I was sweating heavily now, and not just from the heat.

"Nod your ugly head if you understand what I'm saying," Pig-nose instructed. Then, he pointed with his shorter arm to the individual I'd been concerned with. "You see the person?" He asked.

I briskly nodded my head in agreement.

He continued, "That other worker is busy sorting skins by color. His job is none of your concern. I shall teach you a lesson. This lesson is to be concerned only about your own duties." In a swift, fluid motion, pig-nose unsheathed his large, curved knife.

"Wait, wait wait," I babbled as I backed away, "I've learned my lesson!"

He wrapped a massive hand around my throat and stifled my pleas. As I gasped, he forcefully pinned me against one of the bins. I didn't even bother to try escaping from his powerful grip (mostly because I knew I wouldn't be able to). However, I had also learned from prior experience that it was best just to get punishments over with quickly.

As he held me in place, I could only watch in horror as his curved blade swept toward me. My eyes followed the gleaming edge of the knife as pig-nose brought it down and pressed it against my left thigh. He hesitated for a moment as he were savoring my fear. I shut my eyes. The monster held me tight as he start to sawing away at my thigh, along the length of the muscle.

I screamed while I kicked my legs about. I squirmed and beat my fists against him in a blind fit of desperation. Blood poured down my leg.

When I was finally released, I collapsed against the side of the bin. Pig-nose had reduced me to a whimpering wretch. A large piece of skin from my left thigh had been hewn off. Pig-nose now dangled it in front of me to show me what he'd done. I clutched my wound and attempted to put pressure on it. I was later told by a co-worker that I cried something like, "my leg is fucked, my leg is fucked!" although I don't remember saying anything.

Pig-nose addressed me as he waved the strip of my skin in front of my face. I was dizzy form blood loss and it was difficult to focus on what he was saying. If I failed to pay attention, I'd likely be punished again. As difficult as it was, I did my best to listen. I remember him shouting something along the lines of, "See what you've done now?" He blamed me for having been carved up like a holiday feast. Next, I remember him tossing the strip of my skin into one of the metal bins. That's when I fainted.

When my eyes opened, I was still light-headed. The searing pain in my leg was the only sensation I felt. Looking down at the injury, I was surprised to learn that someone had packed it with maggots (which there were plenty of). Whoever had helped had also bandaged my leg with one of the many strips of skin that were also easily obtained. I looked up. Pig-nose was nowhere to be seen. Across the room, a nearby worker gave me a thumbs-up. I returned the gesture. Likely, he was responsible for helping me. He grinned for a moment. Then, his face turned to fear. He hastily went back to sorting skins (or whatever he'd been doing).

Pig-nose had returned.

I expected another punishment. Oddly enough, pig-nose didn't yell or shout. As he addressed me, he spoke in a manner that was quite calm. He was nonetheless distressing.

"You've made more work for that other vile, disgusting slave," he let me know, "Because of your selfishness, he had to go out of his way to put your skin in its correct container. He received a punishment as a result. He is not pleased with you. You don't want to make enemies here. From now on, stick to your work. Remain busy at all times. You will be happier that way."

I tried to take in the depth of his insanity but it eluded me. Shocked as I was, I had to affirm my understanding. I wholeheartedly decided to focus on my own duties from that point on.

All I can relate to the plight of my co-workers was that their tasks sucked at least as much as my own. I couldn't be positive, but I had a suspicion that our skin-canteens were manufactured in my workplace. I believe this due to the availability of materials, but I never confirmed if it was the case.

I was too busy dodging Overseers (pig-nose in particular, who had developed a fondness for making my afterlife more miserable), and attending to my duties to explore as the months dragged by.

My world soon became a hazy blend of sweat, blood, and pain. My general, day-to-day suffering was afflicted on me by the Overseers. However, my Overlord was also a cause of suffering that is worth mentioning.

Other than my Overlord's daily lecture (and the redundant, morning, city tour that it always gave for the new people), my Overlord very rarely addressed us. It felt that humans were beneath it (they all felt that way). I only heard it speak to any of us when it was issuing a command or handing out a punishment. In truth, my Overlord only showed up sporadically. I most often saw it during our day-off competitions, or once in a while when it popped its balding, misshapen head into The Factory for what I assumed was an inspection.

Whenever my Overlord came by to inspect my workplace, I noticed that it engaged in regular, one-on-one conversations with the Overseers. It was as if the two of them were good friends on a coffee break together. I eavesdropped on their bizarre discussions as often as I could. This gleaned some interesting facts.

For one, I discovered that my Overlord lost most of its teeth from chomping on people's skulls; it liked to suck the blood from our heads. It particularly enjoyed a good drink around midday. I used this knowledge to my advantage to avoid becoming a human-slurpy and made it a point to steer clear of my Overlord around then.

I also learned that my Overlord liked the texture of human livers. Fortunately for all of us in The Factory, the livers it took were from slaves in The Kitchen. They could enjoy the smell of fresh bread all they wanted, I was happy to keep my liver.

My Overlord also enjoyed a ritual called 'morning puncturing.' This involved the random torture of someone immediately after the work day began. It was designed to motivate employees. The term, however, was rather misleading: a variety of persecutions actually fell under morning puncturing. Not all of them involved sharp implements. The torture varied according to each Overlord's personal preferences. Plus, it wasn't necessarily held every morning.

My Overlord preferred to use sandpaper in diabolical ways.

In spite of this, it wasn't a glutton for punishment like some of the other Overlords. Throughout most of Hell, it was widely considered one of the better masters to be owned by. One reason for this was that my Overlord didn't make morning puncturing a daily occurrence: it usually only pursued the activity when in a more foul than average mood.

Another reason that my Overlord was considered "nice" was that it wasn't often prone to random cruelty. Whereas many Overlords (and certainly Overseers) were unpredictable in their violence and methods, my Overlord adhered to a loosely-defined rule set. Everyone under its authority knew the rules. We could be reasonably certain that as long as our tasks were accomplished, no punishment would be exacted.

On the other hand, there was a downside to this: if a task weren't done to its liking, the rage of my Overlord knew no limits.

I was set free from the enslavement of my Overlord and my Overseers at precisely the same time each day. The end of every workday was marked by the barking of wild hell-hounds that waited to be fed outside. Each looked like a starved Doberman but had a longer, sleeker body, patchy, disheveled fur, and bloodshot, rabid eyes. The hounds knew when we were all getting out of work. They were just as hungry as we were.

Thus, we were released from our duties and had to fight these roving packs off. Someone on the edge of the crowd was always dragged off and devoured. In that instant, the rest of us ran away from the distracted hell-hounds.

This mad rush clogged the streets with pedestrian-traffic. I hated traffic on Earth, especially on the way home from work. In Hell, the pedestrian traffic was longer than any line at Disney World. Everyone was irritable and impatient. We didn't need cars to have road rage. All it took was a slight bump to start fists flying. Sometimes, small riots broke out. These delayed the trip back to the Residential Area for an hour or more. The hell-hounds then capitalized on our dissention. They always caught back up to our crowd and dragged more people off for a meal.

Fortunately, once we exited the Work Area, this traffic began to disperse and the hounds were usually too fat and full to pursue us further. One by one, the host around me disappeared. I was always left walking alone. That was okay by me: I viewed everyone else as a potential threat. I would have preferred to be locked inside a Smart Car with an angry badger than trust anyone in Hell. People were as unpredictable as our Overseers. We tended to avoid each other.

These moments alone were the best part of each day…at first.

I loved that I didn't have to look over my shoulder every two-minutes. That was as refreshing as a cold drink on a warm day (though I was beginning to forget what that felt like). I never stopped loving that, really. However, as time went by, my attitude about this period of alone-time shifted: I became immersed in my own head.

I recalled how the guy I'd met on my first day had cried as I'd tried to run away from him. I began to understand why. Normally, I tried to avoid thinking about my situation at all costs: the day to day torment was simply too much to handle. Yet being all alone made it impossible to do that. Thoughts crept into my head like a stalker lurking in the shrubs. The loneliness was unbearable. By the time I came to The Thorn Patch, I was always depressed.

The stabbing barbs soon replaced my mental suffering with physical agony. However, the loneliness returned right after I crossed the obstacle. When I arrived at Slaver Square each evening, I was usually on the verge of tears or outright weeping about my miserable, despondent existence.

On evenings when I cried, I always wiped the tears from my face and paused to collect myself (which could take up to fifteen minutes) before I entered the square. To let anyone else in Hell see weakness was to invite calamity. The people here were worse than vultures and they'd pick a person's bones just as fast. To make sure I didn't fall victim to those vultures, I smudged a handful of dirt on my face before I entered the Residential Area. This tactic helped me to hide the tear-trails that ran down my soot-covered face.

Granted, I wasn't the only one who cried: I often saw many other slaves with telltale, bloodshot, reddened eyes and unmistakable tear-trails. I never asked them about their problems nor did anyone ever ask me about my own. Sympathy was another weakness that was best avoided. Besides, even if I'd asked someone what the matter was, and really given a shit about their answer, they would have denied there was any problem.

Once I arrived back home (or what constituted home), I had a period of free time before dinner: usually between thirty minutes and one hour. The time varied daily, and was mostly dependent upon traffic and hell-hound distractions. This free chunk was one of the only unsupervised parts of my day. This could be a blessing or curse, depending on what went down.

There was certainly occasional violence. People fought over the best place to rest, or for a spot where they planned to sleep that night. Sometimes, people tried to steal a skin-canteen from another slave. In general, though, this was the most peaceful time of the day for all of us. The reason for the peace was simple: we were too tired and worn from our twelve hour shifts of torture to have enough energy to bother anyone. Therefore, we often isolated and tried to rest. Sometimes, we congregated in small groups when the loneliness became intolerable.

During the few social occasions we had, I discovered just how different my former life had been from the lives of many other slaves. I talked with a banker who was sent to Hell for embezzlement, a cold-blooded killer who had murdered his own family, and even a perverted priest who took advantage of little boys. As far as our past lives went, I had very little in common with anyone.

The main trait that we shared was hope that we could avoid future pain. We also wanted to find ways to gain extra food rations, or to earn an Overlord's praise. These things were certainly on my mind. In addition to them, my true dream was to find a way back to my beloved wife and son, but I wasn't about to tell anyone that secret desire. I reserved a spot in my heart for a faint glimmer of hope that it could happen.

Another thing we talked about were tips to avoid pain. I heard about one great tip a month after I entered Hell. It was intentional suicide. It sounded insane, but in reality made sense. The reason it worked was that we were transplanted into a new soul-body at the Communal Room in the Residential Area. By killing off an existing soul-body at the end of a work day, people avoided the long trip back home. This spared them a walk through The Thorn Patch. Other times, intentional suicide was done if a person's current soul-body was so badly injured that their chronic pain was too much to take. This exploit was so effective that some slaves made it a regular occurrence to take their lives.

Suicide in Hell depended on where a slave worked. Some slaves were so fortunately situated that they could just leap to their deaths. In The Factory, the best way to do it was to stick your head into a compactor. Some slaves didn't have a reliable (or pain free) method. These people preferred to recruit someone else to murder them, often with a blow to the head.

Our masters frowned upon this abuse of the Communal Room. They wanted us to suffer as much as possible and it irritated them that we had found a loophole. They did their best to prevent our suicides and threatened us with all kinds of punishments. Like on Earth, though, people found ways to die if they wanted it bad enough. As long as we were successful in our efforts, our masters had no way to punish us: they didn't know what our new soul-bodies looked like and there was no tracking process in place.

The final common thread I held with other slaves was the idea of freedom from our terrible existence. Much like Mel Gibson in Braveheart, we wanted to overthrow our cruel masters and rid ourselves of the agony that shrouded us like a fog. No one came out and outright said as much (doing so would have invited the worst kinds of problems) but this was evident in the tone of a person's voice when they spoke about their Overlord. People hinted at perceived ways to injure or kill an Overlord. Some wondered how many slaves it would take to bring down an Overseer. I heard people talk about ways to make effective weapons out of the materials we had available. We knew that as large and imposing as our masters were, they were not impervious to injury.

I once listened to an intriguing rumor. It claimed that an Overlord was killed when it slipped off a narrow ledge inside a building called The Chamber of Raging Hormones, where the lustful were punished by having their groin's mutilated. This was located in another section of the Work Area, right next door to The Satisfaction of a Lower Nature Department. Through random chance, the Overlord who died was rumored to have pierced its belly-mouth by landing on a metal exhaust pipe that stuck out of the floor below. No body was recovered because the genitally-deprived slave who told the story insisted that the Overlord had dissolved into crimson colored jelly the moment it died.

I wasn't sure if I believed the rumor or not. Yet even if it were true, a coordinated strike against the Overlords would not be enough. Their orders came from a central intelligence. We all assumed it was Satan. The Overlords received instructions and passed them to Overseers. In turn, we carried out the instructions in the form of our duties.

The source of the Overlords instructions had to be taken out if a revolt was feasible. Just what was that source? Did it go by the name of the Devil, Satan, Lucifer, or Beelzebub? Was a fallen angel of unimaginable power, supposedly cast down to rule this forsaken realm, the true master of Hell? And, if so, could I be set free from Hell if this ultimate source of evil was removed?

FIFTEEN: A CHANGE OF HEART

The mere notion that anyone could overthrow the devil in his own realm was laughable. It couldn't be done. Nothing like an organized revolution had ever taken place. The last person who even suggested a revolt was turned in to an Overlord by a co-conspirator before their plan had even developed. That Overlord handed the guy to a group of Overseers who made a public display of him in the middle of Slaver Square. No one knew for certain what that man's name had been. Everyone now simply knew him as Marlowe. His name had become synonymous with bad luck.

His story was known as "The Story of Unhappy Marlowe." It had achieved legendary status. Most people knew it by heart because it was repeated so frequently. In a way, it served as a sort of twisted fairy tale. "The Story of Unhappy Marlowe" served as a chilling reminder of what happened to anyone who was deemed problematic. When I first heard about it, I drew two conclusions: first, it had to be horrendous. I figured this because nearly every fable within Hell revolved around gruesome torture. Second, I knew the story had to be true. Marlowe's fate had been so impactful that it made a lasting, vivid impression. In that way, it stood apart from the rest of the gossip.

Marlowe's final moments had been so terrible that they made any day at The Factory, The Hospital, or The Hall of Tedium seem only mildly distressing.

For his crimes, Marlowe had been stretched between two wooden posts and tied by his wrists and ankles so he was suspended about a foot above the ground. Once he was arranged to the Overseers liking, in a suitably-painful position, the real torture began. The first thing they did was twist red-hot screws into each of his fingertips. Next, they sliced the webbed part of skin between all his fingers with a thin strip of metal. Immediately after, Marlowe's hands were forced into buckets of salt that had been taken out of The Kitchens.

Marlowe was then left there for an unspecified time. The duration depended on who told the story. Some people claimed it was a few hours. Others believed it was a few days. Whatever the real truth, it was considered a fact that the Overseers stoned his toes and ankles until the bones were all but disintegrated. When the stale wind of Hell had blown through afterwards, it was said the remnants of his feet flapped around like wind-socks.

The rest of Marlowe's torture was lengthy and gruesome and the details of it aren't really necessary. He ended up bleeding out while hung upside-down from one of the poles as if he were a cow in a slaughterhouse. This was after Overlords pulled Marlowe's skin off with meat-hooks. His screams had kept everyone awake for eight nights. On the ninth, someone finally got sick of losing sleep from listening to him: they snuck over to where Marlowe was staked out and removed his tongue. When Marlowe was revived in another soul-body at the Communal Room, the Overseers were waiting. They whisked him away. No one ever saw him again.

It is generally assumed he is still being tortured under the direct supervision of Satan.

The co-conspirator who turned Marlowe in was given reduced labor for his part in the plot. He was also allotted an extra ration of water each day. No one could blame him for making that choice. However, everyone *was* rather envious of him. He became a marked man and had painted a massive target on his own back. This made him the victim of constant insults, beatings, and even rape (which happened anyway, but more so to him). Although every slave was subject to horrific incidents all day and night, he received three times the abuse that the average slave dealt with. Sooner or later, he could no longer endure it. He requested to be transferred somewhere isolated, away from the populace.

One of the Overlords granted his request for some unknown reason. Like Marlowe, he vanished, never to be seen again. One rumor of his fate claimed that he was locked away in a dark cell for eternity. Another alleged that he was being kept as a pet by the Overlord who had granted the request. What actually happened was anyone's guess.

Regardless of what actually befell the co-conspirator, or the person now known as Marlowe, "The Story of Unhappy Marlowe" was sufficiently powerful enough that it prevented any more organized plots. Marlowe's martyrdom epitomized what everyone in Hell feared.

After I heard this, I never mentioned revolution again; it just wasn't worth the price. I also became more stringent with what I said to others, regardless of the topic. Loose lips sink ships or get you flayed and stoned. Yet the silent thought of freedom (which resounded in my heart) never went away. It was a flicker of light in the darkness as surely as my dream to see Jessica and Kurt.

Once dinner-time arrived, all semblance of sociality we shared was cast aside like a used condom. Dinner was worse than Friday Night Fights. It was worse than breakfast, too. Dinner was considered peaceful when the casualties were under four hundred. As usual, everyone gathered in Slaver Square when the food bell rang in the distance.

Instead of Overseers serving us (like they did for breakfast), dinner was the job of the Hospitality Workers. These people worked 2nd shift, from just before dinner, until after it was served. Their role was to get loaves of stale, moldy bread from The Kitchens and to transport those loaves to the general population.

Immediately after the dinner-bell sounded, the Hospitality Workers came rolling in on convoys of wooden, eight-wheeled carts that looked like something medieval merchants once used. The carts had three large, spiked handles on each side. Each worker painfully clasped a handle to move their cart, which did not move easily: the wheels were more octagonal than circular.

When the dinner carts finally arrived, we were supposed to form orderly lines and wait for the Hospitality Workers to hand out all the loaves.

Imagine how that worked out.

The carts were mobbed almost the second they appeared. They usually got overturned in the frenzy. The workers pushing them were most often crushed by the carts as they flipped, or they were killed in the ensuing stampede. Dinner was a melee for each and every morsel.

The first time I attended dinner, I went hungry. I was unable to get to a cart in time. I also watched someone get hit square in the face with a rock. I remember him falling down with a twisted-expression as he clutched the bread that he'd salvaged to his chest. Three other slaves immediately leapt atop him to get that bread. I swore an oath to myself that evening that I'd never sink to their level. I would go hungry before I smashed someone with a rock and stole their food. Their actions repulsed me.

For a number of dinners afterward, I ate nothing at all. Sometimes, I ate nothing but crumbs. My stomach growled in constant pain. I was soon malnourished beyond belief. It didn't take long until each new soul-body I received thinned out. Whenever a new soul-body lasted a few weeks, which was pretty rare, I could always see my ribs. Even if I'd been able to eat a whole meal, the rations we were allocated were hardly enough to satisfy my appetite. Obesity was unheard of in Hell. I suppose that was the only positive thing about it.

As I starved, I thought back to the gray-eyed man I'd first met. He had shared his bread with me! Having seen and experienced the tortures here, including the torture of hunger (which was one of the worst kinds), I couldn't understand why he had offered me food. I devoured anything that was remotely edible the instant it was in my possession. The concept of sharing made no sense.

When I eventually ran into someone else who was assigned Routine March Duty, I asked him about that. As it turns out, the gray-eyed man hadn't been generous for any noble reason: those assigned to Routine March Duty were given extra bread. They were under strict orders to provide that bread to the newcomers they rescued. If they failed to do so, they were punished. The same held true for Hospitality Workers caught smuggling extra loaves at dinner.

Every night, whether I had eaten or not, I dug my nightly hole where I slept. There weren't many suitable tools to dig with. Anything that even resembled a shovel was often hidden away by other slaves. I could usually find a rock to dig with, but if not, I was forced to use my hands. The time required to do this averaged half an hour. My fingernails were habitually mangled and bloodied once I'd finished. Having dug myself a decent place to sleep, I crawled into my hole and scooped a few large piles of dirt atop my body to help conceal myself.

Getting some Z's was a nightly problem. There was no comfortable way to sleep, no matter how I tried to position myself. I never slept for more than an hour at a time. I considered a good night's rest to range from three to five hours.

Every night, I worried that someone would try to stuff my ass like a turkey while I slept. As a consequence, I kept one eye open, as a popular Metallica song suggested. On a regular basis, I was jarred awake by the unmistakable sounds of rape.

Following a close call myself, I decided to keep a pointy rock within easy reach. I wasn't about to fall victim to someone's insane lust without a fight. Of course, as Murphy's Law is prone to kick in, the night after I elected to keep a pointy rock for safety was when I was violently stirred awake. I am convinced if I hadn't taken the extra precaution to carry a pointed-rock I would have been fine. Nevertheless, a few months after I had entered Hell, I was jolted up by two thugs as they pulled me out of my sleeping-hole. I reached for the pointy rock but was thrown aside and kicked in the head a few times. I was barely conscious as I continued to fight them off. They quickly overpowered me. What happened next is something I don't care to recall.

The shame I felt the next day was worse than any I had ever known. If suicide had made any sense, I would have committed it once again. Instead, I was forced to cope with my shame. I cried openly and didn't care who saw. I never let anyone in Hell see me cry, but now I couldn't contain my emotions.

Even The Thorn Patch lost some of its sting that morning. As sick as it sounds, I almost welcomed the physical abuse. I felt that I deserved it. I went through work that day like a mindless zombie. My spirit was totally broken. I sorted through a pile of skins, nearly oblivious to what I was doing. Even the repulsive nature of the work didn't bother me. I could have been doing the laundry for all the thought I gave my work. I'm not sure how many mistakes I made. Through nothing short of a miracle, I somehow got through the entire day without incurring an extra punishment from an Overseer.

The next day, my emotions started to return. Well, seething rage, at least. My anger spiked to levels that I had only known once, after that death of my family. I analyzed every aspect of my situation on the walk to work that morning. I grew angrier by the minute. I thought about my life and the unfair turns it had taken. I swore out loud as I recalled my wretched childhood. I stewed over the loss of Jessica and Kurt. I mentally worked my way through every, single injustice I had suffered in Hell. I couldn't understand how all these terrible things had happened to a nice guy like me. The words of the old scribe at the gate of Heaven replayed in my head like a skipping CD.

We appreciate the amount of goodwill and service you've done. However, your final act was one of extreme selfishness. The Lord created you. Therefore, your life isn't your own to destroy. When you did that, you were playing God.

The more I thought about what I had been told, the more I filled with rage. My resentment festered all day like one of the many wounds I typically bore. I recalled how I had been sentenced to purgatory so swiftly and harshly.

The scribe didn't even let me plead my case. Who was he to judge me?

I knew I had gotten screwed. With each passing day, I grew angrier with God.

How can there be a loving, kind, forgiving God if he did this to me? How could I have been sentenced here with these other, horrible people over one simple act? These people deserve to be here. They are criminals and killers. I worked my whole life! I served God and tried to do good deeds! Look where it got me! What a bunch of complete bullshit! God has no mercy. If only I could see him, I would show him no mercy.

Thoughts like these filled my head daily. I began to act like the selfish person the sage had told me I was. I did it solely out of spite. My behavior gradually grew worse each day. I welcomed the new changes. I vowed to become the hardest, toughest, and most cruel person in Hell. I told myself that I would never be taken advantage of again. Piss on anyone who messed with me.

When dinner came one particular evening, I was so hungry and miserable that I stopped at nothing to get my fill. As I ran to the bread cart, I angrily pushed someone else out of my way. He fell face-down in the dirt in front of me with a loud groan. Without thinking or caring, I stepped hard on his back and pressed him further into the dirt. I laughed at his pained cries. He was nothing but filth to me. I used him as a mat on my way to the dinner-cart. I reached the cart just as it was being overturned.

I snatched two loafs from the ground and crammed one into my mouth right away. I took a step backward. I felt someone claw at me from behind. They were trying to steal the rest of my food! Before I knew it, my hand shot out in a tight fist. I busted the thief's nose just like I'd done to Monroe in elementary school.

Then, almost without my own permission, I began to scream in his face, "I'll teach you to take what's mine!" Before I knew it, I was choking him unconscious. I still had my other loaf of bread, though, so I was very pleased with myself.

There was once a time when I wouldn't have been capable of that kind of thing. That time had passed.

About half a year dragged by. My deeds became more barbaric.

I broke a man's wrist in a breakfast skirmish. The day after that, I rammed my thumb deep into someone's left eye for trying to take my bread. I blinded him. As if that weren't enough, I stomped on his throat because his pained yells annoyed me and I wanted to shut him up!

While these acts were despicable unto themselves, none resulted in a death. Two more months passed and that changed. It started when I didn't get to the dinner-cart in time. I didn't want to go hungry. My plan was to beat someone up for their food.

As I scanned the area, I saw a very thin and very frail person nearby. He had somehow gotten a hold of food, despite being one of the weakest looking people I had ever seen! He reminded me of the starving children I used to try to help. This weakling was making a cardinal mistake: he wasn't being cautious with his meal. Rather than hiding it, or being secretive, he all but waved his loaf of bread around as if he were showboating. As he sat down to eat, I noticed his hands were trembling. He was so weak that he almost couldn't lift the bread to his mouth. His arms looked like toothpicks. It was obvious that he'd been in the same soul-body for a long time. I wasn't sure how he'd managed to not die or get killed.

He was the perfect prey.

I headed in his direction.

He turned and looked at me with a horrified expression on his withered face. He knew what my intentions were. I suppose I had an evil glint in my eyes. He grabbed the bread to his chest in both hands, as if it was a baby, and then he tried to flee.

You son of a bitch! I thought. *That's my fucking bread!*

I tackled him to the ground. His head narrowly missed hitting a rock the size of a football. In spite of that, I still landed atop him with so much force that I felt one of his ribs break. He wheezed and let go of the bread. It rolled a few feet away.

As I sat atop his back, I felt the thrill of victory. It was a primal moment of conquest where the strong were taking what they wanted from the weak. He moaned like the frail person he was. I heard him issue a straightforward plea as I pinned him facedown, "Please....take the bread.....please....just..... leave me alone."

I snarled in a fury. I can't explain what it was about his weakness that made me see red. Maybe it had something to do with the weakness I felt in myself after the two thugs had violated me. Maybe it had to do with the sage at the gate of Heaven, and my inability to do anything about my sentencing.

Whatever it was, I grabbed the rock we had just fallen next to and hefted it over my head with both hands. Before he could say another word, I slammed it down on the back of his head with all the leverage I could muster.

There was a sickening crack as I felt his skull crunch. I then felt his body go limp. The last gasp of air hissed out of his lungs. I let the rock drop out of my hands. It rolled to the side with a dull thunk.

I looked at what I had just done.

I should have felt sorrow. I should have felt regret. I felt nothing at all. The only thought I had was of the bread he'd just relinquished. I reached over to pick it up. My bread was gone! Someone had snagged it as I had caved the man's head in! I hadn't even noticed. I'd been so preoccupied with the act of murder that I had let another slave swipe my prize.

It was only then that I felt regret. Not for the man I had just killed, or for the state of my soul, but rather for the lost food.

Following that episode, I lost any hope that I would ever see Jessica or Kurt again. It really sank in that I was stuck in this dreadful realm, and I'd become just another, terrible soul. I knew that even if I saw my wife or child, I had changed so much they wouldn't know me. I certainly didn't expect that either one of them would love me. Was it even possible for me to readjust to any sort of normal life after what I had been through? How could I expect myself to carry out the role of a loving, devoted parent when I had just brazenly smashed a feeble, defenseless man's head in with a rock? How could I look my wife in the eyes and tell her what I had done? I had killed for the pleasure of it. The bread had been a lower priority. Jessica would never understand what I suffered through. I couldn't place such a burden on her.

It was impossible for me to return to my former self. I had killed the old me as surely as I had killed that feeble man. This loss of hope was disheartening and it only made my hatred stronger. The ideals I once strived to uphold vanished in a wave of blood and violence. As years went by, any compassion I once felt was now replaced with contempt.

The years in Hell became a blur. I no longer felt sorry for people when I saw them dragged away to be punished. I started to laugh silently to myself as I listened to their pleas for mercy and heard their piercing screams of agony. Their pain was a source of amusement. They were worthless maggots. It thrilled me to see the fear in their eyes as they anticipated their unrelenting torture. I enjoyed watching them squirm like helpless minnows used for fishing bait.

ANDREW CORMIER

The thoughts I once considered evil were now commonplace. They had wormed their way into my head like an annoying musical jingle for an unwanted product and they were there to stay. Once I reached that point, the breaking of my spirit was complete.

Sometime in this indescribable period of indistinct, meaningless, years, my Overlord noticed how much enjoyment I was taking from the torture of others. It had been monitoring me throughout the years. My attitude hadn't escaped its attention. To my great surprise, one day after 'morning puncturing,' it approached me with another slave in tow. Its rat-like tail was wrapped around the slave's neck.

"This slave is to be punished at The Pain Fields," my Overlord let me know. "You are invited to join as I administer his lesson."

A broad smile crossed my face. "Of course I will attend," I offered. The glee I felt was about equal to when Jessica said she would marry me.

I followed my Overseer to the Pain Fields.

Once we arrived, which was no more than a few minutes later, the other slave's wrists were shackled to a wooden post. His bare back was exposed to me. My Overlord handed me a whip.

"You may do the honors," it told me, "You will whip this slave for a minimum of thirty times. You may continue to whip him for as long as you choose."

I took the handle and uncoiled the whip. For a moment, all I could do was stare at the marvelous device in wonder.

The slave tied up in front of me turned and looked over his shoulder. "Why are you working for them?" He asked me.

I remained silent. I didn't see a need to respond.

"You traitor! I'll make you pay for this, I swear I will!" He threatened.

I continued to ignore him. His threats turned into appeals for mercy. I could see the fear in his eyes. "You don't have to do this! Please reconsider!" Seeing how I continued to ignore him, the slave then tried to petition my Overlord, "Please master, I promise I'll do better work next time!"

My Overlord looked at me, "Proceed when ready," it said.

"This one reminds me of a greedy little child, deprived of a new toy," I commented in reference to the slave.

My Overlord laughed like Jabba the Hutt. It curled and uncurled its claws in anticipation.

I laid into the slave with the whip.

As he screamed, I taunted him, "Take your punishment like a man! You are a pathetic coward! You sicken me!" I whipped him until my arm was tired. My Overlord was practically beaming. We suddenly had something in common.

The thoughts of revolt or revolution that I had once romanticized quickly faded. Over the next two years, they became nothing but a distant memory as I bonded with my master over the other slaves' pathetic pleas for mercy.

I received immediate benefits from this situation. The best one was that I was regularly excused from my work at The Factory to attend and administer punishments in The Pain Fields.

At first, my master always accompanied me for these sessions. After about four months I was allowed to go about my own business. The morning after I performed my first crucifixion (at the end of those two years) my master approached me again.

"Halt your activities," it commanded.

"What could I possibly have done wrong, master?" I inquired with concern as I wiped blood off my hands. "I allowed this scumbag to suffer for extra long, just as I believed you would have done. If I can do better, I beg you to please show me."

My master waved its t-rex arms in a crisscross manner as it answered, "You have done nothing wrong with this one. You are told to halt by order of The Dark Lord. He demands your presence. Prepare yourself to conduct business. An Overseer will be here to escort you in short order. You may consider this the highest of honors."

I grinned from ear to ear as I waited for my escort.

SIXTEEN: TO FACE OBLIVION

When at last the Overseer who was to be my escort arrived, I was told in no uncertain terms to follow him. We left the Pain Fields and entered the Overlords Dwellings. As far as I knew, I was the only one who had ever been allowed into that section of the city.

The road there was paved with carved, granite squares that were charcoal-colored. Each square measured five feet by five feet and they were placed in rows of three. The granite squares had been sanded smooth. This road formed the first real, careful construction of any type that I had seen in Hell. Within the Residential Area and the Work Area, most everything looked half-assed. This road gave me the feeling that I had crossed over to the right side of the train tracks.

I counted the squares as we traveled (for lack of anything better to do). I was up to sixty when we came to the first of many rows of gigantic, obsidian houses. They looked like miniature volcanoes, but with doors, windows, and flat roofs. The front door of each house was similar to the one at The Factory. The windows were oval and crafted from the same deep-red, stained-glass that I had seen everywhere else.

On each roof, a banner of crimson hung from a wooden frame. Every banner bore a symbol painted in black: I saw a yellow moon, an eye with a nail in it, an upside down animal with no head (it could have been a dog or horse), and more. I figured each symbol marked the Overlord's rank or clan.

Some of these miniature, volcano-homes even had a garden of rotted fruit or vegetables planted out front. Many of the gardens were surrounded by little fences of bone. This was the first sign of any culture that I observed of the Overlords. I was also surprised to see that some of their yards had hell-hounds on chains out front.

An equal curiosity was that many hell-hounds even had doghouses! These were made from a number of materials that included rotted, mildewed wood, gray brick, and a material that looked like it could be human skin. Some of these doghouses (or hound-houses) actually had little, painted signs nailed to them. They displayed names like Ripper and Toxin. I didn't see any Cerberus, though.

The pet hell-hounds barked and snarled frantically at me as I strolled past. I returned the favor as I barked and snarled back. I laughed at them as they lunged at me and were stopped by their chains. I wanted to kick them (or worse), and I would have done so, but my Overseer escort was keeping watch on me. He just glanced at me with annoyance before he finally told me to shut up. I figured it was in my best interest to let the hell-hounds bark and ignored them.

Once beyond the houses of the Overlords, the familiar, dead underbrush and featureless landscape stretched in front of us. We got further away from the city. The roar of machinery and the screams of the tormented vanished. Eventually, another obsidian building popped up in the distance. It appeared to be a guard house, and resembled a barn. It was built into the large bone-fence that surrounded the entire city.

Two Overlords came out of a barn door to meet us as we approached. My Overseer escort ordered me to halt. He then went off to meet the two Overlords. I could see them talking just outside the guardhouse but couldn't decipher their words. They allowed me to pass a minute later.

Ahead, the neatly-lain slab road turned back into a dirt path. The solitary, giant mountain that dominated the landscape loomed into the sky. The ever-present, swirling clouds circled near its top while lightning flashed overhead.

I was escorted to the mountain and then up a ramp that corkscrewed around the outside of it. I went up this ramp until I came to a ledge that was a few hundred feet below the summit. It took about forty five minutes to get there. Here, my escort stopped and signaled for me to enter a doorway which was carved into the mountainside.

I paused to catch my breath and took a drink of water from my skin-canteen. As I took this quick break, I surveyed the view. I could see the entire city of Hell from here. Hundreds of smokestacks belched forth dark matter in an incessant stream. It was later in the afternoon, which meant that everyone would be busy working now. It felt great to be exempt.

I moved inside the massive doorway and my escort headed back down the ramp. I found myself in a grand amphitheater with more spherical lights suspended from vulture-like claws along the cavern's ceiling. A lengthy set of stairs ran down the middle of the room in front of me. Another set of stairs led back up on the opposite side. I looked down. I noticed, to my total amazement, droves of females! Every single bench of the amphitheater was packed with them. I would never have envisioned that many women in one place unless it was at a lesbian convention or some sort of men-hater's protest rally.

These women weren't rallying all that well. They were rather lethargic. An eerie hush pervaded the room. My footsteps echoed loudly in the quiet, vast amphitheater as I started down the steps. Immediately, a thousand heads all turned to look at me. I heard the buzz of hushed murmuring as the women whispered to one another. Their faces showed absolute bewilderment. It was as if they hadn't seen a man walk through the area in many years, or longer, and couldn't believe I was really there. I also noticed a great deal of sadness in their eyes; they told a story of unimaginable cruelties and perversion. I had no doubt that these women had suffered as much as anyone here, but I noticed no visible signs of physical abuse on their bodies. Even the tell-tale signs of starvation (that was rampant throughout the men in Hell) was lacking in the women.

I must say, the bodies of the women looked pretty good. Very good, in fact. I would even go as far to say very, very good and delicious! I almost forgot how much I missed titties until I got to see them again!

Most of the women weren't naked, though some were. The majority were rather scantily clad in two-piece slave bikinis. Each woman was chained to their spot. In that sense, they reminded me of Princess Leia when she was held captive in Return of the Jedi. Many of these women appeared to be chained together. The chains wove their way around their feet, and up through a number of iron rings that were fastened into the stone benches they sat on.

I looked the women over as I walked slowly by. Some managed weak smiles. I nodded at them and they nodded back. Some of the bolder ones licked their lips. None of them spoke to me. I got the impression they were afraid to be seen interacting with me. As I got further down the stairs, I noticed that some of the women looked pregnant. The further down I went, the larger their bellies became. I noted the oddity of this but their plight was really no concern of mine.

I went up the opposite stairs. Next, I passed through a massive, stone archway. It led to a hallway. Another row of sphere-lights lined the hallway ceiling. The sides of the hallway were full of alcoves which were separated by red-stained glass. I looked into the first of these alcoves and was shocked by what I saw within. There, a naked woman of medium build was hung upside down, suspended by ropes and chains. Her back was arched against some sort of wooden device like a medieval torture rack, and her arms were tied to the base of it. She was breathing heavily and appeared to be in a great deal of discomfort. I had the distinct feeling she had just been sexually mistreated.

The rest of the alcoves were filled with similar scenes. Some of the women were down on their hands and knees. They were being taken by one or more Overseers. Others were being submerged in water and then hoisted back up. Many were being violated with all kinds of sick objects. None of the women looked like they were enjoying their experiences.

I felt like I had just stumbled upon some bizarre pornography website or studio. I was glad that the thick, red glass of each alcove was soundproof. I made my way quickly through the veritable orgy and kept my eyes ahead. Although I felt nothing for the women, and figured they were just whores who had brought this on themselves, I had no desire to witness their degradation.

At the other end of the disturbing hallway, I entered an enormous throne room. On each side of the room, to my left and my right, a mammoth fireplace was nested into the walls. An entire kitchen set could have fit within each fireplace! Massive logs were currently ablaze within them. Clerestory windows of red-stained glass were set on each side of the two fireplaces. Additional fires burned within braziers of gold that lit the main path which led up to a throne. All these fires cast flickering shadows along the walls and floor. The throne at the head of the room was atop a dais. It was made of the familiar, twisted, black metal I had seen so often.

A blood-red demon that could only be Lucifer sat atop the throne.

Although the room was reasonably lit by the braziers (and a half-dozen sphere-lights that were attached to the ceiling), the demon somehow appeared to be hiding in shadows. It was like he had the ability to choose whether or not I could see him. Even sitting, he was the largest creature I had yet seen in Hell, or ever, for that matter.

The throne that he was perched upon was easily two-stories tall. His prodigious, dragon-like head came well above the top of it. His eyes were black and piercing as they looked me over. His mouth was full of razors. He had four arms. Each ended in a curled claw. Unlike the Overlords, his arms were massive and powerful. They put even Hulk Hogan to shame. Dark red, almost brown colored swirls, like some sort of tribal tattoos, ran down the lengths of his arms. Two colossal, black wings, like those of a bat, sprouted from between his shoulder blades. They were semi-folded as he sat on the throne. I was willing to bet that they'd reach to both ends of the throne room if he were to open them wide. His back and shoulders were adorned with two-foot, curved spines; these were the same color as his arm tattoos. Due to the spikes on his back, he kind of reminded me of some sort of movie monster.

The hair on my back stood on end as I walked up to him. I trembled but tried not to show my fear. Satan merely sat on the throne, still as a statue. The only sound was his powerful breathing and even from halfway across the room I could feel the heat of his breath.

When I neared the throne, he stood up. I looked up at Satan in awestruck terror. His head almost reached the ceiling (which looked a lot like one of the old churches I had seen while in France). I noticed a number of large, gargoyle statues. They were perched along a lip around the circumference of the room, where the ceiling and walls met.

Satan took two steps forward. I observed as a trail of hot fire sprouted up from behind him. He crouched down and brought his enormous head within inches of my face. His breath reeked like burning tires. Beastly, unholy eyes blazed into my own.

After a moment, he stood upright. He then rumbled one word: "Human."

His voice shook the braziers on the floor. I folded my arms and put my hands under my armpits to stop from shaking. I waited for Satan to speak again or perhaps eat me. The tension in the air was palpable.

"You must wonder why I have summoned you here."

I thought there was a pretty fair chance I was about to become a meal for the Lord of Darkness. I prepared myself to face oblivion.

SEVENTEEN: THE BOSS, EXTENSIVE

When Satan's spoke again, his tone was candid, although his voice still boomed, "You have caught my eye, tormented soul. I have reviewed your life. Many events have led you to this moment: none were coincidence. There is a grand design at work in the universe. You are affected by good and evil forces in ways you cannot even begin to understand."

I began to get the impression that I wasn't here to be tortured. I relaxed just a little and lowered my hands to my sides.

Satan continued, "The source of good comes from God in Heaven. I am the source of evil. This is widely accepted by many religious denominations. Nearly every human has some belief in a power of good or evil. In reality, there are very few atheists."

"I personally believe atheists are egomaniacal and full of delusions," I injected my opinion as I felt a bit more comfortable.

If the Devil was capable of an expression, I would have guessed his would have been one of incredulity. I had actually interrupted his introduction and had been fairly forthright about it! I had to be out of my mind. In that instant, the Devil could have reached out and snapped me in half, or gobbled me down as easily as if I were a mini-cupcake. He didn't even threaten me. Nor did his tone change.

"Most people," he continued unabated, "Believe they are the center of the universe. They feel so self-important that they swell full of pride at their meager, human accomplishments. They do not grasp a grand scheme." He paused for a moment, in what I believed was deep thought, and snickered in a tone so sinister that even Rambo would have shit his pants. "Yet like all living things, humans cannot stop death. Those who enter my realm and witness my vast and unimaginable power tremble like reluctant soldiers facing combat for the first time."

As he continued to speak, I felt the hatred that was inside of me come to the surface. I added, "It must be great fun to watch their horror. People are weak and foolish. They are a model of cowardice."

Satan nodded, "Ahh, yes, I derive great enjoyment as I break them of their pride. I crush them mentally, physically and emotionally. In due time, they conform as obedient servants."

"I hope I have proven to be a good servant, master."

"I am pleased with you. Tell me why it is you wish to serve me."

This felt like a defining moment. I knew that much hinged upon my answer. I thought carefully before I provided Satan with an honest reply, "I was treated unfairly by the scribe in Heaven. I was not even given an opportunity to speak my mind. God sent me here. It is His fault I have suffered like this. I performed good works throughout my life and they amounted to nothing,...at least for me. I made sacrifices. I gave away my time and money to other people. All I received in return was ingratitude and a trip here. I have been paid back with brutal beatings, mockery, humiliation, and the repeated death of my soul-body. All this has been because of one, final decision in my life."

"So you do not blame me or my minions for your suffering?" Satan quizzed me.

"Not at all."

"Why? Has not it been us who have been the source of your misery?"

"I had believed you were, but not anymore."

"Why is that?"

"You and your minions were doing the jobs you have always done. Your rule is harsh but just. Bad deeds cannot go unpunished, nor can good deeds go unrewarded. I did not like the punishments I received, but I learned to accept them. When I started to view your kingdom as the Overlords do, I began to receive rewards. In contrast, the sage at the gate of Heaven didn't even allow me to see Jessica or Kurt, or even speak to either of them. By the rules of God, I was judged and condemned. I received not an ounce of what I deserved. That is why I wish to serve you."

Satan paused. I felt his breath in my face and the weight of his gaze upon me. Seconds ticked by. I looked at him with apprehension as I waited for his reaction. At long last, he made a simple statement, "The lessons you received have strengthened your character."

His approval made me beam.

"You will make a fine servant," he let me know.

"Thank you for the lessons, master. I cherish the opportunity to show you my worth."

My words were not just lip service to the Devil. I meant them with every fiber of my being. I was my own man, making my own choice. Before, I had placed my faith in the wrong hands. God had failed me all along; I shouldn't have been so blind! I'd spent so much time trying to be charitable. All the while, I'd been serving a master who cared nothing for me. This time, I would serve my new master diligently. I wouldn't be treated with such injustice.

"You learn well, young one," Satan informed me while stretching his wings. "You may be worthy for an important task. Before I assign it to you, I must ask a few questions: do you wish to learn more about how your world is governed? If so, I can teach you much about myself, and much about God. If you want to hear more, you can learn more than any human has ever been privileged to know. All you have to do is agree."

I replied without hesitation, "Yes, master, please continue."

Satan seemed pleased with my response as he started to speak. Although I still couldn't see an expression on his visage, my intuition made me think as much.

He told me, "Many religionists believe in the power of prayer. They are correct in that belief. When a person takes their concerns to God through prayer, that person shows faith in the forces of good. Likewise, when someone refuses to pray, or prays for dark things to happen, they show faith in evil forces. Once a person displays such faith, the corresponding deity, myself or God, is able to intervene and influence them.

"God has three common ways to influence humans. The first is by spreading goodwill. The large-scale evidence of this is the various charities and organizations that spring up to help assorted groups. To counteract goodwill, I use negative messages."

"How so, master?"

"Imagine you are watching the device you call television. A commercial reaches your eyes and ears. It asks you to send a monthly donation to a poor child. My influence would be evident in a simple thought, perhaps as simple as: *I don't need to send money to them.* Or, maybe I make the thought more extreme, something like: *fuck them.* Maybe I just supply the notion to change the channel and fill you with disgust. Such is my doing."

Satan let me think on this for a moment. Once he seemed confident that I had processed the information, he continued his message, "The second, major way that God influences humans is by providing fortunate circumstances. An example of this would be getting fired from a job, only to subsequently find a better one. Should that happen, it is a blessing, and commonly thought of as such. I respond to God's blessings with misdirection. Should I get my way, you get fired from your job and your circumstances worsen. Perhaps, you remain unemployed and lose everything you own. On the other hand, maybe you fill up with spite. You become vengeful and go back to your old workplace to shoot people who you think deserve it."

"So you warp the minds of the weak or foolish, master?" I clarified as I tried to follow along.

"Yes, exactly: I plant sick thoughts in human heads. This is done to force a variety of outcomes that I deem satisfactory." Satan flapped his wings slightly. The flames within the braziers on the floor shifted from the breeze he generated.

I watched a bunch of sparks flutter up to the ceiling as Satan continued, "Finally," he said, "The third, major way that God is apparent in human lives is through the creation of miracles. A miracle is the absolute greatest display of power that God can use. An example would be this: you fall off a bridge and shatter your skull. You are in a coma for four months. Your family is told you will never walk or talk again. If you come out of the coma, you will be brain-dead. Yet before you know it, your recovery is rapid and unprecedented. You are eventually restored back to normal. That is the healing power of a miracle."

"And you counter them how?"

"I reverse the miracle. I make it so you do not recover from the coma, or, if you do recover, you are never the same again. I oppress people and destroy their faith in all things good. Once they lose faith, it is easier for me to influence them. It is incredibly difficult, if not impossible, for me to corrupt someone who frequently prays or performs good deeds on a consistent basis. On occasion I succeed, but the effort expended is hardly worth it.

"When I find a prospect that seems easy to influence, I begin to corrupt them. This usually happens very slowly, over a period of years or decades. In the average person, this may produce only white lies or petty theft. The results are stronger if the person is easier to sway. When my malign influence is stronger then the influence of good, they have been corrupted. Once corrupted, they lose any sense of morals or values that were instilled in them. They also lose their compassion for others; they thrive on misery. The individual may become a thief or they may turn into a murderer or a rapist. I then claim their soul upon their death. This is part of an ancient agreement I have made with God. Each of us honors it: he gets the good souls, I get the bad ones."

"People can change and be redeemed, though," I added. "People can do evil and learn from it to become good. In my case, I feel that my soul was generally good. Did God have a choice to take me, or not?"

Satan snorted. A breath of fire flew over my head and nearly singed all my hair off. "I hate when that occurs," he growled. "And yes, it can happen. On occasion, an extreme and direct act of God can restore a soul to His graces and allow God to claim them. More often then not, they are beyond help, and I get to claim their soul. If there is a gray-area in the matter, the choice belongs to God."

"So he did reject me," I established.

"Yes," Satan affirmed.

My hatred for the sage in Heaven and for my rejection felt stronger than ever. I focused intently on Satan's continued words, "And now you know how we impact your world. It is time you learn what happens here. There is a constant struggle for power between myself and God. As there are wars on earth, there is a war in the afterlife. Sometimes, I've been on the winning side, or else the tide is turned against me."

"Is there any way to tell who is winning?" I interjected.

"When peace reigns, so does God. When chaos reigns, that is my influence expanding. When the history of mankind was at the darkest, I was being the most productive: World War II, the collapse of the Roman Empire, and the bubonic plaque were results of my efforts. Even the flood of Noah, which was actually caused by a meteor strike, and generated a massive tsunami, was my doing. Of course, God is a tricky nemesis. He managed to turn that calamity to His own cause and used it to grow His following."

"God is a great deceiver," I surmised. "I know He deceived me. I followed Him and He banished me."

The Devil smirked. I felt he was keeping something from me, but I wasn't sure what it was. "Indeed," he conceded. "Another time when God outdid me was the renaissance. I tried to corrupt His church. My goal was to turn it into a force of evil and persecution. He swayed that period toward growth and revival. He bested me during the Industrial Age as well: I tried to turn the world into war. I was successful for a period. To my astonishment, God gave men insight to create new inventions that improved their lives. He also gave them unity to oppose oppression. Thus, He thwarted my bigotry and secured another, temporary victory."

"This all makes so much sense now that you've explained it, master."

I thought closely about current events on Earth. Everywhere people were killing one another for various reasons. People locked their doors at night for fear of being robbed. For similar reasons, they carried weapons for protection. Racism was rampant. Graveyards and churches were vandalized with no respect for the dead. Nearly everyone's sex conduct was shameful. Children were being kidnapped, raped, and murdered. Kids in Africa were turned into militia soldiers. The Chinese labored in sweatshops. North Korea was a virtual prison. The Middle East was one big battleground. The morals established by God were all but ignored as everyone selfishly pursued lust, greed, and self-righteousness.

"All the worst problems of the world now are your doing?" I asked.

Satan nodded.

A moment later I offered him my praise, "It seems that God is too weak to stop you. His foolish morals are crumbling in His face."

Satan smiled at me, though it was more of a snarl that showed off his vicious fangs, "And He never allows for any real fun, either. Ultimately, it is the greed inherent inside people that makes it easy for me to sway their minds. Humans always want something for nothing. They are reluctant to help others unless they get something from the exchange. Your world places far too much emphasis on money.

"Pharmaceutical companies are a powerful example of this: they withhold the knowledge to cure various diseases because they make more money off long-term treatments or prescription pills. They are happier profiting from suffering than they are for curing sick patients. Large businesses also use their greed to sway lawmakers to conform to their own agendas. While all this goes on, God and faith is forgotten or pushed aside."

"Most people don't know what to believe anymore," I agreed, "Their faith is scattered among many different gods that don't exist. Even religious works meant to help us live happier lives are being interpreted as an excuse to kill. Instead of working for peace, everyone is trying to force their own beliefs down the throats of others."

Satan laughed. "I sowed those seeds of discontent myself over the course of many centuries. It's one of my proudest works on Earth."

"You have done well, my Lord. The moral fabric of society is rapidly unraveling."

"Your sentiments are appreciated, not that they are necessary," Satan replied. He paced to a massive, arched window nearby and looked out over Hell for a moment before he turned back to face me. "Normally, this mayhem would be a good thing," he said, "It would mean I am far stronger then God. However, the circumstances behind this surge of power are different this time. You see, I am fighting for my life. I am desperate.

"God is winning the long-term battle for control over the universe. The universe has a tendency to head towards good and oppose evil. In spite of all I do, and everything I try, God is naturally stronger then me. The unified good has a sneaky way of always triumphing."

"That just doesn't seem fair."

"It is not!" Satan roared in a rare display of emotion. The whole throne room shook and the sphere-lights above me rattled. "The Angels of God and his saints are tougher than my Overseers and Overlords by default. They can fight longer, are faster, and can sustain more damage. This unfair advantage makes it difficult, if not impossible, for me to succeed, even with triple the souls here that are in Heaven."

"So you have actual warriors that fight one another?"

"Yes, we do. As long as God and I have existed, we have fought this battle for control. The whole time that we have influenced the events on

Earth, we have also fought one another in this dimension. Our warriors engage in combat in a neutral space between Heaven and Hell. Our two dimensions meet there. Neither of our armies have yet had sufficient power to break across the realms. It has been, for the most part, the largest game of chess ever played. It has turned into a gargantuan stalemate."

I suddenly knew my purpose for the meeting. "You are trying to break the stalemate and want me to help."

Satan nodded once more, "You are wise. That *is* the reason you are here. I need your assistance to accomplish my vision. I need an Earthly body to do things there that I cannot. God did this through His son. I need a son of my own. You burn with a hatred that consumes you. You can fulfill great works for me."

"You want me to destroy the world?"

"I want you to increase the death and suffering that already exists. I want you to bring plague, sickness, war and injustice in unheralded heaps. The mention of my name fills all who dwell in this realm with fear. Your name must do the same on Earth. It must carry the opposite effect as the name of Jesus of Nazareth. While the world is so filled with sin, I need millions, or possibly billions, to die. I need their souls to be sent here. They will swell the ranks of my army and fuel our economy for war. These extra souls, and the expanded influence they bring, will give me the leverage to triumph against Heaven."

I thought about this for a moment and asked, "How will I achieve this?"

"I will give you supernatural abilities and be your guide. I have great power and fury, but it is not infinite, like many would think. My power comes with a price. I thrive on destruction like some type of vampire. It isn't that I want to do terrible things to your world. I have been cursed to do them in order to maintain my existence. It is a curse that has cast a shadow over me since I was cast down from Heaven. To break this curse, I need to completely annihilate Heaven. In doing so, the natural balance of good and evil will be all within my control. I will gain complete dominion over the universe. I can then do whatever I please."

"So I help break your curse and you inherit the universe?"

"Yes."

I thought about the proposal. The implications of it were staggering. One question entered my mind. It was more important than any other (as far as I was concerned).

"If I were to succeed, would you then have the power to restore Jessica and Kurt to me?"

The Devil nodded at me. "I would be able to do that with ease. Once I have possession of Heaven, all the souls within it would belong to me. You could once again live in harmony with your family, friends, and anyone else you wished. I would even give the Earth to you as your kingdom."

I was almost too stunned to believe my ears. My greatest hope was still possible! I just had to reach out and make it happen. The words were hardly out of Satan's razor-toothed maw when I replied, "I will do this for you."

Satan rubbed his massive claws together, "That pleases me. Now, let us review my plan."

With a wave of a claw, Satan motioned to a consortium of female slaves nearby. They dragged two, massive, wooden thrones to us. The larger one was clearly Satan's: it took eight women to move. They strained with great effort and their breasts heaved as they pushed the throne over to where Satan stood. My throne was identical (but smaller) and only took four slaves to move.

When we were both seated, some of the female slaves pushed a round, wooden table to us. Others placed a number of charts written on papyrus atop it. They positioned skulls on the corners of each chart to hold them down. Two women then kneeled at Satan's massive, clawed feet. He used each one as a footrest.

"Would you like a footrest as well?" He asked.

I declined. As I watched the female slaves being utilized as furniture, I thought about all the pregnant women I'd seen earlier and decided to inquire about them.

"Master, what was with the many, female slaves in the other chamber? A great number appeared to be pregnant. None of the men I have met down here have seen any woman since we entered Hell. Unless I am mistaken, no human is responsible for these pregnancies."

"You are correct in that assumption, my servant. The Overseers and Overlords breed these women to grow my army. Their ill-gotten offspring become new Overseers or Overlords. In that way, these women are punished for being adulterous on Earth."

The punishment sounded truly abominable. I guess it answered my question as to which gender the Overlords were. I didn't want to know how they mated (my assumption was that it involved their belly-mouths in some disgusting manner.

"Because I am pleased with you," the Devil continued after he'd answered my question, "If you wish for any of the women here to satisfy your needs, all you have to do is ask. I will grant any request you may have. Just point out which women you want and consider them yours. You may even pick several at once if it suits you."

I seriously considered the offer but again declined, at least for the time being. We had important business to discuss. Satan shrugged (as best he could with all the spines and the wings) and pointed to one of the charts on the table. It was in some archaic language with unusual, swirling symbols and a number of triangles painted in blood on it. Therefore, I had no idea what it said or illustrated.

As Satan studied different items on the chart, he informed me, "I will drain power out of my realm to raise you from the dead. You will return to Earth in a flesh-body. I have had the strength to do this for millennia but have been waiting for the right human to come along. I only have one chance at this. So, once you are back on Earth, your first goal is to collapse the Catholic Church."

"Why them?" I wondered.

"They are the major institution that reminds society of right from wrong. They have the largest influence and the strongest public presence. In addition, they have been faced with past scandals so their reputation has already suffered a serious setback."

"Okay."

"You will need to start small, but I will help you get into a position of power. I need you maneuvered so that you can influence decision-making. Once you become an important icon, you will abuse your power and tarnish the good name of Catholicism. I will leave it up to you to decide how to go about this. Do whatever it takes to accomplish your goal, but be careful you don't compromise your position."

"Yes, master."

"When people see how they have been betrayed, I predict the church will begin a rapid downward spiral: people will lose faith in religious leaders, church attendance will drop off, and clergymen will become widely criticized. With all of those issues hindering them, the source of income for the church should decline until the church goes bankrupt. When its doors close forever, the center of goodwill that it once stood for will cease to be. The house of God will be shattered. As a final blow, society will begin to forget their ethics. The number and severity of sins will rise. In turn, this will allow for my power to grow until I cannot be challenged."

"Master, your vision sounds difficult, but not impossible," I commented.

"I know this can be done," he confidently told me, "I have been at this for millennia. Once you break the church, we can begin phase two."

"Which is?"

"You shall set nation against nation. You shall sow seeds of doubt amongst world leaders. Never before has the time been so ripe for a massive war on Earth. With a little prodding, you can bring it about. The misery that mankind has seen before will be nothing compared to the era I will help you unleash upon them. No one will be spared. Together, we will twist the entire world until God's kingdom collapses."

"Hell on Earth," I whispered.

"And you shall stand at the center of it," Satan told me. "Of course, you must accomplish your work swiftly. My strength will only be at a peak for a short while. If you don't work with reasonable speed and prudence, God could counter these plans. If God can perform enough miracles to help the church survive and allow society to recover, it will be my undoing. The warriors of Heaven could rage through here and slaughter this realm. My minions and I would assuredly be put to the sword. Even if failure doesn't meet with such severe consequences, you must not fail. I will not tolerate failure."

I thought about the implications of Satan's chilling warning. "I know I will not fail," I told the Devil, "And nothing would please me more than to cleanse the world for you. Mankind is reaping what they have sown. They are long overdue for their judgment."

"Do you have any questions about what you must do?"

I couldn't think of a question and it felt like I really should ask one. I recalled several job interviews on Earth as I struggled to come up with something. While I thought, I leaned back in my chair and looked up at the ceiling. That was when I noticed the sphere-lights again.

"I have no questions about my mission," I replied, "But may I ask a general question?"

"You may."

I pointed upward and inquired, "What's with those light? I see them a lot, but I don't see how they work. What powers them?"

The devil pointed to the ceiling with his two, upper arms, "I know all that happens in my Hell. I will satisfy you with a response. Those unique lights were installed after Hitler was sent here. They were specially made for him."

"Hitler gets special lighting, master?" I asked a bit dumbfounded.

"No, not as a reward," the Devil clarified, "As a punishment."

Now I was rather curious. "What fate was assigned to him?"

The Devil paused for a moment. He started to speak then stopped. A tiny puff of dark smoke wafted out of his nostrils. As it drifted around his head, he said, "It is in your best interest not to know. I will just say that Adolf is hooked to various machinery that keeps him alive. That same machinery does a number of other things to him on a constant basis. One of its functions is to power the sphere-lights by harnessing his constant screams."

I was sure Hitler deserved whatever they were doing to him, but even I felt aghast at the Devil's vague reply. "Would you say he is worse off than Marlowe?" I inquired per way of comparison.

"Ahh, Marlowe," Satan reminisced, "Or at least the name everyone knows him by. I alone know his true name, not that it matters. Did you know that his tale is always recited mistakenly? If people realized the great pains I go through to impose such delicious torment on him, they would be more punctilious."

"And?" I asked after a brief pause.

Satan snorted, "Hitler is much worse off than Marlowe."

I silently mouthed the word 'wow' before I told him, "I have no more questions. I am ready to go now, if you wish it."

Satan spread his four arms wide and extended his claws. In some sort of bizarre blessing, he added, "Go forth now with rage and contempt. Let the world feel your presence. You shall be the catalyst who will bring me the kingdom of Earth and the kingdom of Heaven." He then reached out and touched a massive, clawed finger to my forehead.

I felt as if my body was being cooked alive from inside. The burning sensation flowed through me. I was overwhelmed. My eyes rolled back in my head. Right before I collapsed, I heard Satan say, "Make me proud, my son."

EIGHTEEN: BECOMING THE BISHOP

I came to dizzy and disoriented. My vision was totally blurred. It was a few minutes before I could see straight again.

Blue sky now replaced the red, stone, cavern ceiling I had grown accustomed to. Clouds replaced the spherical lights. Green grass was abundant. The landscape was no longer featureless and barren. The sun was out. I had forgotten what natural light looked and felt like. I was also fairly cold. After years of ninety-two degree temperatures, I supposed even if the temperature was now in the seventies I'd be cold.

I looked around. It looked like spring-time. There were flowers of red, pink and white in bloom. I saw no snow or signs of wilted plant life. Had Hell been a dream? If so, where was I now? How had I gotten here? I examined my body. Much to my surprise, I had a new set of clothes. I was wearing a black overcoat, a blue dress-shirt, tan khaki pants, black socks, and black dress-shoes.

Even more of a surprise to me was that my skin was a different color. I was much darker than I had been before. I looked Mediterranean. Fortunately, no one was around to see my reaction to my new body. It would have been quite a spectacle.

My surroundings were as unfamiliar as my body. I was not in a place I knew of, or had traveled to. The road next to me was unpaved. It was very narrow. Fields stretched to my right and left. Rolling hills spanned for as far as I could see. A large building overlooked the valley that I was now standing in. It was perhaps a mile away. The architecture was unfamiliar. It was stone, in shades of tan and gray, with one large tower in the back. It seemed Romanesque. Above the main doors, there was some sort of large, carved circle, although I was too far away to see what is said or depicted. The building resembled a church, but from this distance, I couldn't be sure. In any event, it seemed like a logical place to head towards.

I arrived there in short order. Several, middle aged tourists were standing outside of a thick, stone wall that encircled the church-like building and some other little buildings. I knew they were tourists because they were taking pictures; either that, or they were photography buffs. Whoever they were, I approached one man who was wearing a fancy, brown sweater.

"Excuse me sir, can you tell me where I am?" I asked politely.

He raised an eyebrow at me. His response was in Italian as he said, "I'm sorry, I don't understand you."

Bizarrely enough, I knew what he said.

The voice of Satan rang in my mind: *human language is no longer a barrier for you.*

I repeated my question in Italian, which I spoke none of until that moment.

This time, the guy replied, "Ahh, this is the Basilica of Saint Francis, in Assisi."

"Thanks," I waved goodbye to the gentleman and proceeded to locate a bathroom.

Upon looking in the mirror, I nearly fainted. I was around the same age as I had been when I died on Earth. Otherwise, all resemblance ended there. I had short, black hair in a buzz-cut. My eyes were brown and I had thin lips. My ears seemed too small for my head and too high up. My nose was also a bit too big. I knew people altered their lifestyles, and went through mid-life crises, but shit! This was a bit much!

How did I get this body? Who is this person?

Satan answered my thoughts again: *your consciousness has been transported into a body that was born of dust. You have been made from nothing. Such is my power.*

"What's the next step in my mission?" I asked aloud, though I wasn't sure if the Devil could hear me.

Again, he spoke: *you will use your knowledge of theology and of legal matters to become a lawyer of Canon Law.*

Not one to question my master, I agreed and immediately began my mission. I sought out the information I needed by talking to a local priest. From there, I proceeded to Rome. I was soon accepted into an International Theological Seminary, with very few questions asked. I attributed this good fortune to supernatural powers.

The timing of my arrival on Earth just happened to be in the middle of a semester. This turned out for the best. It allowed me to keep a low profile for the first months of my return. More importantly, it gave me a reasonable interlude to readjust to my new life. During this phase, I lived at the seminary and performed various chores to earn some income.

Understandably, I found the transition from Earth to Hell to be one of great difficulty. I had a variety of psychological issues to work out and they really rattled my confidence at first.

Nightmares were the worst of my problems. I was plagued by recurrent visions of my time at The Factory, the Overlords, and the brutality I had faced. Every night, I awoke screaming and soaked in sweat. Sometimes, I discovered I had wet the bed. This was quite an embarrassing discovery for the son of the Devil.

In addition to these issues, I was very paranoid and anti-social. I continually expected people to hit me when I asked them a question. I thought that anyone who was walking to close behind me was following me.

One concrete example of this early phase was when I dropped a bag of groceries on the way to the shoddy, one-room apartment that I rented. As they spilled out of the bag, I cowered within my doorframe and expected to hear the malicious voice of an Overseer tell me how I was about to be punished for screwing up.

As it dawned on me that I was in Italy instead of Hell, I started to pick up the groceries. A neighbor noticed this and came over to help. Out of instinct, I cried out, "Get the fuck away from me!" I even cocked back my fist to lay her out.

Her look was of bewilderment and sheer terror. When I realized what I had done, I lowered my fist and profusely apologized. This was followed by her saying, "Okay, okay, it's alright, hun, I'm going to go on my way now, okay?" She hastily made her way back to her own apartment down the hall and fumbled the key in the lock as she frantically tried to open the door. When she finally got the door open, she disappeared inside and slammed it shut. I heard the deadbolt and chains lock. She never approached me again. It took several minutes afterward for my breathing to return to normal and my pulse to stop racing.

There were, certainly, other oddities I had developed. Some were subconscious. Others were more obvious. I avoided open-flames and converted my stove from gas to electric. I bought a ridiculous amount of rat-poison and pesticides. I stayed away from knives, scissors, and any sharp implements that looked painful, both for my own safety and for the safety of those around me (I still envisioned the tortures I planned to inflict on everyone I met). I shaved with disposable razors and wouldn't even consider a straight-edged one. It was actually rare when I did shave, and even then only to maintain appearances. My silverware was all made of plastic. The spork became my dearest companion. I didn't own a blender or anything with whirring blades. And, much like any woman I had ever met, I all but shrieked whenever I saw a spider.

It will sound odd, but another major change was feeling good. I hadn't felt anything close to decent health in decades. I sometimes thought there was a problem if I wasn't hungry or in pain. Once, I even cut myself in the kitchen and was surprised when my wound totally healed within a week! In Hell, anytime I had an injury, it never healed before my soul-body died. Although soul-bodies possessed accelerated healing (that could endure extreme abuse), most injuries grew worse over time. Injuries often became infected. Whenever they had been close to healing, most Overseers had taken great joy in reopening them.

Then, there was the subject of people: they were there to be utilized before they could be barbarized. Satan had made that clear to me. I once acted just like them. Now, their mannerisms seemed foreign (and not just because they were all Italians).

People on Earth weren't overly concerned with excruciating torture or starvation. I never once heard any mention about unnecessary surgery or being force-fed feces. Most people talked of things like electric bills, relationships, and employers that did not maim them. I viewed such things as petty grievances, nothing more. I found it difficult not to kill or torture them as I had done in Hell just out of sheer frustration.

To appease my dark thoughts, I often took home prostitutes. I figured Jessica would never know about this. I also figured that if she did learn of it once I had her back, she would have to mind her place. After all, I would soon deliver Earth and Heaven to the Devil. The world was my playground now. I could do whatever I pleased. This philosophy made it easy for me to abuse the prostitutes I picked up. Plus, society turned a blind eye to them. No one noticed or cared about the well being of street-walkers. I performed sick acts on them. I often sodomized them and cut them with razorblades (the only sharp objects I allowed myself to have, and only because they were little and non-threatening). I did this to them with relish. Oh, and I speak of enjoyment, not the hotdog type. I didn't slather the prostitutes in a pickle-based substance. That would be truly depraved.

In any event, these types of sadistic activities kept me from rampaging throughout Italy at random. Furthermore, the darkening of their souls aided the Devil.

By the time my Theological Seminary studies got underway, I was reasonably more adjusted. I had feared that my many issues would get in the way of my mission, but Satan kept assuring me that I was doing just fine. I was allowed to heal in my own time. The confidence I had felt throughout my final days of Hell returned. I could conquer my own problems and thus the world. I was still perfectly capable of striking fear in all those I met. I would make humanity pay for their deeds.

The results of my new studies exceed my hopes.

I found I had been granted the uncanny ability to memorize everything I read. I felt like some sort of human calculator. I committed everything to memory and it stuck. I aced every course. I hardly had to try. Teachers and students alike viewed me as a prodigy.

Within a year, I caught the Vatican's attention. I wasn't even close to graduating.

The next thing I knew, I was interning for them. I helped their lawyers with misconduct cases and I became their go-to person in almost no time at all. My vast, prior experience with law, and mastery of every language on Earth, proved useful to no end. Of course, I couldn't reveal to my superiors that I knew every single language. I let them believe I only knew English, Italian, Spanish, French, and German. My command of those languages was more than sufficient to make me a valuable asset.

It was because of all these skill (and some interference from the Devil) that I became an influential canon lawyer within just three years. All the while, I pretended that I genuinely strived to provide dioceses and religious institutions with unbiased assistance. I acted as if I were supporting parishes with caring methods for resolving conflicts. If the fools even suspected what really went on in my head, they would have locked me away for countless exorcisms and used the very canonical law I was practicing to put me away!

I carried out that role with unprecedented efficiency for another year. I felt that Satan's plan was moving too slowly. He kept reassuring me that his time was different from Human time and we were right on schedule. He let me know that time in Hell passed differently than on Earth: every day in Hell only amounted to a half an hour on Earth. I'd spent untold years in Hell, but only a few months had passed here since my death!

I was granted access to vast droves of canonical doctrine. That allowed me to alter much of my official history. I made it appear that I'd been a bishop for ten years at a church that was now closed. Making that change was really as easy as crossing out the name of a long-deceased bishop and inserting my own. Satan gave me that idea, so I can't really take the credit for it. It was due to his interference that no one really asked about my past. In my defense, I had also been smart enough to never bring it up. Therefore, when I was eventually asked about it, I was able to make the claim that I was a bishop. No one had any reason to doubt me. After all, I was a holy man doing good works, not some lying street-scum.

As I aggressively built my reputation, I also built a network of associates. These included a large number of priests, some bishops, a handful of archbishops, and sixteen cardinals. All of them placed their utmost confidence in me. They knew me to be pious and unwavering in my faith. I was considered knowledgeable and a genuinely pleasant person to be around. I was so well-versed in theology by that time (plus I had been to Heaven and Hell and they could only theorize about the two places) that we often had lengthy debates about scripture. I became friends with a number of these people. We associated with one another outside of the church. I even spent time at their house's.

While these friendships solidified, I planned a way to bring the whole structure crashing down on their heads. My ultimate goal was to meet and befriend the pope. It was through him, the most public face of the Catholic Church, that I figured I could do the most harm to their institution. In order for this to happen, I still had to expand my network. My worth had to be proven without a shadow of a doubt.

It was through guile and patience that I rose through the ranks of the church in the year that followed. That, and of course, unholy power that allowed me to cheat. Later in that year, I finally met the pope through some of my cardinal connections. He took an immediate liking to me. I wasn't privileged to see him very often, but through the help of the Devil, I capitalized on the moments when we encountered one another. The influence that the Devil and I we were able to exert on the pope was undeniably powerful. So much so, that when it came time to appoint a new cardinal, I was the name on the tip of the pope's tongue.

He later told me that he couldn't place why he'd wanted to elect me. He said he felt a bit fuzzy on the situation and had a lot of trouble thinking of anyone else. But, whenever he thought about me, the idea of boosting me up just made sense. This was, naturally, the Devil's doing. The clouding of the mind was an easy trick for him to pull off.

With my new position and responsibilities, I was busier than ever. I also had direct access to the pope. This allowed us to chat. We soon become friends. At first, I avoided spending too much time around him. This was to parlay the suspicions of other church officials. If everyone suddenly noticed that the pope was always hanging around his brand-new cardinal, I figured they would think something was up. It may sound peculiar, but even office politics at the Vatican could get very catty.

Granted, I had supernatural forces directly aiding me. I was sure that Satan could help me to sidetrack any suspicious holy-folk. That was until Satan assured me that even his trickery wasn't foolproof. Therefore, I played my cards close to my chest. There were a lot of very intelligent, God-faring people in Rome. If enough of them suspected anything was amiss, I knew there was a chance God would be called into play to answer their fears or suspicions. They had the power of unity and goodwill. Such things could break through most evil, or so Satan had led me to believe. Plus, I had a hunch that any direct prayers about me to God could alert Him to a spy.

I moved slow and deliberately. Every action I made was calculated. If rumor of any scandals arose within a diocese, I often handled them in two ways. Either I procrastinated and did nothing, or I pushed the blame off to other church individuals who I deemed were threats. When I procrastinated, I discovered that many issues faded into the background or got lost in the shuffle. When I blamed others, I was deliberately trying to make situations worse, but not to the point where they were out of control, and never in a manner that was traceable back to me. These subtle political actions ever so slowly weakened the foundation that the Vatican rested upon.

All the while, I continued to talk with the pope and to gain his trust. I was biding my time until the moment was right. According to Satan, I would know what to do when that time came.

It was no more than three months later when that fateful moment arrived. I was ready. I caught wind of an incident that involved a group of bishops who had been driving drunk! They had ran over and killed an eighty-five year old war veteran who'd been a pillar of the community! I had no doubt that Satan pulled a few strings to make that calamity happen. It was instantaneously front page news.

I checked all the facts on the case before I did anything. I learned that there was almost indisputable proof that the bishops had been intoxicated and could be placed at the scene of the accident. I noted there were at least ten witnesses to the event, and enough were reputable that it could be a serious problem. I then saw the video. It was utterly embarrassing for the church.

Taken on a shaky, cell-phone camera that night, the video started with an up-close view of the eighty-five year old veteran stuck under the bishop's car. The camera zoomed out to show the bishop who was driving. He stumbled out of the vehicle, still in his official garments, and fell down on his hands and knees. In slurred speech, he then blurted out, "Oh my God, I killed that guy."

Simultaneously, another bishop exited the back seat of the car. This one held a golden collection plate in one hand. In a drunken stupor, that bishop meandered over to the person filming the accident. The camera zoomed in on him as he drunkenly asked, "Have you seen this collection plate?" The bishop then pointed at the plate and laughed nonsensically. Of course, what was actually heard on video was, "Have you pee'd this selection cate?" A second later, he projectile vomited. All told, the video was twenty one seconds long. It exploded online and went viral in hours. Comments on it were disabled because there were simply too many.

The scope of the scandal was massive. I wanted to make it worse. I made sure that we denied everything when it first broke. I knew that denial would cause the most backlash. To achieve this, I drew up a public statement and looked it over. In the statement, I made the far-fetched claim that the church believed the video was a hoax. Until further proof came out, we had no opinion on the matter. It was a fairly callous response to the problem, but not an outright cover-up. In itself, the statement wasn't enough to ruin the reputation of the church (but it was a good start).

When this announcement was simulcast on TV and the Vatican Radio, people questioned if the event really was fictional. As was typical, the public had a very short memory for events that didn't immediately impact their lives. This questionable period only lasted until the next day. That was when the victim's family came on TV and denounced us. They were joined by the doctor who had pronounced the victim dead. He had also conducted the autopsy. It was a sad moment for them (not that I cared). For the church, it created a maelstrom of anger.

It was time for me to up the ante. I drew up another statement as media around the world condemned the bishops and our handling of the situation. The world demanded answers. Rather than confess the obvious truth, and deal with the matter in a professional manner, I generated an outright lie. I fabricated an absurd claim: the church was of the firm conviction that the bishops had been college kids posing as bishops after a night of drinking. We believed these college kids had broken into a church and stolen all the church items.

I knew that no cardinal in their right mind would approve my announcement. It fell upon my shoulders to read it to the world. I counted heavily on Satan's assistance to make this happen. To cover my tracks, I drew up a different, safer press release. This was the one I showed to the cardinals who were handling "the drunken bishops," as they had come to be known. In that statement, I made a number of provisions. I called for the swift and immediate removal of the drunken bishops. I announced to the Italian courts that the church would fully cooperate with their criminal trials. Lastly, I declared that we would work with the victim's family for financial compensation.

The panel of cardinals wholeheartedly approved my official statement. I volunteered to be the one to read it. No one objected to this. A few hours before I was due to announce our position to the world, I placed the good copy of my speech (as far as the church was concerned) in the desk of my secretary.

To the rest of the world, I read my version of the speech. It was horrifying to all who watched. It painted the leaders of the church in a terrible light. Media around the world turned us into a laughingstock. Angry cardinals (and other church officials) approached me about it. The pope himself left me an enraged voicemail! I played ignorant. I laid all the blame on my secretary. I told my accusers that she had given me a different speech on the way to the podium. The cardinals who read my good speech all vouched for me. None could even conceive that I had done such damage on purpose.

The desk of my secretary was searched, despite her protests that she knew nothing about what had happened. My original, pre-approved speech was found. She continued to maintain her innocence, as I had known she would all along. I immediately terminated her. She started to cry. I had her escorted out of the premises by security. For extra measure, I even added, "The Lord will punish your misdeeds, Cynthia! Pray for forgiveness and repent."

In the back of my head, Satan congratulated me on a job well done.

The backlash that followed rocked the church. Newspaper headlines around the world lambasted us. Opinionated callers on talk-shows hurled insults. People called for the trial, arrest, and imprisonment of many church leaders. Prior sex abuse scandals were brought up again. It became a tornado of problems. It was apparent that the crisis wasn't about to fade away over time. It only intensified the more church leaders tried to ignore it as they went about their duties.

Behind the scenes, I pulled strings like a puppet master. I used my access to the Vatican Secret Archives to become an 'unidentified source of information at the Vatican' for one particular news station. With the utmost of diligence to protect my identity, I fed a specific journalist documents that showed proof of sexual misconduct. These leaked documents implicated many well-known cardinals. The Vatican had kept this information hidden away for decades, but now these crimes were as exposed as a stripped wire. I, of course, was the Golden Child. My record remained unblemished: not a single, negative event or deed could be traced to me.

When daily protests started in Rome, I awoke with a smile each morning. The plan I had formed with Satan was, so far, an unparalleled success. In no time at all, protesters were throwing eggs and rotted fruit at Vatican officials whenever they went out in public. This included me. I didn't want to get hit with produce, so I stayed indoors and had my new secretary do my shopping.

One of the more rowdy protests started early on a Friday morning. By 10:00 am, at least three thousand people had gathered for it. They carried picket signs which read: 'leave the altar boys alone' or 'God said thou shall not touch.' Some protestors worked together to carry lengthy banners with the names of abuse victims written in thick marker. Others had obscene effigies of straw or wood which they had dressed like corrupt church leaders. In truth, some of the creativity the protestors had put into their signs was impressive. Secretly, a number of us had a good laugh at a few signs (it was the priests and bishops, etc, who didn't laugh that we figured were guilty).

The Dean of the Sacred College of Cardinals didn't find these protestors as amusing as some of us. In one of the biggest embarrassments of his life, on both a personal and professional level, he became the victim of a humiliating protestor attack. On his way into work that morning, as he shuffled through the mob, he heard someone shouting his name. He turned around to see who it was, thinking it was someone asking for a prayer or perhaps someone he knew. This was a big mistake. Right as the dean turned, he saw an overweight, balding, middle-aged man who was holding something unusual in his hand. It was, of all things, a full colostomy bag!

"Here's a bag of shit for a bag of shit!" The guy exclaimed. He then heaved the medical bag at the stunned dean. It landed right at his feet with a gross, splatting-noise, and exploded all over his shoes, soiling them.

This action incited the crowd even more. A round of rip-roaring laughter rippled through the protestors. Seconds later, people started to chant "Poop shoes! Poop shoes!" as they pointed at him.

The man who threw the colostomy bag at the dean was immediately apprehended by police. He was later charged with vandalism and malicious mischief. The dean practically ran into the Vatican to get out of the public's eye and escape their taunts.

I sat in my office and laughed about the event for the whole day afterwards. I couldn't even look at the dean for the next week without needing to stifle my laughter. Two of my favorite headlines about the incident read, 'this administration stinks' and 'dean doused in doo-doo.' Both articles were accompanied with pictures of his messy shoes.

After the pope read the same headlines, and had finished being both amused and infuriated (in about equal parts), he called me into his office. "What should I do?" He lamented.

"About poop shoes?" I asked.

We both laughed for a few seconds until his face and mood turned serious again. "Not just that," he said, "Although the dean's unfortunate pooping is a concern...I speak about the general situation that that church is dealing with. In my whole time as pope, I have never been faced with such adversity. I have prayed to the Lord for guidance in this matter and I am still unsure what, if anything, can be done to resolve it. Have you any wisdom, friend?"

The voice of Satan rang in my head again: *Tell him to step down as pope.*

"I think you should step down as the pope. It is the only logical decision for you to make. People want action. Your resignation will show them that the church is committed to a change. It may be the only way we can restore the public's faith."

The pope nodded at me with a look of sadness on his face. "I was afraid you would say that, my long-time friend. You have never led me astray. If you think it is for the best, than I believe I will go along with you."

I was shocked by how well the suggestion worked. The influence of the Devil was functioning even on the holiest of men!

"Yes," I told the pope, and tried not to sound too enthusiastic, "I do think it is for the best. The sooner you do it, the better for all of us."

"I suppose that is what I will do then," he said with a sigh, "Oh, and I'm sorry about that angry voicemail I left you. I said many things unbefitting of the pope."

"That's of no concern," I let him know with a pat on the back, "I don't hold grudges."

The pope resigned by the end of the week.

An emergency Papal Conclave was held. It was time for the College of Cardinals to vote in a new pope. With many other cardinals now jailed or removed from office, I was one of the front runners. When white smoke billowed out of the Sistine Chapel, the official announcement was made: I was the new Earthly head of the Roman Catholic Church.

NINETEEN: THE FALSE PROPHET

In my new role as pope, I vowed to do everything within my power to modernize the church. I also promised a new, zero-tolerance policy for any individuals who neglected the rules. I guaranteed the watchful public that through the Lord's guidance, we would overcome our obstacles together as a community. I promised that I would transform the church into a revitalized beacon of hope for all.

The first way I showed my commitment to change was by ousting hundreds of officials, from deacons to cardinals. By the time I was done, fewer than forty cardinals remained of the original 193 who'd held office at my election. I did this so I could setup my own base of power and garner my own supporters.

Whilst many church officials and leaders protested such drastic overhaul, the general public was vastly supportive of my reform. This allowed me to continue to establish my authority unchallenged. My false promises were blinding the world as surely as if a large spotlight had been shined in their faces. The public adored me.

Many of the new officials I brought it were yes-men. They allowed me to usher in another phase of changes. This involved the reform of many canonical laws. Among them was an allowance for women to become priests, and a provision so that priests could get married. These moves brought me widespread public praise. I was hailed as the man to bring the Catholic Church into a new era. One major newspaper even proclaimed me as the savior of the little children's assholes. Granted, they worded it more discerningly, but that's what the article basically said.

I also altered (or put laws in effect) that took power away from the cardinals and archbishops. This made me the final authority in most matters. With those changes in place, I decreed that every cardinal should now live at the Vatican, and conduct duties with technology instead of going abroad. I did this not to make matters more efficient, but rather to gather everyone to a place where I could find and monitor them.

With Satan's help, I had maneuvered myself into a position that let me turn the Catholic Church into a true dictatorship. Unwittingly, the rest of the church had let it happen. By the time anyone realized how powerful I'd become, it was too late for them to do anything about it. With so much weight to push around, I was like a poker player with all the chips. I used the wealth of the church to fund a movement that I called "Soldiers for God." The mission statement for the group was to help fight oppression around the world. In reality, this became a tightly-disguised military operation. I had started a literal army funded by religionists.

My Soldiers for God were at first made up of just professional soldiers that were hired as a contracting service. I started with just a few, small groups. I had them trained and recruited in secret locations all around the world. They were setup in such a manner that even if one became compromised, the paper trail was so difficult to follow that it would be nearly impossible to track.

In this way, I was not just working on Satan's scheme to collapse the church and create more sinners (with the goal of inevitable war). I had actually taken the plan a step further. I was developing the ability to fight that war! I was a son that my new father could be proud of. His voice constantly encouraged my progress.

As my soldiers trained, I used my position as pope to influence a number of world leaders. I ate lunch with a different president at least once a week. I made these scheduled luncheons seem like missions of goodwill. Who would question the pope's intentions, anyway, especially the pope who was becoming a hero to all? It was easy for me to pretend to hold peace talks and to act as if I were trying to improve society.

Instead, I listened to each president's concerns. All of them were worried about their public persona. They all had an agenda they wanted to spin. I allowed them to do this and didn't interfere. What they didn't know was that I was paying careful attention to their foreign relations. Every leader was troubled over a number of other countries. I couldn't fault them for those worries. I merely stretched the truth when I had to, but often this wasn't necessary.

If the possibility of a real conflict loomed in the foreseeable future, I made sure to mention it often. There were leaders who had more to lose than others from such potential wars. I tried to persuade them that whatever conflict they dreaded was right around the corner. I even told outright lies about foreign leaders to one another. I often heard it's not what you know, but who you know. Well, I was familiar with all the major players who counted. I knew just enough about each one to make my lies scary.

As world leaders placed more trust in me, the power of my lies became more believable. This allowed me to stretch the truth just a little more. I helped to affirm their fears. On one occasion, the president of the US outright asked me, "Holy Father, I know it's not your duty, but I really think Russia is plotting against us. What is your view on the issue?"

My answer was so bold and blatant it was almost laughable afterwards. "Of course they are, my son," I told him. "Just pray for guidance in the coming conflict with them and I'm sure God will tell you what must be done."

The president didn't even blink! I had just about promised him a war and he was suckered right into the deception. My malign influence, combined with that of the Devil, had warped him just enough to eliminate rational thinking. The time was set for conflict.

I met with the Russian president a month later. "I have some news that I fear concerns you," I told him.

"What is this news?" He asked.

"I should not pry, but I feel the Lord is asking me to supply you with aid. The US president has told me that he plans to ally with other nations in Europe to force sanctions upon you so your economy will be crippled for good."

"Is of no worry," he snickered, "Russia is strong. We will not be bullied. We will crush our enemies."

"Well that's good, because he planned to strike you by surprise," I divulged. Then, for good measure, I pretended that I had let that information slip out by mistake. I immediately corrected myself, "Oh uhhh... I mean he was worried about surprise strikes."

The Russian president looked at me askance. I could see the legitimate concern on his face.

"I am afraid I have said too much," I let him know, "I need to be going now. May God watch over you and bless you until we meet again."

We parted ways and I let that conflict simmer for a while. As tensions grew between the nations, I decided the time was ripe to announce my Soldiers for God to the world. I deployed two companies of them to certain problem areas in Africa. This showcased our presence in a part of the world where chaos reigned. Most of the world didn't give a fuck about Africa and had long since given up on the continent. Those attitudes helped me to endorse my soldiers as leaders in the fight against oppression. They were bringing freedom, and the love of God, to people who were incapable of doing it on their own.

I claimed that the soldiers I sent in were the entire military of the Roman Catholic Church. This allowed me to keep the exact size of my operation a secret. I also dubbed them experimental to lessen the impact of this news. Finally, I explained that The Soldiers for God were under strict orders to fight only sinners, such as guerillas and pirates. My men were, in fact, fighting some very bad, violent Africans. This was all to my advantage: my position was so widely revered, and Africa so known for problems, that almost no one fussed about the military action.

When I saw that I was unhindered once the campaign got underway, I took things a step further. An advertising campaign for the church's new fighting force was aired around the world.

Through clever, biased commercials, we showed The Soldiers for God capturing prisoners. The prisoners truly looked like filthy, disheveled animals – the worst kind of men you could imagine. Although I am not racist (I hated everyone the same), I will mention the fact that all of the prisoners were black. I comment on this because of stereotypes that have unfortunately existed against black people for centuries. As wrong as these stereotypes are, I still used them to my advantage. My television ads targeted many middle-class, white families, who actually had racial biases in one degree or another. My ads asserted that the prisoners had burned down villages, raped women, killed or kidnapped children, and committed other vile acts. Whether or not any captives had committed such atrocities was inconsequential: my Soldiers for God looked pristine. They were clean shaven. They stood up tall and smiled for the camera. They bore the flag of the Vatican City on their right sleeves with pride. They made the lie look even more real. It was a call to enlist for all holy Catholics and those who wished to convert.

If any church leader had tried such a wild scheme just a decade before, the church would have been doomed. It would have emptied out faster than if someone with smallpox had just been discovered sitting in a front pew. Not only am I sure of that, but I am also positive that church leaders would have been investigated (and likely imprisoned) for a plethora of crimes.

As things now stood, I had become such an icon that my new military was hardly a big deal.

Not everyone was on board, of course. A reasonable percentage of people were wary about the change. Many worried about the future implications of a religious organization having real firepower. These concerned citizens voiced their opinions, and I continued to play my role as a loving pope in response to them. These negative voices were rapidly shut down by the horde of people who I coerced into accepting my revolutionary ideas. The majority of the populace was pleased to see the church doing impactful work that the whole world could appreciate. People started to call me a patriot. They referenced me as a man of vision. TIME Magazine even dubbed me the man of the year!

One, unintended side-effect of this was that Church membership picked up. Donations from generous parishioners started to increase, especially among white, middle-class people who had seen my TV advertising. Satan wasn't too happy about this, and he let me know it. He said it was hurting his war effort because too many people were being nice and generous. I told him not to worry; I was using all the money to strengthen my Earthly military. He allowed me to have my way in that regard.

When at last the time came when a conflict erupted between Russia and the US, largely due to my meddling, I was overjoyed! Instead of trying to restore peace, I reached out to some of the world leaders who had utmost trust in me. Within two weeks, I had North Korea and China committed to a war alongside Russia, against the US.

To even the odds against the US military, the mightiest fighting force in the world, I knew we had to cripple their dependence on technology. We had to strike first and strike hard, or all would be lost. I first suggested this to Chinese leaders and they accomplished it through thousands of hackers. They knocked out every satellite system and overloaded the US power grid. Within an hour of that digital attack, coordinated strikes were launched.

North Korea drew first blood. By this time, they had developed the capability to strike the US with nuclear missiles. They did so without me even needing to ask or suggest it.

With their primary defense system offline, and no way to track the incoming missiles, the US West Coast was hit by two warheads. The first one struck LA. The second one decimated Las Vegas. Hours later, as confusion reigned and the US struggled to deal with the magnitude of the disaster, the Chinese Military invaded northern California at a series of major shipping ports. For the first time ever, foreign troops had landed on US soil!

The Chinese accomplished this through secrecy and careful planning.

They mainly transported their soldiers with a fleet of well-disguised, ultra-large container vessels, or ULCVs, that posed as commercial ships. Each boat was 1,200 feet long and equipped with a crane. These ULCVs rapidly unloaded convoys of armored vehicles and thousands of soldiers per vessel. The Chinese moved fast. They were soon interspersed throughout major cities in California and areas of Oregon. They indiscriminately slaughtered thousands as they pushed further inland.

The sneak attack, and lack of satellite coverage, made it difficult for the US to coordinate a counter offensive. They managed to stall the Chinese advance, but lost many military bases and radar installations by the end of the day. The following day, Canada immediately pledged troops to help fight the Chinese invaders. They sent their soldiers into the western US and bombed the Chinese with whatever air support they could muster. The week after that, Japan sided with the US and sent troops into China. The next week was when Australia and South Korea declared war against the volatile North Koreans.

By now, the Chinese had gained a foothold throughout much of the western US. Their forces were quite heavily entrenched there. Current statistics reported that the Chinese had more soldiers than the Americans had bullets, and the casualty count was ticking up so fast that a super-computer was needed to stay up to date.

The Americans quickly realized they had two options: they could either hit many of their own cities with nuclear weapons to take out the Chinese, or they could fight a massive battle on the ground. The president was too afraid of the backlash that would occur if they used nuclear weapons in a domestic manner, so he gave the order for the ground battle. It became the largest tank and infantry battle in history.

This unprecedented clash lasted for the next seven months. It was fought along one, massive front (which avoided most of southern California and Nevada due to the radiation from the nukes). Aside from those two areas, the front stretched all the way from southern Arizona, up through Salt Lake City, Utah, and made an arc to Seattle, where it stopped at the coast.

The US fought for their very lives and the Chinese threw body after body at them in an endless stream. By the time the battle ended, US troops proved superior. Their air support was able to turn back the Chinese and prevent a total collapse. The cost was immeasurable. Some estimates put combined losses at more than 20,000 tanks and armored vehicles. The death toll, which included civilians, was estimated in the tens of millions. The number of wounded was several million as well, though it was less than the number of dead (due to an inability to retrieve the wounded on both sides).

At the same time, Russia engaged the US East Coast with a series of targeted missile-salvos. These were intended to knock out key installations. Most of them failed because the US recovered their satellites in time to shoot the missiles down. The few Russian missiles that did get through wrought havoc. They claimed thousands of lives. It was reported that the governor of Virginia and a number of US congressmen were among the dead.

The US responded to the Russian attacks by launching their own ICBM's at specific, Russian targets. Other than those missiles, the US was so overwhelmed by the Chinese invasion that they couldn't take any offensive action against Russia.

This whole mess was really a delight for me, though it did leave me wondering who from my former life, if anyone, had been killed in the violence. I was well aware that Mr. Whigham, Mr. Fosworth, or even my parents could now be rotting in the ground. Not that I would shed a tear one way or the other for any of them. It was intriguing, however, to speculate about the fates of those who had once been a part of my life.

While I formed hypotheses about how former friends and family may have perished, the warfare spilled into Europe. It was like watching a kettle boil over. I was able to sit back and watch as one by one, other countries chose a side or opted to abstain from the conflict. As expected, Great Britain, France, Germany, and Spain all vowed to support the US with military actions against its enemies. Many of them began to engage Russian troops. Russia mounted a massive counter-invasion into Europe.

I was very pleased as I kept up with all that progress. I had no doubt that all these embattled souls were going to the Devil. I could feel his influence getting stronger as the world went to shit. Bear in mind, I did not sit idle while that fight raged. I made many public appearances and condemned the violence. I warned of the problems the world would face as world leaders allowed their greed to rule them. I preyed on public fear.

It was this fear that drew hundreds of thousands to my Soldiers for God. The military of the church gave them a way to feel safe. They considered my military a neutral force that would be left alone by the warring countries of the world. I ordained that all able-bodied parishioners should be signed up for service. I declared this to be the new direction of the church. Through firearms and numbers, we would provide a safe haven for all who sought us out. I built my unholy empire as other empires crumbled.

By now, the Italian president was consulting me on a daily basis.

"Holy father, what side do you believe I should take in this conflict?" He worried. "I fear that my people will suffer greatly if I choose wrong."

"My son, I think the answer is clear," I reassured him. "You should

ANDREW CORMIER

withhold from the conflict."

"But the US and Europe are screaming for my help," he argued. "How can I not come to their aid?"

I paused for effect before I replied, "Because to do so would invite calamity. This is not a conflict that will end fast, or without repercussions. You will destroy Italy if you get involved. For now, make it known that you will defend yourself if attacked, but you will not engage with any country otherwise."

The president rubbed his forehead and a pained look crossed his face. "But Father," he added, "Italy lacks sufficient strength to prevent a Russian invasion. If they attack us, we will fall. I do not believe they will honor this peaceful stance."

I laughed loudly. He looked at me as if I were a madman.

"You find this amusing?" He asked with irritation.

"Ye of little faith," I told him, "Do you doubt that I, your great friend and counselor, and a servant of the Lord, would step up and offer you my support?"

"I cannot ask you to do so, Holy Father."

I dismissed his claim with a wave of my hand, "I am not asking you to persuade me. I am telling you now: the Soldiers for God will defend Italy. Together, we have the strength to oppose any military in the world. No one will attack Italy while I remain the pope."

"I don't know how to thank you enough," the Italian president said. His eyes even started to dampen. He took my hands in his and kissed them several times. I allowed this heartfelt gesture although it sickened me. I could put up with his foolish display of gratitude because I had just usurped Italy from him and he didn't even realize it.

"No need to thank me," I smiled and tried to look sincere. "I do this for the good of Italy and for our friendship. It is the right thing to do."

I waited patiently as world events unfolded. It didn't take long for the situation to worsen. I can't recall everything that went on, but there were notable events.

One of the most tragic was the fate of England: Russia nuked them early to get them off the board. There was no longer a British Empire. In fact, Ireland, Scotland, and Wales were all collateral damage of that strike. The Russians pulverized the tiny islands. I expected that the region would remain a wasteland for a few centuries.

In addition to that destruction, Egypt broke its peace treaty with Israel. This occurred when several Middle Eastern countries determined to conquer the tiny, Jewish nation at last. Never a nation to be indecisive, Israel's response was immediate and unrestrained: Cairo was leveled by a warhead. I could almost feel the blast from my seat in Rome. As it was written in the Book of Ezekiel, the heart of Egypt had melted. I was fulfilling prophecy.

The war in the Middle East lasted for two years. Near the end, some country of unidentified origin exploded a nuclear weapon in the Mediterranean Sea. It became a toxic cesspool of death, incapable of sustaining any life. Water started to become a precious commodity, especially where I was located. A massive drought followed as one of the coldest winters ever set in. Crops and livestock died throughout much of the world. Hungry people in the worst afflicted areas resorted to cannibalism. That year, many more souls were claimed by my master.

What followed was a rapid shifting of borders and many, smaller countries were simply wiped off the map. This occurred mostly in Europe. Due to the presence of my army, no one dared to invade Italy. We escaped much of the carnage, other than intermittent food shortages and water rations. In other regions, there were areas where entire populations were simply gone. Cities were toppled and were replaced by smoldering ruins. Ghost cities stood in spots where people had either fled the violence or left in search of food. Countries fought each other bitterly around the world. Many exhausted their supply of soldiers and provisions. Russia's military collapsed entirely. The people of Syria revolted and overthrew their dictator; it collapsed into total anarchy. In a show of total surprise and horror (for everyone but me), the US went ballistic on China. As soon as they could, they nuked the Chinese into virtually nothing. Half a billion people died. A comparable death toll was the result when Pakistan also nuked their long-time enemy, India.

After this indescribable violence leveled off, most of the world's super-powers had vanished. Many nations which were once great now had no organized military or even government. The countries that still had soldiers fought with whatever limited capability they could muster. In contrast, I had sole possession of the largest, most well-equipped military on Earth.

For a long time, I had been a bystander while many of the events that I had helped to shape had unfolded. I was weary of waiting to make my move and eager to use my army. I had contributed to the flow of mankind's blood indirectly. I decided that I would now make a direct contribution. I picked up my phone of solid gold and called my second in command. When my Colonel answered the phone, I said, "We know that the whole of creation has been groaning together in the pains of childbirth until now."

His response echoed into my receiver, "Roger that, mate." I hung up the phone.

The secret code phrase that I had used to activate my Soldiers for God was a passage from Romans 8:22. I took it directly from the bible. The passage was dedicated to future glory, and I interpreted it to refer to my future glory. Plus, I was in Rome, so it was easy to remember.

My Colonel was charged with the day to day handling of my Soldiers for God. He was nothing but a puppet to me, but his loyalty was unwavering. That was the main reason I'd made him into a leader. His military record with the British SAS prior to entering my service had been exemplary. Once he proved trustworthy, I gave him more responsibilities. Through him, the Soldiers for God had grown over the course of six years. They now numbered over a quarter million troops. My fighting force had the best possible equipment money could buy. I also had a vast amount of air power and armored vehicles.

With a simple sentence from ancient scripture, he put all of my planning into action. He was eager to get revenge for what had happened to his homeland.

Immediately after I hung up with him, he issued a number of specific commands to various subordinates. The commands called three elite groups into action. Each had been trained for this moment. They knew precisely what was expected of them.

The first group let the Italian president know that I was now in charge. They did this by filling his body with lead. His cabinet was informed likewise. My military, which was now much larger than the Italian one, issued a simple order to the leaders of the Italian military: they had a new president. It was me. They would comply or they would resign. Their resulting cooperation was 100%.

The third group rounded up other high-ranking officials and judiciary leaders. As before, a similar directive was made known. Those who did not follow me were permanently removed.

The final action that was related to my Colonel's initial orders was the brutal extermination of all the cardinals. I wanted to be sure that there was no one left in power within the church to question me.

The Vatican turned into a killing ground. My loyal, best-trained commandos smashed down doors as they burst into room after room to shoot, stab, or beat the cardinals to death. I watched as one cardinal was thrown down the stairs and then beaten with the butts of M16 rifles. I saw another tossed through a stained-glass window to plummet to his death. I was pleased to finally be rid of these yes-men and pencil pushers.

Six of the cardinals, whom I had originally retained, escaped my eradication process. Two of the escapees were later hunted down. The first was killed outright by my soldiers. The other was brought to me in St. Peter's Square. This occurred right as I was about to give what I hoped would be an inspiring speech. I had an entire, new battalion standing at attention, facing me while I was all dressed up in my papal regalia (which included my papal tiara).

I had added my own touches to the pope's-outfit, of course. The first was a set of reflective sun-glasses so no one could look right into my eyes. I felt this added mystique. The second improvement was a leather belt with a saber sheathed on one hip and a Colt 1911 .45 on my other hip.

I was just about to begin my speech as two soldiers dumped the captured cardinal at my feet.

"Why have you done this thing?" The beleaguered, unkempt cardinal asked as he looked up at me in all my finery.

I adjusted my sun-glasses and told him, "I have done all that is necessary to reshape this world." I didn't let on that I was doing it for the

Devil. I didn't want my troops to think that they had been deceived.

To my great surprise, the cardinal seemed to know my plans already, or else just made a logical assumption. "You serve Satan." He accused me as he knelt at my feet, "And you have all along. We never needed an army. We never needed so many progressive changes."

"Whether I serve God or the Devil is no concern of yours," I let him know. "If you had done your duties all along, you would not have left the church in a position where I could walk in and take it. This was your doing as much as it was mine."

The cardinal shook his head at me, "You are misguided. You are no pope of mine. I do not expect mercy, but I ask that you think about what it is you are doing. The Lord will still forgive you, if you repent."

I drew the golden-handled saber from my belt and exclaimed, "I don't need His forgiveness!"

I plunged my blade deep into the last cardinal's stomach.

He bent over in pain and groaned while the saber jutted out of his gut. With a pained gasp, he coughed blood up all over his crimson robe. I let go of the saber's handle and forcefully kicked him in the shoulder. He fell onto his side then rolled over, onto his back.

While the impaled cardinal coughed up his life, and bled out onto the stones of St. Peter's Square, I turned back to my men. I addressed them while I pointed at the dying cardinal.

"Do you all see the fate of those who stand in my way?" I hesitated for a moment to let my message sink in. Then, I bellowed, "You will go forth now and set this world of madness right. We will retake the world and make it safe again. There are those who would rather hide inside their bunkers or lock themselves inside of rooms than fight. These men would let others fight for them. We will not be among them! I will not be among them! For the glory of God and the good of humanity, we shall go forth and spread the wings of victory! May the saints and the angels guide us!"

My speech was met with a raucous cheer that lasted for a few minutes. As the cheering ceased, the cardinal at my feet croaked one last time and then moved no more. "I declare this man a saint," I said over the now-quiet throng. "Those of you who wish to be blessed in his blood may step forward. May it offer you divine protection and be a symbol of your devotion."

As surely as if the gathering was an official service, a line formed. I dipped my fingers in the blood of my newly christened saint and made a quick swipe along the front of each soldier's helmet as they approached. We would make our enemies tremble before me.

TWENTY: SOLDIERS FOR GOD

My secret army revealed itself for the first time once my impromptu ceremony ended. Thus, my genocide began. I held no vendetta against one specific ethnic group or nationality: I persecuted everyone I came in contact with. In my mind, there was no such thing as an innocent victim.

As my new battalion filed into the various transport trucks that lined the edge of St. Peter's Square, or else hopped atop the twin columns of C1 Ariete tanks that led up the main road, I jumped into my new Popemobile: a white-painted Humvee that had a .50 cal machine gun mounted to its roof. From there, I travelled alongside my grand militia as we pushed into Switzerland and Austria and killed everyone we came across. I even took a few turns at the .50 cal (so long as no one was shooting back). My aim was surprisingly decent!

Other than my antics with the machine gun (which was mostly for sport, and nostalgically made me recall the Gatling gun I had once owned), we hammered both countries by ground and by air before they knew what had happened. In a serious display of military might, they both surrendered the same day. It was the city of Vienna that incurred the worst of my wrath.

As I settled into Vienna, my officers and I made ourselves at home within the surviving, west wing of Schönnbrunn Palace (the entire east wing was leveled). I also sought out souls for my master. I setup a base of operations within The Mirror Room. Though many of its fabulous, crystal mirrors had shattered as a result of nearby explosions, I still appreciated the Rococo decorations that were left intact.

While I looked out a window that faced south, at smoking craters and charred patches where the gardens had once been, I watched my soldiers string barbed wire around a statue. They were making the area around the Neptunbrunnen (meaning Neptune Fountain) of the palace into an outside prison. Even as they worked, I watched some other soldiers corral the first of my prisoners. I gazed up at the Gloriette and a cloudless sky beyond. After I admired the beautiful scenery for a minute, I went over to a table to review a map of the region.

As I sat on a sixteenth or seventeenth century stool with a red cushion, I planned my next move and also put on an audio tape that I had stolen. It was one of the guided tour tapes. I learned that a six year old Mozart once gave a concert to Empress Maria Theresa in the room I now occupied. Well, either that or one of the adjacent rooms.

A few minutes later, as I listened to the tour guide ramble, the Colonel who had initiated my original operation entered the room.

"Sir," he said as he saluted me.

"Yes?" I asked as I looked up from my map.

"Where do you want your interrogation area setup? Some of my men weren't sure what you had in mind. They were thinking of fencing off a spot near the Grand Parterre."

I intended to create a separate area where I could take my prisoners for random torture. I didn't expect them to know anything. Then again, that wasn't the reason I felt like torturing them. It had been far too long since I had handed out a punishment. I wanted a suitable torture chamber and had to give the area a name that wouldn't sound as dreadful as its intended purpose. Otherwise, my men would begin to question why I was killing civilians and what my motives really were. Hence, the interrogation area.

"I think it would be best to set the area up in an existing room in case it rains," I told him after a moment of deliberation, "That will also keep prying eyes away and muffle any screams."

"Understood, sir," my Colonel answered. "I'll have the men clear out a few rooms. Do you want them to save any of the fancy, Austrian, historical stuff?"

I shook my head, "Not necessary," I let him know, "And thank you, Colonel." He saluted me and turned to leave. Before he did I added, "Oh, and Colonel, please have someone sweep up the floor here. I keep slipping on bullet casings."

"Affirmative, sir," he let me know.

The next morning, after I awoke, I looked out a window of the Mirror Room at a massive host of Austrian captives. They were a pitiful bunch as they huddled together, packed into my prison. I felt like a true king. I went into the adjacent Rosa Room and was served a breakfast of corned beef, toast with apple jelly, and a glass of orange juice. The breakfast arrived on the finest of sparkling silver.

When I ran out of orange juice, I had a prisoner (who I had made into a servant) refill my glass. As he did, one of my captains entered the Rosa Room.

"Sir," he said as he saluted, "I wanted to make you aware that your new interrogation area is ready. We set everything up within Emperor Franz Joseph's birth-room and two adjacent rooms."

"Thank you, Captain," I said. I dabbed my cheek with an embroidered napkin and then told him, "Please meet me outside, by the Grand Parterre, in ten minutes. I still need to take my morning shit and make myself look more presentable. That is all for now."

"Yes, sir," he said and then left the room.

I attended to my business and then joined him outside where all my prisoners were gathered. They stared out from the barbed wire at me with looks of apprehension, fear, and hatred. Their faces were dirty and haggard. Their hair was disheveled. Couples held hands. Children clung to mothers in terror.

"This man," I said as I pointed to a random prisoner, "Is due for interrogation."

The bewildered prisoner protested, but was soon placed in fetters and hauled off. Once inside my interrogation area, he was shackled to a make-shift, iron pillory that my soldiers had welded together the night before. I started his interrogation by refreshing my archery skills. I hadn't practiced since high school and this was as good a time as ever.

My first arrow went right through his left calf. The next one penetrated his right palm. The final one pierced his foot and pinned it to the floor. I made a mental note to have my soldiers find more arrows.

For the next, three hours, I hacked the prisoner up with a variety of implements amid his screams and pleas of mercy. When I finally left the Franz Joseph birth-room, the entire floor was slick with blood.

I paused to eat a traditional, Austrian lunch of Szegedinerkrautfleisch (even with my vast array of languages I found it difficult to pronounce). It consisted of a diced, lean, pork leg, cooked with sauerkraut in a paprika sauce. I had this with warm bread and butter, and a glass of red wine.

After lunch, I interrogated another prisoner. As I continued these private tortures, I also instituted frequent public executions. I ordered these held three times a day, for five prisoners at a time. The method was hanging. I officially deemed the individuals criminals against the state and charged them with conspiracy.

My soldiers built a solid gallows and carried out my orders flawlessly. As part of their sentences, and for my enjoyment, I also forced prisoners to make their own nooses. The result of this was that many didn't have a correct slip-knot. Often, the condemned strangled to death instead of fracturing their neck. Some tried to cheat the system and had very loose knots, which hardly strangled them at all and did no damage. I had these cheaters cut down and then put into a Chinese device called the Tiger Bench. It was a fairly simplistic method, but that was why I liked it.

The Tiger Bench was traditionally made from a board or two chairs. It positioned a person upright, with both legs extended in front of them. Once in place, the person then had bricks (or other materials) piled on top of another board, or into a bucket, or directly atop their legs, until their legs eventually snapped from the weight. In my version of the device, I preferred to elevate each victim's feet about a foot higher than their waist. Often, I had my soldiers force members of the victims' family to do the work. I had them either pile the bricks atop their family member, or sometimes instructed them to sit on the victims' knees until the knees gave out.

After a stint at the Tiger Bench, I had the victim (and any family members) buried alive. This was done in the prison area by the other prisoners. It saved my soldiers the trouble of burying bodies later.

Within a few days of these public and hidden tortures, prisoners started to refer to me simply as "the demon." I rather liked the nickname. I had turned Austria's most famous tourist attraction into my favored seat of judgment.

The prisoners tried to revolt one evening but my men cut them down with machine gun fire and grenades. The soldiers violent show of aggression left about a hundred prisoners dead and several hundred wounded. We left them where they fell, either to heal on their own, or to die. The grounds around the palace that evening were tinted red with blood until a heavy rain storm washed it away later that night. Nine of my soldiers were killed in the rebellion. I made sure to pay the prisoners back threefold for it. They didn't rebel again.

A month or so into my stay at Schönnbrunn Palace, as I reviewed a ledger of prisoner activities, my Colonel approached me with tidings.

"Word of the capture of Austria and Switzerland has spread to the US and also France," he let me know.

"Took them long enough," I commented.

"Well sir, communications aren't what they used to be. The internet has been down for a long time now, and the telephone lines in many countries are damaged or irreparable."

I sighed, "I may not have a computer with me, but I'm aware that there is no internet, Colonel. Please get to the point. What do the US and France want?"

"They have supplied explicit orders to cease your hostilities. They have threatened war if you do not relinquish both conquered territories and return to Italy to reassume the role of a neutral pope."

I dropped the ledger on a table. "Do they know about my prison camp?"

My Colonel shook his head, "They say nothing of it, so I cannot be sure. They are most certainly aware that you command a sufficient military force. France has been monitoring the steps we've taken to fortify the region. We've seen a buildup of French troops near the border of Switzerland."

The news was mixed. It was bad that we had another upcoming conflict so soon, but also good that they hadn't discovered my camp. The less other countries knew about my gruesome tortures and mass executions, the better. "As far as the US is concerned, they talk bold but they are bluffing," I let my Colonel know. "They are nothing more than an aging dinosaur and all but extinct. They just can't admit that they've been beaten. The scope of their domestic problems is ferocious; you know this as well as I."

"Yes, sir," my Colonel confirmed, "I'm in total agreement. The aftermath of the Chinese invasion and that nuclear attack has crippled them. I've heard ongoing reports that the remnants of their military are still fighting roving bands of Chinese who are causing trouble from coast to coast."

"And there is also the matter of their economy, which I have tried to keep abreast of," I let him know, "It was already floundering before the war and now it's in turmoil. The US cannot afford another conflict."

"May I suggest an action regarding the US, sir?" My Colonel inquired.

I motioned for him to go ahead with a wave of my hand.

He cleared his throat and continued, "I would be surprised if a number of other countries do not swoop in for what I anticipate to be an easy land-grab. I recommend we do it first, and as soon as possible. I can have men on the ground in Washington, D.C. within three weeks."

"I thank you for your offer, Colonel, but I have others plans for now." I tapped my finger on the table a few times as I thought. "The US can be ignored. They pose no danger and can do nothing to hinder our progress. The threat of France, however, has to be taken seriously."

In World War II, England had proven to be a big thorn in Germany's side and France fell to Hitler in about six weeks. The situation now was vastly different. France had escaped the worst of the mayhem from World War III. They were one of the few countries left that still had a very capable military and infrastructure. My order was simple, "We will demand the immediate surrender of France and ask that they recall all troops. Make it clear that they are to comply by the end of the month. If not, I will bring the full might of the Soldiers for God against them."

"Understood, sir," my Colonel confirmed, "I will write up the demands myself."

"Good. I expect France will give up without bloodshed. If not, we will engage them. They will learn what it means to challenge us."

To my surprise, the frogs showed some backbone. They didn't comply with my order. Instead, they rallied Germany to their cause. The Germans were equally concerned about my intentions. They had also come through the prior chaos relatively unscathed. Together, the two nations figured they stood a reasonable chance at repelling me.

Both fought my forces with all their ability. They French weren't about to just turn belly up for me. Likewise, the krauts were as stubborn as always.

My Soldiers for God held France off and overwhelmed Germany, but the conflict took half a year and resulted in a sufficient loss of life. I chocked up every lost soul as a victory for Satan. France plagued my men for another year before the French gave in to the inevitable. All the while, I remained in Austria with a sizeable contingent of elite troops. We continued to punish the ever-shrinking number of malnourished, Austrian prisoners. By now, each prisoner's gaze was a hollow stare. They just about shuffled from place to place with no will to live. They hoped for death.

With victory established in France and Germany, I granted their wishes. I planned to oversee the reconstruction of both nations and move my base elsewhere. Therefore, my prisoners were no longer of use to me. I ordered them killed to the very last man. This happened in one blood-filled day. When it was complete, I ordered the remnants of Schönnbrunn Palace demolished and the bodies burned. My next stop was France, where my Colonel awaited.

Once there, I noted the destruction of Paris. The smoke and dust in the air was so thick that I don't think I saw the sun for the first three days. The loss of Paris was my only regret to the campaign against the French. It had been unavoidable. The bulk of their splendid monuments, artwork, and cathedrals (all items I'd once enjoyed) were annihilated.

Many fires still raged out of control and most of the buildings were now slag. All of this annoyed me, because I wanted to tour the country again once I finished conquering everyone. Now, there really wasn't anything worth seeing. The French could have avoided this tragedy if only they had surrendered peacefully, like I had asked. I made a mental note to put up new monuments in my honor once rebuilding got underway.

My first, official act in Paris was to have a real éclair. There is nothing quite like a real, French éclair. I ordered one brought to me and was delighted when it arrived. Following its consumption, I attended to the French leaders that my Colonel had rounded up. I personally disemboweled them in front of their families. I subsequently disemboweled their families and christened my troops with their blood. All their bodies were then decapitated. The heads of the French leaders were put on spikes at the site where the Arc De Triomphe had once stood (it was now just rubble).

With France appropriately punished, Germany was my next destination. In a similar fashion, I had the heads of the German leaders also impaled and made them visible at the Alexanderplatz in Berlin. I started a second prison-camp there and implemented a variety of tortures and forced-labor upon the Germans.

Europe was now under my direct control. My new prison camp kept me occupied like a kitten with a toy mouse. It was what I considered to be a thriving community. My soldiers needed to be kept busy, however: a lazy soldier gets no killing done. Such was the motto I thought up while in Berlin. In my estimation, a good soldier needs practice to stay efficient as surely as a good gun needs oiling.

Per the guidance of Satan, I gave The Soldiers for God plenty of practice. At his suggestion, I ordered them back into Africa. This time, they literally walked right in and claimed it. No one wanted more violence there. Russia fell two months later with just mild resistance. At that time, I had exhausted my supply of German prisoners and I returned to the Vatican. I then renamed it to Jessica City, after my lovely wife, and I held an official ceremony for the occasion.

While I partied and reveled in the spoils of victory (which included a sex-filled romp with a number of college-aged Italian women in the actual Popemobile), Japan was being conquered by my soldiers. At the end of the year, a now dictator-less North Korea (I have no idea what transpired there), was up for grabs. I took it without a fight. I allowed South Korea and the Philippines to remain under their own governments because they agreed to subservience under my rule.

The world was left in complete devastation but I ruled most of what remained. I figured at least seventy percent of the world's population had thus far perished. This only meant that fewer people were around to complain about my rule. Those who did complain were silenced. From my standpoint, I gave the world a punishment that was warranted. I had fulfilled the agreement I had struck with Satan and delivered more souls to him than even Hitler, Stalin, or Pol Pot.

Nonetheless, like Shang Tsung (who I knew of from Kurt's Mortal Kombat video games and a series of bad movies), my thirst for souls was legendary. There was still more to be done. From my seat at the Vatican, I agonized over my next move. As my paranoia grew (or at least that's what rumors said was happening), I fostered the nagging notion that I had ignored potential threats. There were still countries in the world that could cause me harm, despite their repeated assurances of peace and their pledges of mutual assistance to restore civilization.

I could not trust them. Any potential threat had to be removed for good. I felt like a greedy player of Monopoly. I didn't have *all* the real estate and I wanted it. When I reviewed my maps, and looked at Europe, Asia, and Africa, I saw that I was missing one very important tile: Israel. It was, to me, the Boardwalk of the game. It had the power to make or break me...for good.

Israel, with its military proficiency and arsenal, was the last country within my new domain (which I renamed to Kurtopia) that was not under my control. Despite unbelievable odds, Israel had bested all their neighboring enemies and had come through the conflict bent but unbroken. I had to take Israel in order to solidify my grip on the region. Once that was done, I could then decide if actions against the Americas or Australia were warranted.

When assessing the military capacity of my new target, I learned that Israel's air force had been depleted. Their nuclear capability was now non-existent. All they had left were infantry and armor, and not a great number of either. I knew their tenacity would be the biggest stumbling block. Israel would fight to the last breath, like some classic pugilist going fifteen rounds.

I gathered my overwhelming forces and marched for the Holy Land. I was eager to have all of Europe, Asia, and Africa to call my own. My military massed at their borders like one immense swarm of insects. The Soldiers for God were comprised from hundreds of thousands of men, but that day we were one big, living, entity. Israel was a may-fly by comparison. I stood at the head of this army, dressed in my papal regalia and tiara with my saber and sidearm at my side. Even I was amazed. The tanks, infantry, and helicopters I had brought for support stretched for miles in every direction. I ordered the attack to commence. My troops flowed into Israel like a tide. Attack helicopters led the way. I waited for the massacre. Then, something went wrong.

The brightest of white lights filled the sky. It enveloped everything and I had to close my eyes and shield them with my hand to avoid going blind.

Someone had set off a nuke!

I waited to vaporize. I realized I was mistaken.

That wasn't a nuke, I thought, *what else could be so bright?*

I opened my eyes as the light faded. My helicopters dropped out of the air as if an EMP had simply shut them down. Below them, my glorious, armored vehicles just fell apart as if the bolts and screws had been removed. As if in a cartoon, the drivers of vehicles were left clutching steering wheels with nothing attached. Soldiers tumbled out of APCs and Humvees as the benches and floors gave way underneath them.

"What the fuck is this?" I screamed. I ripped my papal tiara off my head and tossed it to the ground. As I stamped on the fanciest hat in the world, I yelled, "Would someone please tell me what kind of weapon that was?"

My soldiers looked confused. I drew my pistol and shoved it up into the chin of a nearby Captain. "Tell me what just happened," I ordered.

"I....I'm sorry, your Holiness," he stammered as he gazed down the bridge of his nose at the firearm, "I....I don't know. I swear it. I would tell you if I did."

Enraged at my loss of heavy equipment and troops, I pulled the trigger.

Nothing happened.

I looked down at my Colt 1911. It had never misfired. It was widely considered the most reliable handgun ever made. I cleared a round from the chamber and stuck it to the side of the Captain's head. He was practically whimpering and frozen in fear. I wanted to see someone die. I pulled the trigger a second time.

Again, the gun misfired.

It then began to glow with brilliant light. It became so hot that it burned into my palm. I shouted and dropped it to the ground. It started to sizzle and dissolve. When I looked up, I saw my living swarm, my impressive army, laying down their weapons as one.

"What the fucking are you doing!?" I cursed at them. "You maggots! You are the Soldiers for God! You serve me! I order you to keep fighting!"

I then saw a bright figured bathed in light. He was looking directly at me and coming my way, ever so slowly. In his right hand, he held a flaming sword of pure light. The throng parted for Him as He came forward. I knew who He was before He was even close enough to discern.

"Jesus Christ." I said it half as a swear and half because it was Jesus Christ.

As prophesized, He had conquered death and returned to divinely intervene and save the world. This was the ultimate miracle of God at work and I hadn't seen it coming. Satan certainly hadn't counted on it. My soldiers bowed down at His feet. Almost as one, they crossed themselves. I heard murmured prayers of repentance as they begged Him to forgive their horrible deeds. Satan raged in my head as he realized he had lost all of their souls, likely for all time.

As the Christ approached me, I felt my body lock up. I was frozen in place just like my Captain had been a moment before.

"You will not hurt my flock again," He stated simply. There was no hate or anger in his voice. It was peaceful and calm, like the ocean on a still day.

I could have responded, but was dumbfounded. The holy power of the Christ was simply too much for any evil to stand against. He touched the sword of light to my chest. I felt all the malice, hatred, and negativity of Satan leave me. I was the Devil's only son. I was defeated.

EPILOGUE: THE END OF THE END

I haven't heard the voice of Satan in my head since that day. Nor did I hear any other voice, except for one occasion: immediately after the sword of light touched my chest, I heard a voice of love and joy. It was a voice of peace. These were the exact words:

"Pawn of Lucifer, you did your best to bring your doom to my Heaven. Know that you have failed and that my armies have repelled those of Satan. Our eternal struggle shall continue, but know that I have been victorious for now. You have played your tricks, and I have played mine. Know that I am merciful. You can be forgiven, but you shall never grace my kingdom. Your destiny is to face Lucifer soon. His vengeance will fall upon you as a hammer strikes an anvil, and, like the smith working metal, he will warp your body with his rage. Your torment will be without end."

Such were the words that resounded in my mind. My torment will be without end. I have a feeling those words will stay with me for eternity. I have been consumed by them since the moment I was locked in this cell. As I look out through bars, I realize it is probably the last time I'll see blue skies. For my crimes against humanity, the world governments have sentenced me to die by firing squad. My execution is only hours away.

I never imagined how my life would change because of a few decisions. I never wanted to be evil. I didn't expect that I would become the Antichrist mentioned by antiquity. Unfortunately for me, God was right; he was right all along.

I need to pay for my crimes. I know that now. I will never see Heaven. I will never see Jessica or talk to her. Kurt, too, is lost to me forever. I won't even get a chance to apologize to them for the person, no the vile creature, that I've become.

When I get back to Hell, the Devil will still be there waiting . He will be *very* angry with me. He warned me not to fail. The punishment he has in store will likely be the worst ever conceived. I imagine it will make me wish that I could be assigned to The Factory, or hooked to machines and used as some sort of living light-bulb. I suspect that my tale will replace The Story of Unhappy Marlowe; assuming it isn't so severe that no one wishes to dwell on it.

Looking back on what has transpired, I can't believe I was so misled! I once believed that God was The Great Deceiver. Earlier, in my Earthly life, I had thought the deceiver was Satan. I suppose to an extent he did manipulate me. Yet even if he pulled some strings, it was still ultimately my choices that wrought my fate. I am the victim of my own delusions. They have bought me eternal damnation.

THE END

ALTERNATE ENDING

The world was left in complete devastation but I ruled most of what remained. I figured at least seventy percent of the world's population had thus far perished. This only meant that fewer people were around to complain about my rule. Those who did complain were silenced. From my standpoint, I gave the world a punishment that was warranted. I had fulfilled the agreement I had struck with Satan and delivered more souls to him than even Hitler, Stalin, or Pol Pot.

Nonetheless, like Shang Tsung (who I knew of from Kurt's Mortal Kombat video games and a series of bad movies), my thirst for souls was legendary. There was still more to be done. From my seat at the Vatican, I agonized over my next move. As my paranoia grew (or at least that's what rumors said was happening), I fostered the nagging notion that I had ignored potential threats. There were still countries in the world that could cause me harm, despite their repeated assurances of peace and their pledges of mutual assistance to restore civilization.

I could not trust them. Any potential threat had to be removed for good. I felt like a greedy player of Monopoly. I didn't have *all* the real estate and I wanted it. When I reviewed my maps, and looked at Europe, Asia, and Africa, I saw that I was missing one very important tile: Israel. It was, to me, the Boardwalk of the game. It had the power to make or break me...for good.

Israel, with its military proficiency and arsenal, was the last country within my new domain (which I renamed to Kurtopia) that was not under my control. Despite unbelievable odds, Israel had bested all their neighboring enemies and had come through the conflict bent but unbroken. I had to take Israel in order to solidify my grip on the region. Once that was done, I could then decide if actions against the Americas or Australia were warranted.

When assessing the military capacity of my new target, I learned that Israel's air force had been depleted. Their nuclear capability was now non-existent. All they had left were infantry and armor, and not a great number of either. I knew their tenacity would be the biggest stumbling block. Israel would fight to the last breath, like some classic pugilist going fifteen rounds.

I gathered my overwhelming forces and marched for the Holy Land. I was eager to have all of Europe, Asia, and Africa to call my own. My military massed at their borders like one immense swarm of insects. The Soldiers for God were comprised from hundreds of thousands of men, but that day we were one big, living, entity. Israel was a may-fly by comparison. I stood at the head of this army, dressed in my papal regalia and tiara with my saber and sidearm at my side. Even I was amazed. The tanks, infantry, and helicopters I had brought for support stretched for miles in every direction. I ordered the attack to commence. My troops flowed into Israel like a tide. Attack helicopters led the way.

My great victory, at the site of Tel Megiddo (which in Greek translates into Armageddon), was over within hours. Actually, that's not quite correct. The Translation, I mean, not my crushing victory. The Greek word for Armageddon is derived from Hebrew; Har Megiddo, which means 'the hill at Megiddo.' This is the site where my Battle of Armageddon took place, just as prophesized in the bible (and that

Armageddon movie got everything totally wrong: an asteroid had nothing to do with it). In a splendid stroke of irony, I forced Israel's leaders to surrender the Holy Land to me there before I dismembered them. In that glorious moment, the remnants of the civilized world came to an end.

All nations thereafter recognized my supremacy. It had finally dawned on everyone else that I could not be beaten. Their only option to avoid bloodshed was to surrender and accept me as their ruler.

Within a week of Israel's defeat, the last of the world's free leaders bowed down to me as I signed their unconditional surrender. The new world that I had forged was mine to shape any way that I wished.

ALTERNATE EPILOGUE

Hence I sit upon my throne with all the nations of the world subservient to me. Even as I stare out over the Sea of Satan (I renamed the Tyrrhenian Sea to the West of Rome), a consortium of slaves is finishing this memoir. Thousands of other slaves around the world are building monuments to me in every capital city. Tithes from other nations are being heaped upon my doorstep almost daily. Most of these nations are now being ruled by my officers: that was their reward for their exemplary service.

As promised, Satan offered me the Earth. The next time I heard from him was after the golden gate of Heaven had been knocked down. He personally appeared to me once he got done ripping the wings off the Angel Gabriel. I was sitting in Rome at that time, in my newly christened throne room. Satan shook my two hands with two of his own, and congratulated me on my achievements.

He let me know that his victory was total and complete, and that he alone now ruled the universe. This revelation was followed by the news that I was now immortal, and so long as I wished, neither myself nor anyone I chose would ever need to die (and if we did, everyone automatically went to Hell). I was then told that Hell and Heaven were in the process of being modified to be more Earth-like. Satan wanted both regions to be a bit more neutral and passive; he didn't see a need to enforce relentless torment anymore. One of his big projects was getting everyone in the Afterlife adjusted to the changes.

After relaying this news, he offered me the first of two gifts: it was the sage who had rejected me at the gate. He came into my throne room in shackles, escorted by two Overlords. He was beaten and bloodied, and his crimson, gold-trimmed robe was now all ripped to shreds. He looked like a beggar.

The Overlords knelt at my feet to pay homage before they hooked the sage's shackles to an iron ring that I had installed in the floor a few feet from my throne. Rather than have the sage tortured or killed, I opted to keep him as my servant for all time. I wanted him to know how it felt to be humbled. I took a page out of Satan's book and now use him as my personal writing desk. In that way, his misery goes on every day. I find it a most pleasing form of revenge.

The next gift that Satan offered me was the fulfillment of my deepest desires: he reached out of thin-air and plucked the souls of Jessica and Kurt out of that emptiness. He returned them both to me, though in different bodies. Jessica was now a tall, blonde, Norwegian woman. Kurt was Mexican. These were both slight adjustments, but I was just glad to have them back.

At first, they were both shocked and could say nothing. If I were still capable of tears, I suppose I would have had some. Instead, I embraced them both. Their arms just hung limply at their sides as I did this. I assume they failed to return my embrace due to the overwhelming emotions they must have felt.

I spent the next week getting to know them again. They told me about the joy they had known in Heaven. They mentioned how all the beautiful things they had seen there were now gone. They told me about how loving God was, and how tolerant and merciful he was, and how they wished he were still around so they could feel that kind of peace again.

I listened to their stories with an abundance of joy and awe. I can only imagine those type of things! I haven't told them anything about Hell yet. There isn't much to say about it, and I think they've both formed a general idea about how much I suffered whilst there. I briefly mentioned that I was the pope for a while (I dissolved the church officially after everyone had surrendered). I also told them about the nice things I'd seen in Austria (and other places I'd visited) since I returned from Hell.

My family was getting along so well that it came as a total surprise to me when both Jessica and Kurt tried to escape. It was perhaps less than two weeks after our glorious reunion. I had gone through so much just to free them from Heaven and return them to me, and they repaid me with ingratitude! I was stunned when the guards hauled them back to my throne room and told me what had transpired.

I couldn't punish either of them, of course: they were family and they were all that mattered to me. I was, however, forced to lock them in their chambers. I regret doing it, but I see them often. We eat all of our meals together, as a family. I also allow them out of their chambers for a few hours a day to roam the palace grounds as they wish. The only caveat is that they must be escorted by guards constantly: I cannot risk that they will run off for some perceived injustice. I will never lose them again.

With so much attention and care lavished upon my wife and son, I find their dissatisfaction quite troubling. The first time I locked Jessica within her quarters she gave me a ration of shit about how the world is a mess now, I'm a tyrant, she doesn't even know me anymore, she hates me, the Devil has destroyed everything, etc, etc, ad infinitum.

I could only laugh at her fanciful imagination. Kurt also shared similar sentiments with me, but I still think he's too young to really know what he's talking about. I suspect that in time both my wife and my son will get over themselves and welcome these changes. After all, these changes are for their own good. In time, we will be the loving, caring, happy family we once were. I am confident of this, because they have all of eternity to adjust.

THE (OTHER) END

Author's Note:

I hope you enjoyed reading this book as much as I enjoyed writing it. I want to thank you for your purchase and support. If you would be so kind, it would greatly assist me if you would go to the website you bought it from (Amazon, Barnesandnoble, etc), and post an honest review. You can also leave a review on my website: author.andrewcormiergraphics.com – Thanks,

– Andrew Cormier

ABOUT THE AUTHOR

Andrew Cormier was born in Lowell, MA. He moved to New Hampshire in 2006. His love of books began around the 3rd grade, when he read Jack London's *White Fang* and *The Call of the Wild*. He has continued to write novels in multiple genres ever since, including fantasy works: *The Winds of Change* and *What Tomorrow Brings*. His other favorite authors include R.A. Salvatore, Robert Jordan, and George R.R. Martin.

In addition to his writing, Mr. Cormier enjoys playing guitar or video games, camping, and football. He is an avid Patriots fan. His notable achievements include a BA in Graphic Design and Media Arts from Southern NH University and a black belt in Shaolin Kung Fu. He also attended a blacksmithing school in NC for the enjoyment of it.

Made in the USA
Charleston, SC
15 May 2014